Praise for the Year-Round Christmas Mysteries

"Delightful. . . . [A] humorous tinsel-covered tale that made me laugh out loud even while keeping me guessing."

—*New York Times* bestselling author Jenn McKinlay

"Delany has given us a story full of holiday cheer, an exciting mystery, wondrous characters all in a place I would love to really visit. Its charm just lit up my day. This is one mystery you shouldn't miss this holiday season."

—Escape with Dollycas into a Good Book

"I delved right into this story—it grabbed me in and wouldn't let me go."

—Socrates' Book Review

"The Year-Round Christmas Mystery series continues to build upon this delightful town inhabited by fully developed characters. . . . [A] smartly funny series written by an experienced author."

—Kings River Life Magazine

"Vicki Delany does a masterful job of creating an inviting fictional small town that is all about Christmas."

—Open Book Society

"Ms. Delany has started a promising new series with *Rest Ye Murdered Gentlemen*."

—Fresh Fiction

"The dynamic characters in this series really are what stands out most. . . . Compelling and kept me guessing. A great holiday read."

—A Cup of Tea and a Cozy Mystery

Berkley Prime Crime titles by Vicki Delany

REST YE MURDERED GENTLEMEN
WE WISH YOU A MURDEROUS CHRISTMAS
HARK THE HERALD ANGELS SLAY
SILENT NIGHT, DEADLY NIGHT

Silent Night, Deadly Night

Vicki Delany

BERKLEY PRIME CRIME
New York

BERKLEY PRIME CRIME
Published by Berkley
An imprint of Penguin Random House LLC
1745 Broadway, New York, NY 10019

ISBN: 9780440000303

First Edition: August 2019

Printed in the United States of America
1   3   5   7   9   10   8   6   4   2

Cover art by Julia Green
Cover design by Sarah Oberrender
Book design by Tiffany Estreicher

To my own friends of long acquaintance: Pat, Jackie, Karen, and Leslie

Acknowledgments

As always, I am grateful to the members of the Canadian crime writing community for their help and support. The idea for this book began at a "writers' retreat" (much retreating is done, little writing!) with Barbara Fradkin, and with Robin Harlick during long walks in the snowy woods surrounding Robin's Quebec cabin.

Thanks also to the great team at Berkley, mainly Miranda Hill and Michelle Vega, and to my wonderful agent, Kim Lionetti at Bookends.

And, most of all, to the cozy community, whose enthusiasm for books and reading, and cozy mysteries in particular, is always an inspiration.

Chapter 1

My mother had been excited for weeks.

Then again, sometimes it can be difficult to tell. Excited is my mother's normal state of mind.

The first of the girls (as she called them) had started arriving yesterday. The rest were due this morning. After settling in, they planned to tour the sights of Rudolph, New York, beginning with my store, Mrs. Claus's Treasures.

I checked my watch. Eleven thirty. "Now remember," I said to Jackie O'Reilly, my shop assistant, "these are long-time friends of my mother, but I've never met any of them before."

"Doesn't sound like such good friends to me," she said. "My mom's childhood pals are more like aunts to me than my own aunts are."

"College friends drift apart. In terms of location as well as moving on with their lives. They've kept in touch over the years with Christmas cards and the like, and some of them visited Mom in New York when she was singing.

Mom and Dad stayed with one of the women when they were in California last year, but Mom says this is the first time since college that they'll all be together. Anyway, the point is, Jackie, treat them well. This weekend is really important to Mom."

"Treat them well. I'll remember that. I assume you mean not like I treat our other customers, Merry."

"That's not what I meant."

"Whatever." Jackie tucked a piece of fresh holly around a giant glass bowl piled high with silver and pink balls. "How's that look?"

I studied it. The display seemed sparse to me. "Fill the bowl up more. It should be on the verge of overflowing."

"If it overflows any more, they'll fall out."

"Another one or two will be okay." In my former life I'd been a style editor at one of the country's top lifestyle magazines. I had a good eye, and I was proud of it.

I left Jackie to it, and went to give a small nudge to a customer who'd been spending a lot of time examining the earring tree. "Those are hand-made by a local jeweler," I told her.

She picked up a pair of earrings. Delicate threads of silver had been twisted into the shape of a snowman, and a tiny red stone provided his nose. "I've been admiring the quality. They are pricey though."

"The artist's name is Crystal Wong. She's from Rudolph and is in her first year at the School of Visual Arts in New York."

"She works here part-time." Jackie placed a pink ball on top of the stack. It did look dangerously unstable. She picked up a silver orb and slowly settled it in place. The display wobbled, and she held her hands out as though to catch them if they fell. Trust Jackie to make her point, even if the entire display collapsed around us.

"You're right, Jackie," I admitted as I remembered that at a magazine shoot we often had displays tumbling around us moments after the pictures were snapped. A photographic display isn't designed for stability or permanence. "Any more balls and the whole thing's going to topple over."

She didn't bother to hide her self-satisfied expression as she removed the last two balls.

"I like knowing the name of the artist and helping support a local community at the same time," the customer said. "I'll take these for me." She handed me the snowmen and then she picked up another one of Crystal's pieces, a gold chain with double links and a small jeweled wreath at the throat. She ran the chain through her fingers and checked the price tag. "This might be a bit too much for a preholiday gift. I'll take these instead." She swapped the necklace for a pair of earrings shaped like wreaths. "For my mother-in-law. I'll call it a Thanksgiving present to get her in the mood for the holidays. I'll take some of those napkins as well. I love your tree."

"Thanks." I gave the tree an appreciative glance. A live Douglas fir, replaced once a month, fully decorated with bells and balls, ribbons and wooden cranberry strings, small, warm white lights, and a glistening silver star at the top, filled one corner of the store. This was a Christmas-themed shop, but that never stopped us from featuring other holidays at the appropriate time. Today the main display was set as if for a Thanksgiving feast, with a centerpiece of real sugar pumpkins, fresh apples, red maple leaves, an orange and brown runner with matching place mats, and turkey-themed dishes.

I took the jewelry to the sales counter while the customer continued to browse. We'd been busy this morning, but the store was emptying out as lunchtime approached.

It was the week before Thanksgiving, coming up to the busiest time of the year. At Mrs. Claus's Treasures, I specialize in locally made crafts and design elements for gift-giving and for decorating the home. The store's located on Jingle Bell Lane, the main shopping area of Rudolph, New York. The greatest desire of the townspeople and shop owners of Rudolph is to be officially designated America's Christmas Town. That hasn't happened, not yet, but we call ourselves that anyway.

Although we celebrate Christmas all year round, the weeks between Thanksgiving and New Year are the busiest, by far, and like all the owners of shops and businesses along Jingle Bell Lane, I was gearing up to do nothing but work for the next six weeks.

"Speaking of Crystal," Jackie said once the customer had left, laden with not only the two sets of earrings and Thanksgiving napkins but a porcelain Mrs. Claus doll dressed in Victorian attire, a chain of bright red wooden cranberries, and a set of the silver and pink balls. "How's she doing in New York?"

"Well, I think." Jackie and Crystal had never gotten on, perhaps because bold Jackie was filled with her own self-importance and shy Crystal was genuinely talented, but I got the feeling Jackie was proud of how well Crystal was doing. "She seems to be enjoying her classes and is making friends. She'll be home for the holidays and is going to do some shifts in here at the busy times."

"That's good," Jackie said. "I could use the help."

She spoke as though I weren't, at this very minute, rear-ranging the jewelry display.

The chimes over the door tinkled and my mother swept in. She'd been a soloist at the Metropolitan Opera and had retired from the stage a few years ago. Now she taught voice lessons, but she was still every inch the diva. Her look was always dramatic with her huge dark eyes and jet-black hair (these days owing more to Clairol than to her Italian mother) and still-flawless olive skin. Today she wore a black wool cape tied with a row of fire-engine red frogs and lined with scarlet silk, a matching red hat trimmed with fake black fur, and red leather knee-high boots with substantial heels.

"Darling. How lovely to see you." She wrapped me in a hug, and I was enveloped in the familiar scent of Chanel No. 5. She released me and turned with a dramatic sweep of her arms. "Girls, come and meet Merry, my eldest daughter. Merry owns this absolutely darling little shop."

The five women who filed in in my mother's wake were a mixed lot. Their clothes ranged from new, expensive, and fashionable to mass-produced, well-worn, and slightly tatty. They ranged in size from short and round to tall and lean. They were all the same age as my mom, but if I hadn't known they'd been college roommates, I might have thought their ages varied by twenty or more years.

They greeted me warmly and gushed over both me and my shop.

Mom made the introductions, and I struggled to keep the names straight:

Constance: designer jeans, three-hundred-dollar haircut, diamond earrings and rings, tall and fit, healthy winter tan

Barbara: average height but powerful-looking in khaki pants, hiking boots, cropped gray hair, a row of piercings through her right ear

Karla: short and plump with pale pudgy cheeks, cloth coat pilling around the elbows and under the sleeves, sturdy brown footwear of the sort my paternal grandmother would have called "sensible shoes"

Ruth: heavily wrinkled, bags under eyes, jeans worn in the knees and hem but not fashionably, scuffed sneakers, an aura of cigarette smoke clinging to her and her clothes

Genevieve: also smelling of smoke but faint and overlaid with perfume, taller than the rest and as thin as the branches of the earring tree, struggling to keep her age at bay with what might have been a facelift, dyed blond hair tied in a high ponytail that was far too youthful for her

Introductions over, the women spread throughout the shop. Almost immediately Constance began gathering things off the shelves and display racks. Jewelry, Thanksgiving napkins and place mats, a set of coasters showing the elves hard at work in Santa's workshop. Genevieve picked everything up, examined it, and put it back again. Karla went straight to the toys, and Barbara studied the Christmas decorations. Ruth stood against a wall, her arms crossed over her chest, and simply watched the others. A deep line had formed between her eyebrows, and she was not smiling.

"Do you know the origins of these pieces?" Barbara

asked me, pointing to a brightly painted wooden nutcracker soldier that formed part of a collection.

"I can tell you almost to the square mile," I said. "The woodworker lives not far from town, and he forages in the woods for broken branches after a storm and follows the crews who maintain the electricity wires when they're trimming trees."

His name was Alan Anderson and he was my boyfriend. I didn't mention that.

"Is everything you sell here local?" she asked.

"Not everything. I source some of the finer things in the city, but I do my best to get whatever I can locally."

"Merry was a design editor with *Jennifer's Lifestyle* magazine," Mom said. "She has excellent taste."

"I can see that," Barbara said. "I'll take the full set of these, thanks. They'll look great decorating my office."

"What do you do?" I asked.

"I'm a lawyer. We specialize in environmental protection."

"Sounds interesting," I said.

"And important."

Karla had left the toy display and come to see the table decorations. "Interfering with businessmen trying to provide jobs and keep their community alive, more like," she said.

"That's your opinion," Barbara said.

"It's the truth."

"I'd like to hear more about what you and your firm do, Barbara," Ruth said.

Karla turned on her. "People like you, who only work for others, don't understand what it's like to be responsible for the welfare of your employees. Some of these environmental people want to bring in ridiculous petty laws that destroy hardworking family-owned businesses. You wouldn't believe the trouble and expense we have to go to before we can begin a project. All to protect some silly turtle."

Ruth lifted her hands. "I'm just asking."

"And I'm just telling you," Karla said.

I wasn't getting in the middle of that. I went behind the sales counter and began ringing up purchases while Jackie followed Constance through the shop, staggering under the weight of the other woman's selections. Ruth went to stand by the door, where she waited impatiently for the others to finish shopping.

Genevieve put a small ornament on the counter. "I'll be back later," she said to me, "and then I'll clean you out. For now, I'll get this charming fellow."

I'd noticed her trying to unobtrusively check the price tags on all the items she looked at. This little ornament, a two-inch-high wooden soldier to hang on the tree, was one of the cheapest things I sold. I wanted to tell her she didn't have to buy something she didn't really want just to please Mom, but that would come across as pretty insulting, so I said nothing.

"Why don't I treat you to a little something?" Constance was examining the jewelry display, and she called across the shop floor to Ruth. "Isn't this necklace absolutely darling? Would you like it?" She held up a chain with glass stones shaped like holiday lights.

"You don't need to do that," Ruth said.

"But I'd like to."

"No. Thank you." Ruth kept her arms folded across her chest. The line between her brows deepened.

"It's not much." Constance ran her eyes over Ruth, taking in the too-large brown jacket, the worn jeans, the scuffed sneakers. "You need a touch of holiday color about you."

My shop's not very large, and voices can easily be heard from one side to the other, but I thought Constance could have shown a bit of courtesy by approaching the person she was talking to, rather than yelling across the room so everyone could hear.

"I told you," Ruth said, "I don't want it."

"I'm only trying to be nice." Constance's tone was sweet, but a sickly sweet. Too much and without good intentions behind it. "You don't have to—"

"Lunchtime!" Mom called. "Complete your purchases, girls. I have the perfect place in mind for lunch. Merry, can you join us?" She lifted her eyebrows to the ceiling and opened her eyes wide, asking me to agree.

"Sure," I said. "That would be nice. Let me check on Mattie, and I'll follow you. Where are you going?"

"The bakery, of course. Where else would one go in Rudolph after a day of preholiday shopping?"

Except for Ruth, the women all bought something. They paid for their purchases and left. I watched them pass the front windows, heading up Jingle Bell Lane toward Victoria's Bake Shoppe. Mom led the way, chatting to Constance, who'd pulled a gigantic pair of designer sunglasses out of her Michael Kors bag as they left the shop. Barbara and Genevieve walked together, Karla behind them. Ruth came last, well behind the rest of the group.

"Are they all staying at your parents' house?" Jackie asked.

"Yes. You know how big the house is. Room enough for them all."

"How's your dad feel about that? A weekend of a houseful of women?"

"He's fine with it. Which might be because he's not here. He's gone to Florida on a fishing trip."

"Must be nice." Jackie looked out the window. The sun was out in a brilliant blue sky but the air was cold, everyone heavily wrapped in coats, scarves, and mittens. Winter was on its way.

"I'll try not to take too long at lunch." Before leaving, I went in the back to check on Matterhorn, my dog. I usually took a break around now to take him for a walk. He's a Saint Bernard, not exactly a small animal, and fully grown at just over a year old. Training's important with a dog of that size, and Mattie and I had worked hard together, with the result that he was reasonably well behaved when he wanted to be. When he didn't want to be was another matter altogether. Fortunately, most of the time he wanted to be good, and so I often brought him to work with me. Needless to say, he wasn't allowed in the shop itself ("bull in a china shop" is the phrase that comes to mind), but he was content to spend the day in the back with the occasional break for a walk, and he never barked no matter how much commotion was going on in the store.

He leapt out of his bed as I came into the office. His big tongue hung out of one side of his mouth, and his entire body quivered in excitement. I scratched the top of his head, and he rubbed himself against my leg. "Can't walk you right now, buddy. Family duties await. I'll try and get back soon." His water bowl was empty, and the carpet was soaking wet. I took the bowl into the staff washroom and filled it. When I put it back down, he ran to the door and stood there waiting, butt and tail wagging. "Sorry," I said.

His head dropped, his ears lowered, his tail flopped, and his entire body collapsed into itself. At that moment, a picture of him could have been used to illustrate the dictionary definition of "crushing disappointment."

"Sorry," I said again, as I let myself out quickly, trying not to feel too guilty in the face of his enormous, sad brown eyes.

Another group of customers had come in, and Jackie was talking to them about the Thanksgiving table. I walked through the shop and stepped outside.

The street was busy with cars and pedestrians. People were wrapped up against the cold, but I hadn't bothered to put on my coat as I wasn't going far. Most of the shops had added Thanksgiving motifs to their usual Christmas displays. Santas with pilgrim hats on their heads, elves playing with turkeys, a cornucopia spilling small gifts wrapped in green and red paper. Cranberry Coffee Bar featured pumpkin-spiced everything, along with their usual eggnog-spiced everything.

I love Thanksgiving. It's my favorite holiday. Don't tell anyone in Rudolph, but I love Thanksgiving even more than Christmas. My mom and dad always make an enormous turkey with all the fixings—walnut and sage stuffing, cranberry sauce, mashed potatoes, gravy, green beans, a squash casserole, two types of pie. It's my chance to take one last long deep breath before plunging headfirst into the madness of the holiday season.

I love Christmas, too—my dad is Santa Claus, after all—but now that I own the store, when Christmas Day itself arrives I'm totally exhausted. That's a day to sit back, feet up, mug of hot chocolate in hand, open a few gifts at my parents' house, and then have a hearty brunch and go to bed early before opening the shop the next morning for the after-Christmas sales.

I was determined that this year, unlike last, I wouldn't find myself inviting twelve people around for Christmas dinner. I don't even own twelve plates much less a table big enough to put them on.

I ran into Victoria's Bake Shoppe rubbing my hands together and was instantly hit by a welcome blast of heat full of the scent of freshly baked bread, warm pastry, spicy cinnamon, and piping hot soup. The room was full, and a lineup waited patiently at the counter. Each of the red and white checked tablecloths had a miniature pumpkin in the center. A plush turkey sat on the high shelf next to the trophy from last year's Santa Claus parade. That reminded me: I still had a lot to do to put together the Mrs. Claus's Treasures's float for this year, and not much time in which to do it. I shoved the unwelcome thought aside.

The big table in the center of the room was piled high with small shopping bags and surrounded by larger ones, while my mother and her friends lined up at the counter. I slipped behind Mom. "I'm here."

"Good," she said. "Why don't you take a seat and I'll place your order."

"Thanks. I'll have the butternut squash soup and a half turkey sandwich on rye." I turned to the group behind Mom. "Everything is good here, made from scratch every day, but the squash soup might be the best you've ever had."

"Thanks for the tip," Constance said. "This place is so charming."

"The whole town is charming," Genevieve said.

"Do they use peanuts here?" Karla asked. "I'm highly allergic to peanuts."

"No peanuts are allowed in the kitchen," Marjorie said from behind the counter. "Ever. One of my nephews is also allergic, and he works here part-time, so that's a principle Vicky sticks to. Although I can't say the same for anything we sell that comes prepackaged." She nodded to the rows of locally produced jams, pickles, and preserves on the shelf. "Tree nuts, however, like walnuts or pecans, are often used in Vicky's baking."

"Tree nuts aren't a problem for me," Karla said.

"Are they different?" Ruth asked.

"Totally different," Constance said. "Peanuts aren't actually a nut, they're a legume." She looked at Karla. "My son is dangerously allergic to peanuts, so I know how difficult it can be sorting out what you can eat and what you can't."

"I'll save room for the dessert special then," Karla said.

I glanced at the blackboard on the wall. *Thanksgiving stuffing bread pudding with caramel sauce.* Just looking at the words, I felt three pounds settle on my hips.

Genevieve eyed Karla. "A little preholiday treat, dear? I bet you're going to be having a delicious Thanksgiving feast at home in Montana."

Karla's smile didn't drop, but it turned very stiff. "I live in Minnesota, not Montana, as you well know, *dear*, and the dessert sounds lovely. I believe in enjoying the pleasures of good food."

Genevieve, as tall and lean as a racehorse, ran her eyes down Karla's short, chubby frame. "So I see."

Karla's smile cracked and her shoulders tightened.

Constance stifled a laugh and then she said, "Order whatever you like, Ruth. My treat."

"I can pay for my own lunch, thank you," Ruth replied.

"I'm only trying to be nice," Constance said.

"Oh, I think we all know what you're trying to be," Barbara said.

Constance threw her a nasty look.

Interesting dynamics here, I thought.

"I thought I heard your voice, Aline." Vicky Casey, owner and head baker, came out of the kitchen, wiping her hands on her white apron.

Mom greeted her with a hug and a kiss on both cheeks. Greetings exchanged, Mom turned to her friends. "Everyone, meet Victoria herself, the artist in charge of our lunch."

"Hi," Vicky said.

Mom's friends all said something along the lines of *Pleased to meet you.*

"How's things?" Vicky said to me. "I hope you've been as busy as we have."

"A good start to the season. Let's hope it continues."

"How's your float coming along?"

My eyes involuntarily turned toward the trophy perched high on the shelf: a two-foot-tall gold-painted reindeer with a big red glass ball for a nose. If Vicky noticed where I was looking, she was polite enough not to smirk. Not too much, anyway. "Extremely well," I lied. "I'm confident of doing even better than last year."

"That won't be hard," she said. "Considering that last year yours was the only float that didn't even get a participation ribbon."

"Thank you so much for the reminder." Last year I'd been determined to win best in parade, but my float had been sabotaged and withdrawn from competition, and Vicky had sailed to victory. I tried not to be too bitter.

Vicky and I had met the first day of kindergarten, when I, the shy one, had stood at the edge of the playground, nervous and frightened, and Vicky, the bold one, had walked up to me, looked down at me from her impressive four-year-old height, and informed me that we would be best friends forever.

And so we had been. Vicky still towered over me, and she's still the bold one, but I like to think I'm not quite as shy as I once was.

"How about pizza and a bad movie one night soon?" she said.

"Sounds perfect. Dad's away fishing and Mom has her old college crowd here for the weekend. Let me find out what her plans are, and if I'm included in them, and I'll let you know."

"Great. How's Mattie?"

"Well. Healthy and happy. Most of the time, anyway. Right now he's crushed because I'm here doing people things and not out walking him."

Vicky grinned. "I'd better get back at it. Catch you later."

Mom and her friends had taken seats around the big table, and I went to join them. They all had hot drinks in front of them. Genevieve stirred a packet of Splenda into her black coffee and threw a look of what might have been envy toward Karla's hot chocolate, topped with a tower of whipped cream and a generous serving of finely grated chocolate. Karla scooped the top off the cream with her index finger and popped it into her mouth.

"There are spoons," Genevieve said.

"Don't get too anxious, dear," Karla said. "Your lettuce leaf will be here shortly."

I glanced at my mom. She rolled her eyes.

The waitress carried over a tray laden with our food. I inhaled the delicious scents emanating from my soup before digging in.

Once I'd come up for air, and the women had all enjoyed

their first welcome bites, I said, "What's the plan for the weekend? Too bad you won't be here the first Saturday in December. That's when we have our main Santa Claus parade, and it's always hugely popular."

"Your main parade?" Barbara said.

"We have one in July also. When Santa arrives for his summer vacation at the lake."

"That sounds great," Barbara said. "You can never have too much Christmas spirit."

"You certainly can." Karla took a big bite out of her roast beef sandwich. "I don't believe Christmas music should be played or decorations put out until after Thanksgiving. It shouldn't be allowed."

"Good thing you don't work for the justice department then." Genevieve poked listlessly at her salad. "Or everyone in Aline's town would be in jail. Her daughter first of all, right, Merry?"

"We're only giving people what they want." I gestured to the crowded restaurant. "No shortage of people visiting Rudolph before Christmas."

"I didn't mean people should go to jail! I simply happen to believe some restraint makes things more enjoyable." Karla ran her finger around the inside of her now-empty mug and sucked on it.

"Some people enjoy the holidays more than others," Ruth said. "That's all. Each to their own, I always say."

"Quite right you are, Ruth," Mom said.

Karla wasn't ready to let the subject drop. "All I'm saying is that I taught my children, and now my grandchildren, that the best things in life are worth waiting for."

I seized on the first thing I could think of to divert the

conversation. "Are you from Upstate?" I asked Ruth. "You have the accent."

She grinned at me. It was the first smile I'd seen on her. "Yeah. I live not far from here, in Rochester." She'd ordered the roasted eggplant and mushroom sandwich with a small bowl of soup on the side.

"Isn't that exciting?" Constance drawled.

"Hardworking, salt-of-the-earth people in Rochester," Ruth said.

"Whatever." Constance had ordered the Christmas salad. The greens were tossed with dried cranberries, slices of red and green peppers, slivers of white almonds. "I don't know how you people can live here. I can't abide this damp cold."

"Cold?" I said. "This is nothing. And it's not even damp. It hasn't rained for days and the sun's out."

"What I hated most about our college years," Constance said, "was the weather in New York. I couldn't get back to California fast enough."

"That's not what I remember," Barbara said. "Didn't you have another reason for quitting in the middle of our junior year? How is Edward, anyway?"

"He's doing well, thank you for asking. Since he took over my father's company, it's grown enormously."

"Is Edward your husband?" I asked.

Genevieve snorted and Barbara laughed. Mom shifted uncomfortably in her chair. Karla's head was down. She'd already finished her sandwich and the side of kettle-cooked potato chips.

Constance sorted through her lettuce leaves and found a minuscule piece of feta cheese. "My husband, Frank, died a few years ago. Edward is our son." The huge square-cut diamond on her right hand caught the light from the celling lamps. It had probably been her engagement ring, and she'd moved it to the other hand after her husband's death.

"I'm sorry to hear that," I said.

"We knew Frank in college," Mom said. "That's where he and Constance met. He was studying philosophy, as I remember. I was surprised when you told us he'd switched to business."

"Simply the more practical choice," Constance said.

"No grandchildren yet, Constance?" Karla said.

"Plenty of time yet," Constance said.

"Don't leave it too long," Ruth said, as if Constance had any say in the matter. "You want to be young enough to enjoy them. I have four children and three beautiful grand-daughters. You can never have too many grandchildren, I always say. My kids are doing so well. Would you like to see some pictures, Merry?" Without waiting for me to an-swer, she pulled out her phone, pressed a couple of buttons, and thrust the screen in my face. "These are my oldest boy's daughters. That's Jewell, she's three. Natasha is five, and Madison one and a half. Of them all, I think Natasha looks the most like me, don't you?"

I could see no resemblance whatsoever between the bright-eyed laughing girl and this woman with age and worry carved deeply into her face, but I said, "I do. They're lovely."

Not to be outdone, Karla flourished pictures of her grandchildren. "Only the two so far, but I've high hopes for many more." She laughed heartily.

Once I'd admired all the photos, Mom said, "In answer to your earlier question, Merry, we'll be getting a start on our holiday shopping over the weekend, but mostly we plan to hang around the house remembering our youth and catching up on all the news. It's going to be so much fun." She gave the group the smile that once lit up the balcony of the Met. Today's smile was as fake as it had been all the times her back ached, her costume was too tight, the tenor had trod (deliberately) on her toes during the duet, and she'd been fighting with the mezzo-soprano in the wings.

She was, I realized, already regretting this weekend. I gave her what I hoped was an encouraging smile.

Chapter 2

When I got back to work after lunch, I was pleased to see the store was busy. I went into the back to put my purse away and check on Mattie. When I came out, intending to tell Jackie she could take her lunch break, she slid up to me. She glanced around the shop, checking that no one was in earshot before leaning in close.

"What?" I said.

"You didn't take a necklace off the display and put it away, did you?" She kept her voice low.

"What necklace? And, no, I haven't moved anything."

"One of Crystal's. The one with two chains and the wreath in the center."

"I know the one you mean. They've been popular, and we have one left. She's promised to make us more by parade weekend. What of it?"

"Stolen."

"When?"

"I noticed it was gone when I was refilling the display

after you went out with your mom and her friends. I hadn't rung it up, so I did a quick check of the floor and the other tables in case it had been misplaced. Nope."

I groaned. "I'll keep an eye out."

The chimes over the door tinkled merrily as more customers came in. I wasn't feeling so merry. Shoplifting was a curse. I didn't get a lot of it in here, maybe because my customers weren't the sort to do that or because the Christmas atmosphere kept miscreants on the straight and narrow. Or maybe it was because a Santa holding his naughty-and-nice list watched over the shop from the shelves next to the curtain leading to the back rooms.

My heart sank when I remembered when I'd seen that necklace last.

It had been here, for sure, before Mom and her friends came in. The woman who bought earrings and table linens had admired it, but she'd not bought it. I thought back. Yes, she'd definitely returned it to the display rack. It cost more than she wanted to spend.

If Jackie noticed the necklace was missing after Mom and I left for lunch, then it had to have been taken while Mom's friends were in the shop. It didn't have to be one of them, though. Other people had been in. Some had bought, and some had not.

I hoped, for my mother's sake, one of her friends had not been the thief.

Chapter 3

"When I said I wanted to watch a bad movie," Vicky Casey said, "I meant bad like bad as in junk fare, not bad as in horrible."

"I agree. Do you want me to turn it off?"

"Yeah. I don't care what happens at the end. I only hope they all end up dead."

I switched the TV off. A pizza box, empty, and two plates, also empty, sat on the coffee table beside two wine-glasses, not empty. Mattie snoozed on the floor. Vicky and I picked up our glasses and settled back into the couch. Her aging golden Lab, Sandbanks, rested his chin on her knee, and she stroked his nose absentmindedly.

"Mom and her gang are having dinner at the Yuletide tonight," I said.

"I hope Grace told Mark to take care of them."

"Mom would have made sure of that."

Grace and her husband, Jack, were the owners of the Yuletide Inn, the nicest place in Rudolph. The restaurant was one of the best in this part of the country, largely due to the presence of Chef Mark Grosse, Vicky's boyfriend.

"It's nice that your mom and her college friends are still in touch with each other after all these years," she said.

"I don't know about that. I got the sense Mom's thinking this weekend was a serious mistake."

"Why?"

"They bicker, all the time."

"We bicker," Vicky said. "That's what friends do."

"But we don't try to be mean. They are mean. Not all of them, and not to everyone, but there's an enormous amount of tension there."

"They're a mismatched bunch, all right," Vicky said. "Did you see the diamonds on the fingers of the one in the Tom Ford sunglasses?"

"They could see those diamonds from space. That was Constance. She has money, family money by the way she was talking, and she wants everyone to know it. She pretends to be generous, but she uses her money as a way to put other people in their place. That's my impression, anyway. It was also my impression that her fake generosity didn't go down well with Ruth, the one in the ripped jeans and old coat, the one from Rochester."

"I recognized the tall one," Vicky said.

"You mean Genevieve? Have you met her before?"

"Not met, but I saw her in a movie, I think. I don't quite remember which one. Might have been something on TV."

"She has the look," I said. "Bone thin, heavy makeup, maybe a facelift, trying to look a lot younger than she is."

"That's a losing battle." Vicky pushed a lock of long orange hair out of her face, showing the gingerbread cookie tattoo on her right wrist. The rest of her hair was deep black and cut almost to the scalp. The orange color was in honor of Thanksgiving and the fall. Most of the time it was purple. She was a good six inches taller than me, and more pounds lighter than I cared to think. Which always seemed very unfair, considering she baked delicious bread, cookies, and pies for a living. And I did not.

"Genevieve's probably an actor," I said. "Mom went to NYU Steinhardt, to study opera. That's very much a school for the dramatic arts, although they have a program of academic undergrad degrees, too. The group roomed together in their freshmen year, so I guess it was like a bonding experience. They stayed friends the rest of the time they were in college, but I don't think they've seen each other all that much since. This is the fortieth anniversary of them meeting, so they wanted to do something to mark it. Everyone wasn't free until this weekend, and because Dad had made plans for his fishing trip, Mom invited them here. I hope she's not regretting it too much."

"It's only a weekend. Regret or no, they'll be gone soon."

"True. Do you have much trouble with shoplifting?"

Her big blue eyes opened wide. "That's an abrupt change of subject. Why are you asking me that?"

"Maybe it's not entirely a change of subject. I had something lifted today. One of Crystal's necklaces. I hate to think it, but it happened when Mom and her friends were in the shop. It might not have been them. Other people were in at that time, too."

Vicky took a sip of her wine. "We don't have much shoplifting, because I don't have a lot of items for sale, and people have to pay for their food and drink before they get it. But it happens on occasion. Like today. When we were cleaning up after closing, Marjorie noticed that the last jar of red-pepper jelly was gone, but it hadn't been rung up on the cash register. And Marjorie can be trusted to know exactly how much of that jelly we have in stock because she makes it. Coincidence? Maybe not."

I thought back to our lunch at the bakery. Some of the women had visited the restroom; some had browsed the items on display. I hadn't paid any attention to who had been where. I'd left while they were finishing their drinks and making plans for the remainder of the day.

"Are you going to tell your mom what you're thinking?" Vicky asked.

"That one of her college friends might be a thief? No, I'm not. But if they come into the shop again, I'll be on high alert."

"I'll tell Marjorie and the rest of the front-room staff there've been some incidents in town, so they should keep an eye out. Let's change the subject. How's Alan?"

"Well, I think."

Vicky wiggled her eyebrows over her glass. "You think?"

"I haven't seen much of Alan lately. He's incredibly busy at this time of year. All those toys and decorations don't make themselves, you know." Alan was a craftsman; he created wondrous things out of wood with his own hands. He also played the role of Santa's head toymaker at our town's Christmas festivities.

Bored with the conversation, Sandbanks wandered off to see if he could find something tasty in the kitchen. Mattie twitched in his sleep.

Vicky eyed me. "I'm busy. Mark's busy. But we manage to find time to spend together. Relationships need nurturing if they're going to thrive, Merry."

I shifted uncomfortably and took a sip of my wine. I liked Alan. Alan liked me. So why was I reluctant to commit? I'd been engaged once, and it most definitely had not ended well. It had ended a second time, much worse, last July, when my ex-fiancé had been murdered in my own store while everyone was down at the lakeside park enjoying the Santa Claus boat parade.

"You obviously don't want to talk about it, and that's fine," Vicky said. "I should be off anyway. We've started the Thanksgiving baking, and I'll be dreaming of nothing but apple and pumpkin pie until Thursday."

I was horrified. "Apple and pumpkin? That sounds awful."

She grinned at me. "Apple pies and pumpkin pies. Plus a lesser number of blueberry, some cherry, lots of pecan. And a surprising amount of turkey potpies."

"People eat turkey in a pie for Thanksgiving? Isn't that sacrilege?"

"To you and me perhaps. A lot of my customers want to pretend they've made the entire dinner themselves. If you were inclined to a life of crime you could make a good living taking pictures of people who sneak into the bakery the day before Thanksgiving and blackmailing them."

"I'll keep that in mind if I ever close the shop."

Vicky got to her feet, calling for Sandbanks, and Mattie started awake. I got the leash from the hook by the door, and Mattie and I went downstairs with Vicky and Sandbanks to walk them part of the way home.

As we parted at the street corner, Vicky said, "Take some advice from me, Merry."

"Don't I always?" I said.

"As if. Don't let things with Alan die because another man done you wrong."

"I'm not—"

"Yes, you are. Alan's a good guy. A great guy. Whether you're busy or not, you have to make time for each other. He's worth it. Good night."

I watched Vicky and Sandbanks slip into the shadows between the streetlights. Mattie sniffed the ground beneath a bush.

Vicky was right—she usually was—and I knew it. When I got home, I changed into my flannel pajamas, made a mug of hot chocolate, and curled up on the couch. When I was settled and comfortable, I made a phone call.

"Good evening, Merry," said Alan's voice, as deep and rich as the chocolate in my cup.

"Hi. I hope I'm not calling too late."

"Never too late. I'm still in the workshop."

"I was thinking about you tonight."

"What a coincidence," he said. "I was thinking about you, too."

Chapter 4

"How was dinner at the Yuletide?" I asked my mother the following morning.

"The food was excellent, as it always is, and Mark came out of the kitchen to ask if we'd enjoyed our dinner, which was lovely of him."

"But?"

She sighed. "The mood was tense all evening. Very tense."

"That doesn't sound good."

"It wasn't. Everyone tried to be on their best behavior, but some people can't stop making snide remarks, and some people can't help replying in kind. I suspect, Merry, that I've been looking back at our college years through rose-tinted glasses. The only thing the six of us had in common even then was sharing a dorm and fear of being alone in the big city. We were all in some sort of performing arts program but with different specialties. Constance had plenty of money to spend, and the rest of us didn't, so she used her money to make friends. Genevieve was ruthlessly ambitious, but Barbara didn't take her courses all that seriously. Even then she was a New York City activist. Karla was a corn-fed Minnesota girl, and Ruth came from a hardscrabble Upstate New York family and was at college on scholarship. There's a reason we all haven't been together since those days. I must have forgotten that. I'm being reminded now."

Mattie put his big head in her lap, and she stroked his soft ears automatically.

I gave her a smile. "Only a day and a half left. They're going home tomorrow, right?"

"Sadly, no. They'll be here until Monday lunchtime."

We were in the back room of Mrs. Claus's Treasures. Jackie was watching the storefront, and when Mom came in, I'd been catching up on paperwork during the morning lull. The friends, she told me, were doing their own thing for the remainder of the day. Constance and Genevieve were shopping in town, Barbara had gone for a hike in the woods, Ruth had stayed behind saying she wanted to read, and Karla hadn't emerged from her room since breakfast.

"What's the plan for tonight?" I asked.

"I'm keeping it light, casual, and most of all, cheap, and ordering in Chinese food. Do you want to come?"

"After you made the company sound so appealing? No, thank you. Anyway, I can't. I'm having dinner with Alan." He and I had talked for a long time last night and arranged a date for tonight.

"Come tomorrow then. We're having potluck. It was Ruth's idea, to save me having to cook, she said, but I suspect the real reason is she's afraid someone will suggest we go out to dinner again, and she can't afford it. It's difficult trying to manage activities for friends who are at dramatically different income levels. I remember the time I was performing at the Royal Opera in *La traviata*, or was it *Madama Butterfly*? And one of the women in the chorus . . ."

I knew from years of experience to nip Mom's stroll down memory lane in the bud mighty fast or we'd never get back on topic. "Potluck? Isn't that hard for people from out of town?"

"We'll manage fine. My kitchen is big enough and fully equipped, and I'll make an expedition out of our grocery shopping trip. I have a chicken casserole in the freezer, and the others can make—or buy—whatever they like. The best potlucks, I've found, are always impromptu."

"It might be fun."

"I hope so. We're meeting this afternoon at three to hit the markets in town to do our grocery shopping. Constance wasn't entirely pleased at the idea, but I suggested she buy something ready-made if she'd prefer. Constance wanted to go out to eat again tomorrow, but . . ." Her voice trailed off.

"But?" I prompted.

"I paid for last night's dinner. The entire bill."

"That must have cost a lot."

"It did. Constance and Genevieve have not only heavy hands on the wine bottle but expensive tastes. Don't tell your father. I'll have to sneak that credit card bill around him somehow. I told Grace not to present us with a check and I'd cover it. I felt that I had to do it, to keep peace in the group. Ruth is, I fear, somewhat down on her luck. The Yuletide's expensive, and Constance would have made a big deal of wanting to help Ruth with the cost, and Ruth would have been offended. I don't know if Karla's all that well off, either. I'll order dinner in tonight, and we'll have the potluck tomorrow."

"Good idea."

"You'll come to dinner tomorrow. No excuses. Genevieve made a crack this morning over breakfast when Karla helped herself to a second bagel. Barbara suggested we all go for a hike, and Constance said she wanted to get started on her Christmas shopping. Barbara said she'd heard that some people considered shopping to be a recreational activity, but didn't we all agree that excessive consumerism was destroying the planet."

"Let me guess, Constance didn't suddenly see the light and decide to dedicate herself to a life of poverty and good works."

"No, she did not. The word 'bleeding heart' might have been employed. Karla then started on, once again, about hoping for more grandchildren, and Barbara turned on her to say the earth was overpopulated as it is. Ruth sat at the breakfast table, not even trying to be friendly, with her nose buried in a book. That seems to be the way she shuts out the world. She's going through a binge phase at the moment, she told me, for classic mystery novels."

"Sounds like a good idea to me," I said. "The shutting-out-the-bickering part."

"I made a point of rising early this morning to serve breakfast and otherwise be a good hostess, and I spent most of the time cowering in the kitchen, trying not to listen." Mom gave Mattie a final pat and got to her feet with a sigh. "I have to get home. I have a student coming at twelve thirty. He's new to Rudolph and looks to be promising indeed."

I stood up also and wrapped my mom in a spontaneous hug. "Hang in there," I said.

"I'll try. The strange thing is, I like these women, all of them, individually. And not just in memory of our youth and our college years. Your father and I had a lovely time visiting Constance last summer, she made us so welcome, and I've had lunch with Ruth a few times over the years when we've been in Rochester, or with Barbara or Genevieve in New York. I haven't seen Karla since college though."

"Is Genevieve an actress? Vicky thought she'd seen her in something."

"Ask Vicky to tell her that. She'll be pleased. She studied acting at Steinhardt and went to Los Angeles once she finished college. Her real name is Joanne; she took on something she considered to be more exotic, hoping it would help with her career prospects. She had some small success at first and had hopes of hitting the big time in TV, but that never happened. She came back to New York several years ago to take a role in an afternoon soap, but that ended before long. I don't think she gets much work at all anymore." Mom shook her head. "Not many roles for a woman once she hits forty, never mind fifty. Poor thing. Genevieve and I are the only ones who pursued a career in the arts. The others went in other directions. Barbara switched to law school. Constance and Karla didn't even graduate, and both went back home to pick up the lives they'd left. Six o'clock tomorrow. Don't forget."

"As much as I might want to, I won't."

She gave me a smile and left. Mattie made a performance of settling himself into his bed on the floor with much turning and huffing and puffing before finally flopping down in an inelegant heap. I hadn't said anything to Mom about the possibility of one of her friends having stolen from me and from Vicky's bakery. What would be the point? They'd all be off for home on Monday.

I gave Vicky a call. If I had to go to a potluck at Mom's, I'd drag her along with me. That's what best friends are for. "You're invited out to dinner tomorrow night. Are you free?"

"As it happens," she said, "I am. That'll be nice. Where are we going?"

"My mom's. And it's potluck."

Vicky's groan came down the line. "I hate potlucks. I cook all day. I don't want to have to provide my own food when I go out."

"It's a command performance for me, so I'm commanding you to come along, and you can't now make an excuse to get out of it because I tricked you by asking if you were free first. Can't you bring something from the bakery? One of those turkey potpies?"

"They're supposed to provide me with an income."

"Please?"

"I'll manage something. What are you making?"

I had to be at the shop until closing tomorrow evening, and I'm not much of a cook anyway. "I'll buy the ingredients and put together a salad at Mom's."

"No packaged salad mix or bottled dressing."

"It comes another way?"

"Most amusing. I'll make an extra couple of turkey pies, and I might throw in some mince tarts as well. Not quite Thanksgiving, but we're baking them already."

"Yummy," I said. "Save one for me." Vicky's mince tarts were *the* best.

*   *   *

Sunday morning I opened the shop at the regular time of twelve o'clock. The previous night, Alan and I had gone to A Touch of Holly, the restaurant across the street from Mrs. Claus's, for dinner. We'd had a nice meal and then gone back to my place to get Mattie before enjoying a long walk on the trails lining the lakefront. Winter was coming, and the night was cold, but no snow was in the forecast yet. The skies had been clear, and as we got away from the lamps of town, the stars above appeared in a blaze of light. We'd held hands and walked in silence, watching Mattie checking out the news of the neighborhood as left under bushes and around trees.

It had all been perfect, and I reminded myself that solid, dependable, kind Alan was not Max, my cheating rat of an ex-and-late fiancé.

The first people through the doors today were a middle-aged couple. The woman's mouth was a slash of red lipstick, and her smile was wide and her eyes warm and friendly. She wore a camel trench coat with a thick belt and a double row of dark buttons stamped with the Burberry brand. The man with her reminded me of businessmen I'd sometimes met with in Manhattan, with his thick silver hair, close shave, and manicured hands. His coat was black wool, and I guessed that it had cost in the two-thousand-dollar range.

"You were so right, honey," she said. "This is darling!"

"Welcome." I gave them a smile. "Let me know if I can help you with anything."

"I love your tree," she said. "Is it real?"

"It is, and it's replaced the first of every month all year round by a local tree farmer. Most of the other greenery in this shop isn't real though. If you're looking for flowers or other live decorations, the florist farther west along Jingle Bell Lane carries that sort of thing, and it's all marvelous and fresh."

She clapped her hands together. "I absolutely love those porcelain dolls. I collect Santa dolls."

"Then you've come to the right place," I said, smiling at her enthusiasm.

She wandered through the store, exclaiming over everything she saw. The man held out his hand. "Wayne Fitzroy. You won't stay in business long if you send your customers elsewhere."

I shook the offered hand. "Pleased to meet you, Wayne. I'm Merry Wilkinson. In Rudolph everyone helps everyone else. Better for us, and better for our customers, meaning people come back."

He flashed a mouthful of white teeth. "That's what I like to hear. Norma and I were heading home after church and she had a sudden urge to pop in."

"Home," I said. "Do you live nearby? I'm afraid I don't . . ."

"We're new to town, only been here a couple of months. We left the big city and the rat race searching for the simple life. I think we've found it here, don't you agree, honey?"

"Oh yes," she said.

They might have left the rat race, but judging by their clothes, I didn't think the simple life would suit these two all that well.

"I want to get actively involved in the town," Wayne said. "Give something back to the community that's made us so welcome. You're Noel Wilkinson's daughter, or so I've been told."

"You know my father?"

"I haven't had the pleasure yet, but you can't go far in Rudolph without hearing the Wilkinson name."

"He's in Florida at the moment, getting a fishing trip in before the parade and the start of the Christmas season."

"Ah, yes. Town Santa."

"That's right." My dad, Noel, played Santa at all the official town festivities.

Norma Fitzroy put three porcelain dolls on the sales counter. Santa, Mrs. Claus, and a female elf, all hand-painted and dressed in hand-sewn clothes and accessories. "I'll take these, please," she said.

Wayne pulled out his wallet with a flourish, and I went behind the counter to ring up the purchases and wrap them.

"It was nice meeting you, Merry." Wayne picked up the paper shopping bags.

"Bye." Norma wiggled her fingers as they left.

She seemed genuinely nice, I thought. As for him, he tried too hard. I'd seen enough of that phony charm and pretend friendliness in Manhattan, and I recognized it instantly. But if they were interested in the welfare of Rudolph, they should fit in nicely. Our small town would soon rub away at his big-city edges.

My next customer was Karla, one of Mom's friends.

"Good afternoon." I peeked around her, looking for the others. No one followed her in, so it seemed as though she'd come alone.

"I'm glad I found you here," she said. "I'd like to get a hostess gift for Aline."

"That's nice of you. I'm sure we can find something suitable. My mom's fond of Crystal Wong's jewelry."

"Nothing too, uh, expensive," Karla said. "Just a token."

I led the way to the jewelry display. "Are you having a nice visit?"

"I guess."

Not exactly a ringing endorsement. She picked up a necklace, checked the price tag, and put it back down.

"You're from Minnesota," I said. "I've never been to Minnesota."

"God's county," she said firmly.

"Are you from the East originally? You went to college with Mom."

She laughed without humor. "What can I say? I followed my dream of being a dancer. The dream didn't last, but I was stuck at Steinhardt." She wandered over to check out the holiday linens display.

"I wouldn't say 'stuck.'" For some reason I felt I had to defend my mom's alma mater. "It's a fabulous school. My mother loved her time there."

"She might have," Karla said, "but I hated every minute of it."

I took another look at her. Her face was pale and plump, but bitterness was carved into lines around her mouth and eyes. She picked up a china cup, painted with sprigs of holly and red berries. I edged away, thinking I'd leave her to examine my goods in peace.

She put the cup down and let out a puff of air. "I shouldn't have come. Here I am again. Stuck with that bunch, exactly as I was all those years ago. I never fit in there, you know. Not with them and their dreams of Broadway or Hollywood. Not in my class, either, with all those beautiful willowy girls. Believe it or not, I was thin once. But I was never tall."

She spoke more to herself than to me, but I found myself

asking, "Why did you come for this reunion weekend then?"

"Because Aline invited me, and my daughter said I should go." She shrugged. "And then Constance wrote and told me she was coming, and so I thought I might as well come, too. I was never one of their crowd of artistic divas. Even Barbara, who ended up being a lawyer, could put on the theatrics when she wanted. Maybe that's why she is a lawyer. The rest of them got an apartment together after first year, but I stayed in the dorm. All that *just us girls* stuff and constantly popping in and out of each other's rooms was always too much for me. I only went into the dramatic arts because my high school teacher encouraged me. She was a fool. Let's just say that being the star of dance class in Northfield, Minnesota, doesn't cut it in New York City."

Mentally, I rolled my eyes. I'd known Karla for all of half an hour and so far everything she'd told me about herself was that all she did was what other people had told her to do. "Still," I said, "it's nice to keep up with old friends, isn't it? I'm sure you're having fun now that you're here."

"Fun, yeah. Great fun." Her tone was sharp, her voice bitter. So sharp and bitter, Jackie looked up from where she was arranging a display of wooden toy trains. "Let's see what we've been doing." Karla counted off on her fingers. "Barbara wants to have us all out of bed with the sun. An invigorating hike before breakfast. If I say I don't want to go, she'll eye my hips and suggest that I could use a bit of exercise, and Genevieve will laugh that evil laugh of hers. Constance will drink nonstop and drop names left, right, and center, every chance she gets, making sure we all know that she moves among the rich and famous in L.A. And

Ruth, poor Ruth, with that layabout husband of hers and the four kids and not a penny to her name. All she cares about anymore are her silly mystery novels."

I said nothing. There was nothing I could say, and it didn't matter. All Karla wanted was the chance to pour out her misery.

"At least when Ruth drones on about the full plot of the latest book she's read, she's not complaining about the place where she works. She's a clerk in a grocery store, can you imagine anything more boring?" I couldn't help but see Jackie, standing behind Karla's back, spinning her finger in the air at the side of her head. I could imagine plenty of more boring things (such as listening to Karla), but I didn't say so. "And then there's Constance. Born to money, silver spoon in her mouth. And don't you dare forget it. The only one of them I can stand, ever could stand, was your mother. Aline, genuinely talented and nice."

I nodded in agreement. My mom and I had our differences—didn't all mothers and daughters?—but I loved her a great deal.

"Your father's name is Noel, right?"

"Yes."

"Nothing came of her and Paul, then?"

"I don't know any Paul, so I guess not."

"'Paul the Doll,' we called him. We all had crushes on him, but Aline was over the top about it. I always thought he was just playing with her. Playing with all of us. His adoring little harem. He did okay, I heard. Landed some good parts on Broadway. I guess we all play around when we're first in college, don't we? It's part of being young and innocent."

"Mom loves the whimsical cocktail napkins I have," I

said, desperate to bring an end to this conversation. I pointed to the display rack.

Karla didn't get the hint. "Not that innocence lasts long. Constance was the only one of us who snagged a man at college. She married Frank Westerton, who was as much a flirt as Paul the Doll. He was a real slimeball, that Frank." Karla's face settled into angry lines. "But Constance couldn't see it. As for me, I went back to Minnesota, which I should never have left, and found a great man who'd been there all along. We had our thirty-fifth wedding anniversary last month."

"Congratulations," I said, carefully avoiding looking at Jackie, who was now imitating a constantly moving mouth with the fingers of her right hand.

Karla droned on. "I was telling the women at dinner last night how well our company's doing. Unlike Constance, who inherited everything, Eric and I built our construction business completely from scratch. We didn't need anyone's help."

"Most admirable. If not the napkins, how about—"

"Funny to see how people's lives turn out. I would have said Ruth was the one most likely to succeed. She was an actor, but her eventual ambition was to direct big-budget movies. Instead, she ended up back in her two-bit town with a drunk of a husband. She's a clerk in a store."

"So you said. Perhaps she enjoys it."

Karla's expression indicated what she thought of that idea. "What a waste of a life. My husband, Eric, and I own the biggest construction firm in our part of the state. I work for us as the head bookkeeper and office manager. I dropped out of my junior year in college, I couldn't see any point in staying, and went to business school instead."

Karla's bitterness filled my shop. *Waste of a life*, indeed.

Karla might have been talking about the others, but I got the feeling she was thinking about herself. I edged to the napkin display and selected a set showing a field of pumpkins at sunset. "What about these for your dinner tonight? Sort of an early Thanksgiving theme."

Karla shrugged. "I don't think so. Maybe I'll just get a card or something. Nothing I can afford will be able to match what Constance is probably going to buy your mother."

"The napkins are five ninety-nine. I'll let you have them at cost. It's the thought that counts."

"So they say. I've never believed it. We'll see you at dinner tonight, your mother said."

"Yes. I'm looking forward to it."

"I'm not. Potlucks are such a risk for me, with my peanut allergy."

"Surely you reminded everyone of that."

"I did, several times, but some people can be self-centered and thoughtless, can't they? Luckily none of Eric and my children inherited the allergy. I checked all the shopping bags when we got back from the market yesterday, just to be sure. Barbara's making some sort of bean thing. Sounds absolutely dreadful." The tone of Karla's voice never varied. A constant drone of complaints.

"You don't have to eat it."

"No, I don't," she said. "I might come back later and get something for my grandchildren. No, that won't work. I'd have to pack it, and I only brought carry-on luggage on the plane."

She left the shop. The bells over the door tinkled cheerfully. They were the only cheerful thing in my shop. Karla's bitterness had seeped into the very walls. I started to give my head a shake to get rid of the feeling; instead, I let out a yelp and leapt into the air. Jackie had dropped the train engine. All the cars in the train, from engine to caboose, were linked together by wooden hooks and hoops, and they fell to the floor in a seemingly endless crashing of train cars.

"Sorry," Jackie said. "I was so busy wondering what she'd find to complain about next, I forgot I was holding this."

Slowly, my heart rate returned to normal. At least the train wasn't made of glass like many of our ornaments.

Chapter 5

The day was busy with people getting an early start on their holiday shopping or stocking up for Thanksgiving guests, and I put Mom and her friends out of my mind.

At six o'clock, Jackie bade me a good night. I locked the front door behind her, switched off most of the lights, and went into the back for Mattie and my potluck ingredients. I greeted Mattie, told him he'd been a good boy today, and let us out the back into the alley.

The bakery closes before my shop, so I'd arranged to meet Vicky at Mom's. Mattie was always welcome there, as long as he behaved himself, which he did. Most of the time. My mom had some nice things, collected when she'd traveled the world singing opera, and she would not be happy if anything got broken. My parents live not far from Jingle Bell Lane, so we would walk to their house. We went slowly, as Mattie took his time and sniffed at every lamppost and raised his back leg at many of them. The night was cool, but the temperatures were above freezing, and the walk was comfortable.

My parents still live in the house in which my three siblings and I grew up: a grand old redbrick Victorian with multiple entrances and a steep green roof, built in the mid-nineteenth century when Rudolph was a prosperous Lake Ontario shipping port. It had three stories, a big bay front window, gingerbread trim, dormer windows, and a wide porch stretching across the front of the house and curling around one side. My dad believes in celebrating Christmas all year round, but in one thing only my mom put her foot firmly down at the beginning of their marriage: the decorations, including an impressive display of outdoor lights, don't go up until the Sunday after Thanksgiving. In this they were in the minority in Rudolph. Many if not most of the houses on their street were lit by a variety of outdoor lights, ranging from tasteful white trim to full-on flashing displays of color bright enough to read by.

Mom's perennial gardens were neatly tucked away for the winter. The stately maples and oaks, many of which predated the house, stood bare and stark, and the more delicate of the bushes were wrapped in burlap. The flower beds had been dug up and overturned, a few tall swaying golden grasses left to provide spots of interest.

As I turned into their street, I saw a small dark compact car backing out of my parents' driveway. It reached the road, turned, and accelerated, heading away from me. It rounded the next corner and was gone. One of Mom's or Dad's friends, I assumed, making an impromptu visit and finding out that Dad wasn't home and Mom was entertaining.

I walked up the driveway to the back of the house and

let myself in through the kitchen door. "It's Merry!" I called. The soft murmur of voices came from the front rooms. The oven was on, and the kitchen was warm and full of the smell of roasting meat. Mattie's nose moved as he took in all the marvelous scents. I took a deep breath myself.

The house might be a nineteenth-century original, but the kitchen is thoroughly modern: glass backsplash, ceramic tiled floor, granite countertops, a large wooden island with chrome and leather barstools pulled up to it. I put my salad bowl and ingredients on the island next to an assortment of covered dishes, serving bowls, and bakery boxes, and took Mattie's leash off. "Now, you be good," I said.

He grinned at me before running around the kitchen, nose to the ground. Because of his size—he was tall enough to rest his chin on a table without stretching—teaching him to leave people food alone had been an important part of his training.

I carried the bottle of wine I'd brought and followed the sound of voices, Mattie trotting at my heels. The walnut table that could comfortably seat twelve, which had been in my Dad's family for almost a hundred years, had been set for eight with Mom's best sterling silver cutlery, gold-trimmed china, crystal water and wineglasses, and Thanksgiving-themed place mats and matching cloth napkins. Glass candle holders containing tall white pillars, still unlit, were laid in a long row down the length of the table.

The dining area opens directly onto the living room, and both rooms are decorated with things Mom collected in her travels. Venetian glass art, Wedgwood bowls, Chinese vases, Tanzanian sculptures, Japanese pen-and-ink sketches, English watercolors. The wood fireplace burned cheerfully, dispelling the touch of autumn chill, and more candles had been set on almost every available surface, giving the room a soft warm glow. Leonard Cohen crooned softly from the Bose speakers. I put my wine bottle on the side table that served as a bar.

The women were seated in comfortable chairs, and two bottles of wine—one red and one white—were on the coffee table next to platters of cheese, crackers, and a thinly sliced baguette. Heads turned as I came in, and glasses were raised in greeting. Mom leapt to her feet and gave me a hug. "Thanks for coming, dear," she whispered into my ear. She'd tried to tone her clothes down a bit tonight, I thought. She wore a plain black dress with a wide black belt under a red jacket, and her only jewelry was red glass earrings that caught the candlelight when she moved. I smiled to myself. My mom couldn't be toned down even when she tried.

"My pleasure," I said, returning the hug.

Mattie ran past me into the room, eager to meet the women. I've always maintained you can tell a lot about a person's character by the way they react to animals. Constance smiled; Genevieve sniffed in disapproval; Karla recoiled and said, "Keep him away from the food"; Ruth gave him a brief pat; and Barbara immediately dropped out of her chair to roll on the floor with him. Vicky, seated in the leather wingback chair next to the fireplace that was usually my dad's chair, grinned.

"My goodness," Genevieve said. "Is that a dog?"

Or a pony, I finished silently.

"Or a pony?" she asked.

"This is Matterhorn," Mom said. "We call him Mattie."

"My aunt breeds kennel-show Saint Bernards," Vicky said. "But poor Mattie here was born on the wrong side of the blanket, so Merry took him in."

Constance laughed, and Karla threw her a look.

Vicky snapped her fingers, and Mattie went to her instantly. She gave him an enthusiastic rub around his neck and then said, "Sit," and pointed to the floor next to her chair. He gave her an adoring look and then he politely sat.

"Can I get you a glass of wine, dear?" Mom asked me.

"I can help myself, thanks."

I did so and then settled into an armchair on the other side of the fire from Vicky. Mattie curled up on the floor between us. "Did you all have a nice day?" I asked. I looked around the room, checking each of them out. I doubted any of these women would be brazen enough to wear an item they'd stolen from me in front of me, but you never know; they might not have realized I'd be coming to dinner.

I didn't see a Crystal Wong necklace.

Constance looked very ladies-who-lunch-after-tennis in a Ralph Lauren navy blazer over a blue and white striped T-shirt and white slacks. Small gold hoops were in her ears, a diamond necklace was around her throat, and a thick gold band circled her left wrist. Ruth wore jeans, a V-necked T-shirt, and no jewelry except for her small wedding band and engagement ring. Barbara was in a brown turtleneck sweater and multi-pocketed khaki pants and sneakers. Karla's brown dress was plain and didn't fit her very well. Either she'd put on weight since she'd bought it or it had shrunk in the wash. For a touch of color, she'd wrapped a blue cotton scarf tightly around her neck. Genevieve wore a silver sheath dress that showed every sharp angle and protruding bone in her lean body, with large silver earrings and a matching necklace. The scent of tobacco hung over her like an aura: she must have been smoking only moments before we arrived.

"A very nice day," Barbara said in answer to my question. "I went for a long hike this morning in the woods outside of town. There's nothing like the woods of Upstate New York for getting back to nature. You lot should have come. Although"—she glanced at Karla—"some of you might not have been able to manage. It looks like it's completely flat around here, but that can be deceiving. It turned into quite an energetic hike. Even got my heart rate up."

"Is that all it takes these days," Genevieve said, "to get your heart rate up, Barbara?"

"What's that supposed to mean?"

"I seem to remember you were one for the boys, back in the day."

"What of it? I was young once. So were you, but I've realized it's time to stop pretending I still am."

Genevieve bristled. I was pretty sure she'd had some plastic surgery: her face barely moved. "You were particularly fond, Barbara, as I recall, of the younger ones. One advantage of getting old: these days they're all younger than us."

Constance wiggled her eyebrows in delight at my mom, and Mom pretended not to notice. Vicky caught my eye and made a small round O with her lips.

"We don't need to rehash old stories," Ruth said.

"Why not?" Karla said. "Isn't that why we're here? We don't exactly have anything in common anymore. Not that we ever did. Whatever happened to David anyway, Barbara? Are you still married to him?"

"As you well know, Karla, that ended a long time ago.

David and I divorced amicably, and I'm now happy with Benjamin."

"And how old might Benjamin be?" Karla asked.

"Whoa there," Ruth said. "That's totally uncalled for."

"Don't worry about it, Ruth. I say, good for Barbara." Genevieve leaned back and crossed her legs. She sipped at her wine. "Some of us, at least, can still attract a handsome man. I saw the pictures of your children and grandchildren you were passing around, Karla. An attractive family. I assume they take after their father?"

Constance smirked and leaned over to grab the wine bottle. She poured herself a generous amount. Karla looked confused. She wasn't entirely sure whether or not she'd been insulted.

"Karla married her childhood sweetheart," Mom said to Vicky and me. "Not long after college. I had to wait a few more years until I found the right man."

"You should be glad of that," Constance said. "Otherwise it might be you keeping the books, of all boring things, for a minor construction firm in the boonies of the Midwest instead of being a hugely successful opera star."

My mom had spent her career in the cutthroat environment of world-class opera. She had been a diva, and she sometimes acted like one, but she knew when not to take jealous digs personally and when to let minor rivalries go. Because she'd worked mostly in New York City, where she kept an apartment, and traveled extensively, Eve, Chris, Carole, and I had been raised more by our father than our mother. Dad was a practical, down-to-earth, small-town Upstate New York man—and proud of it. My parents were totally mismatched in almost every way, but not for a minute did I or anyone else doubt their devotion to each other.

"At least I do an honest day's work for a living," Karla snapped. "My husband and I built our company up from nothing. Together we created a business and a loving, thoughtful, close family. I never asked to have everything handed to me on a silver platter."

"I assume you're referring to me, and I'll have you know I've worked hard for what I have," Constance said.

"You mean you used your daddy's money to work hard for you," Ruth said. "Must be nice." She cut off a thick slice of creamy gorgonzola and spread it on a cracker.

Constance's eyes narrowed. "Careful, Ruth, you're turning green. Even greener than usual, I should say."

Genevieve laughed. Ruth popped the cheese into her mouth and chewed with angry bites.

My mom threw me a pleading look. I passed the look on to Vicky. None of us knew what to say to stop what was rapidly turning into a multi-way argument.

"Did I forget to offer you my condolences on the untimely death of your husband, Constance?" Karla said. "Didn't the newspapers say something about suspicious circumstances?"

At last someone had gone too far.

The women gasped. My mother said, "I don't think that's at all appropriate, Karla."

A vein pulsed in Constance's temple. She gripped her wineglass so hard I feared it would shatter. "How dare you. At least I didn't bore my husband to death with my endless complaining."

"Isn't this pleasant?" Vicky said. "When's dinner? I'm starving."

I wondered if these women had always hated one another and they'd forgotten that as the years passed.

I glanced at my mother. Her color was high and she shifted uncomfortably in her chair. "Let's not rehash old grievances," she said. "We've been friends for a long time, and we've all lived good lives since." She lifted her wineglass. "Let's have a toast to the next forty years."

"Easy for you to say, Aline," Genevieve said. "You did okay in your career before you quit to bury yourself in this backwater of a town."

"Hey!" I said. That dig was as sharp and vicious as Genevieve's long red nails.

Mom lifted her left hand. The diamond on her finger flashed. "I took advantage of an opportune time to retire from performing, yes. I'll admit that I had some luck in my career, also in my choice of life partner and in our children." She smiled at me. "But far from being retired, I teach singing, trying to pass on some of what I learned to another generation."

"Your luck," Genevieve said, "as you call it, was having a voice suitable for an art form that doesn't care how, pardon me, hefty or old a female performer might be."

Mom sucked in a breath. My mother wasn't fashionably thin, that's true, but she didn't fit the cartoon image of an opera diva, either.

Vicky put her wineglass on the table with a loud thud. "That's mighty rude. What's the matter with you people? Aline's invited you into her home for a nice weekend and a chance to get to know each other again, and all you can do is snipe at each other."

"I haven't been sniping," Karla said.

"You haven't stopped," Vicky said. "I'm going home." She stood up. Mattie leapt to his feet. "Thanks for the invitation, Aline, but it's late and I have to work tomorrow."

"Please don't hurry off," Mom said. "Dinner should be ready by now."

I gave Vicky what I hoped was an unobtrusive signal. If I had to suffer through this, the least she could do would be to keep me company. She grimaced but made no further move toward the door.

"Vicky's right," Ruth said. "Let's forget our grievances and have a nice, pleasant evening."

"Easier for some to forget than others," Karla said.

"What does that mean?" Ruth asked.

"For some of us, the past isn't past and we can never forget things that have happened."

"Be that as it may," Mom said, rising to her feet. "I can foretell the future, and I see dinner. Come along, everyone."

The women stood and picked up their glasses. Constance snatched the bottle of white wine and carried it to the table, and Karla brought the cheese plate. Mattie hurried to be first into the dining room.

Mom and I stood back, and Vicky joined us. "Your friends aren't nice," Vicky said softly.

Mom shrugged. "I must have forgotten that." The smile she gave me was tinged with sadness. "Perhaps I didn't forget entirely, which is why I invited you to help smooth the waters. I'm glad you brought Vicky. Please stay for dinner, dear."

"Good food, plenty of wine, conversation as sharp as you'd find in a Broadway play. What's not to like?" Vicky said.

"You have a seat, Mom," I said, "Vicky and I will serve the food."

Mattie knew better than to beg for scraps at the table, but he made sure to curl unobtrusively underneath, just in case something tasty dropped to the floor.

Vicky and I went into the kitchen. She took oven mitts down from the hook and opened the oven door. We were enveloped in a wave of heat, and she pulled out a meat pie, fragrant and steaming, juices bubbling. "Did you make that?" I asked. "Smells wonderful."

"No, I didn't. We were so busy today, I had nothing left over. I brought the bread and the cheese tray we had for appetizers. And some mince tarts for dessert." She next took a covered casserole dish out of the oven. "I assume we're having this, too."

I peeked into the white bakery boxes. One held eight of Vicky's mince tarts and the other a big round chocolate cake. I opened the bag of salad ingredients that would be my contribution to the feast, dumped them into a bowl I found in the cupboard, and tossed all the ingredients together with packaged dressing, under Vicky's disapproving eye. Before I bought it, I'd read the ingredients list on the bottle of dressing carefully to ensure it didn't contain peanuts. Salad made, I helped Vicky carry bowls and casserole dishes into the dining room, and we piled the table high. As well as the meat pie, fragrant with steam, there were several salads, a couple of hot casseroles, and rolls and butter.

That done, I found a seat between Barbara and Ruth. Karla was on the opposite side of me, between Genevieve and Constance. Mom sat at the head of the table, and Vicky took the foot.

The candles on the table had been lit and the overhead light dimmed. The crystal and silverware sparkled, and the women were smiling.

"Everything looks marvelous," I said. "And smells even better. What did everyone make?"

"Cooking in someone else's kitchen's always a challenge," Ruth said. "But I enjoyed it. The duchess potatoes are mine."

"Quinoa and black beans from me," Barbara said. "That's my specialty. It's best served at room temperature. I often make it on backcountry hiking trips because the ingredients are dry and easy to carry."

"I'm sure it tastes like it, too," Karla said.

"You are welcome not to have any," Barbara said.

It was a good thing my father wasn't here this weekend. He would have thrown more than one of these women out of the house long before now.

We began passing bowls and platters around.

"I made the kale salad," Genevieve said. "It would have been a lot better with arugula, but we were too late to the market to get any, so I had to compromise."

"The chicken casserole is mine," Mom said. The bowl was passed to me, and I gave myself a generous helping, thinking maybe this dinner wouldn't turn out to be so bad after all. I love my mom's chicken casserole, made with mushrooms and tomatoes and a generous slug of good red wine.

"I made the steak-and-mushroom pie," Karla said. "It's always been my husband's favorite, and we have it a lot at home. If there's one thing I've learned over the years, it's the importance of keeping your man happy through his stomach."

If that was intended to be a dig at the salad-making women, Vicky destroyed the moment by laughing. "My boyfriend's a chef. He makes himself very happy through his stomach."

"I'll confess that I used premade pastry," Karla said. "It's not quite the same, is it?"

"It smells fabulous." Vicky cut herself a big wedge.

"I'm not much of a cook," Constance said. "So I cheated and went to Vicky's bakery and got a cake for dessert."

When we'd all been served, Mom tapped her fork against her glass. "A toast," she said.

The women lifted their glasses.

"To old friends," Mom said. "Like all people, we occasionally have our differences, but our memories of our past binds us in friendship."

"Hear! Hear!" Ruth said.

"To old friends," the others chorused.

"I prefer to say 'friends of long acquaintance,'" Barbara said, and several of the women laughed.

Formalities over, we dove into the meal. Even Genevieve served herself healthy portions, although her plate was heavy on the salads.

"Your mother tells me you aren't married yet, Merry," Karla asked. "Any prospects on that front?"

That was a startlingly personal question. I glanced up in time to see Vicky stuffing a bread roll into her mouth in an attempt not to break out laughing. "Maybe. Maybe not," I said. "Early days yet."

"You're still young," Karla said. "Plenty of time left."

I didn't bother to reply that I wasn't all that young and time was rapidly passing. I helped myself to a generous serving of curried egg salad.

"Although, I must say, grandchildren are life's greatest pleasure." Karla looked around the table, almost, I thought, daring some of the other women to disagree. "Far more than any successful career."

But the good food must have been making them all mellow, and no one rose to the bait. Genevieve mentioned that she'd had an audition for a new Netflix production and she was confident of getting the role. Mom wished her well.

Ruth asked Vicky what it was like to own a busy bakery, and Constance told me she and her son were going to Paris for the holidays this year. She began telling us how beautiful Paris was at Christmas.

"Must be nice," Karla muttered under her breath.

"Does your family spend Christmas with you?" I asked her. The bowl of curried egg salad sat in the middle of the table, between me and Karla. It was absolutely delicious. I reminded myself there were mince tarts and chocolate cake for dessert, but then helped myself to another serving of the eggs anyway. I passed Karla the spoon, and she also took another helping.

"They're so busy with their own lives," she said. "That's life these days, isn't it? My son's working up until Christmas Eve, and he doesn't want to have to drive to our place at night, particularly if it snows, not with those precious children in the car. My daughter will be spending the holidays with her in-laws this year." She ate rapidly, with short angry bites, barely taking time to swallow. "I'll miss the grandchildren, but there's something to be said for a peaceful, relaxing Christmas once in a while, isn't there? Eric and I will enjoy a nice quiet celebration on our own this year."

Her eyes slid to one side and she patted her hair. She was lying, more to herself, I thought, than to us. A quiet Christmas could be very nice indeed, but only if that's what you wanted. "Children these days can't find a minute to visit their parents." She looked at the woman seated next to her. "You're lucky, Constance, that your son's willing to give up his own plans to spend the holidays with you."

"Oh yes." Constance smiled around her wineglass.

"We're very close. Then again, I worked hard at being a good mother to him."

Karla let out a small moan, and I turned slightly to face Barbara, not wanting to hear Karla's retort. "I lived in Manhattan for a number of years," I said.

Karla coughed.

"It's not for everyone," Barbara said, "but for those who want to be where the action is, nothing beats it."

"That's what I found. I loved my time there, but I knew when it was time to come back to Rudolph."

"Are you okay, Karla?" Ruth asked.

"I . . . I . . ."

I turned to see Karla clutching her throat. Her eyes were wide and frightened, her face red. Chairs were shoved back as the women jumped to their feet.

"Get her a glass of water," someone yelled.

Mom pounded Karla's back as she gasped for air.

"That won't help," Ruth said. "She has severe allergies. She's having a reaction. Did someone put peanuts in their dish?"

"No!" the women said.

Vicky pulled her phone out of her skirt pocket, pushed buttons, and asked for an ambulance. Mattie leapt to his feet and let out a single bark.

"Does she keep an EpiPen?" I shouted. "Does anyone know?"

"She never said," Ruth said.

I ran around the table and crouched in front of Karla. "Can you hear me, Karla? Do you have an EpiPen?" Her eyes were wide with fear, and she gripped her throat as though she were trying to force air into it. She didn't reply.

I patted Karla's hips, hoping to find the medicine in her

pockets, but my fingers felt nothing bulkier than a tissue. "It's not here."

"She's in Merry's old room," Mom said. "First bedroom on the right."

"I'll get it." Barbara ran for the stairs.

Mom blew out the candles and turned up the lights.

"Stay with us, Karla," I said. "Help's coming."

Vicky shouted into the phone, "Tell them to hurry."

Ruth fell to her knees beside me. "Karla! Karla!"

I got to my feet to give her space, feeling totally helpless. I glanced at the women in the room. Some of them were weeping; they all appeared to be in shock. Constance held Karla's hand, and Ruth rubbed her back. Genevieve had gone to stand at the window, where she stared out into the night, her back rigid.

I had no doubt Karla was suffering an anaphylactic shock, and that it had to have been caused by something she ate.

Everyone here knew Karla was severely allergic to peanuts. Could one of them possibly have been so careless as to forget?

Barbara ran into the dining room. "I can't find it! I looked in her purse, in her toiletries bag, under the clothes in the drawer. Nothing."

"She must have one," Mom said. "She knows how allergic she is. Did any of you see it?"

Heads shook and voices said, "No."

"Where is that ambulance?" Barbara shouted.

"It's delayed," Vicky said in a low voice. "Accident on the highway outside of town."

"Did you tell them it's an emergency?"

"Of course I did. She says at least ten to fifteen minutes."

"She might not have that long," Mom said. "I'm going to keep looking for that EpiPen. It has to be in her room somewhere."

"I'll help." Genevieve turned away from the window and followed Mom upstairs.

Curious as to what was going on, Mattie was trying to force his big body between Karla and Ruth. Ruth pushed him away roughly. I grabbed his collar and pulled him into the kitchen. I shouted, "Stay!" and shut the door on him.

Ruth and Constance crouched beside Karla, murmuring to her to hold on, help was on the way.

"Is there anything we can do while we're waiting?" Vicky asked into the phone. She listened to the answer, caught my eye, and shook her head. "Great, thanks." She spoke to the room. "The ambulance is clear of the accident scene and on its way."

"Thank heavens," Ruth said.

I glanced at Karla's place at the table. The remains of her meal showed traces of everything. Like the rest of us, she'd dug in with gusto and had taken a portion of each dish. Meat pie, chicken casserole, potatoes, quinoa and beans, curried egg salad, bread and cheese, kale salad, my green salad. Before serving ourselves, each of the women had proudly told us what they'd made or bought.

I looked at the food again. No one had laid claim to the curried egg salad. It was light brown in color, strongly flavored with curry powder and what I suspected was a touch of mango chutney.

Was it possible the dish contained peanuts ground so finely they could be concealed in the spices? And were the spices so overpowering that Karla would keep eating?

Karla let out one long gasp and fell off her chair.

Constance screamed, and Ruth burst into tears. Barbara moaned.

I whispered to Vicky, frozen in shock, still clutching her phone, "Tell the dispatcher to send the police as well."

Chapter 6

Detective Diane Simmonds of the Rudolph police department and I are well acquainted because of my job and hers—she shops at Mrs. Claus's, and I've been involved in murder cases before.

I had no doubt this was an attempted murder. It might have been an accident—someone playing a mean joke—but that didn't matter. Not if the end result put a woman's life in danger.

Karla had not recovered consciousness. The ambulance arrived first, closely followed by two uniformed officers in a patrol car. We seven women stood against the walls, watching the paramedics work. The faces of the others reflected varying degrees of shock, and I'm sure mine did also. A wineglass had tipped over, and red wine was leaking into the heritage walnut table. Mom made no move to wipe it up, so I picked up a discarded napkin and did so. The napkin could be thrown away—the table couldn't. The serving dishes were mostly empty, and the plates almost scraped clean. Napkins and cutlery had been tossed in a jumble on the table.

The paramedics administered the contents of an EpiPen into Karla's limp arm. One of them said, "This needs to be a fast trip," and they quickly and efficiently loaded her onto their stretcher. A uniformed officer said, "I'll come with you. Officer Reynolds, you stay here."

"I'm coming, too," Mom said. "She's my houseguest. Merry, make sure the police have everything they need. Perhaps everyone would like coffee or tea."

"I think we should stay out of the kitchen," I said.

"Why?" Ruth asked.

I didn't answer. "You go, Mom. I'll stay here until you get back."

She grabbed her coat out of the closet as she hurried away. I went to the front window and looked out. Two patrol cars were there now, and blue and red lights washed the bare trees in our yard. A few lamps came on in the houses on the street, and heads popped out of doors. The ambulance sped past, siren breaking the quiet of the night. As I watched, a BMW pulled up to the curb and Detective Diane Simmonds got out. Officer Candice Campbell, whom I knew from high school, was standing on the sidewalk. She spoke to Simmonds briefly and then they marched up the sidewalk side by side.

Candy lifted her hand to knock, but I opened the door before her hand could fall, and the two police officers came into the house.

"Merry," Simmonds said. "What's happening here?"

She wore no uniform, badge, or other insignia, but despite the mop of curly red hair, wide green eyes, and trim figure, no one could be of any doubt that Diane Simmonds was now in charge here. She wore a black leather jacket, cropped at the waist, and slim jeans tucked into knee-high leather boots with two-inch heels.

Six faces had turned to watch her come in. She studied everyone in turn. Barbara, Ruth, and Constance had dropped into chairs at the dining room table. Genevieve paced up and down across the living room floor. Vicky stood beside me.

The uniformed officer who'd been the first to arrive, so young I wondered if he was shaving yet, had been shifting uncomfortably from one foot to the other, and now appeared relieved to have someone in authority take over.

"My mother has weekend guests," I said. "Old college friends. She—Karla—had an allergic reaction to something in the food. She collapsed, and we called 911."

"I'm sure she's going to be all right," Genevieve said. "They'll treat her at the hospital, right?"

Barbara and Ruth nodded in agreement.

I lowered my voice so only Detective Simmonds could hear. "I don't think this was an accident or carelessness."

She studied my face. "Is that so? I'll talk to you first. Was the meal prepared here or brought in?"

"Here."

"Let's go into the kitchen."

We walked through the living room and into the dining room. As we passed the table, Constance reached for the cheese knife.

"Don't touch anything," Simmonds snapped. Constance's hand leapt back as though she'd touched an open flame. "Officer Campbell, please keep these women company until I get back. No one is to disturb a thing. Officer

Reynolds, we seem to be attracting a crowd. Please go outside and tell folks to mind their own business."

"Karla had an allergic reaction," Ruth said. "That's all. She'll be okay once they get her to the hospital."

"Until I have determined that," Simmonds said, "you will do as I said."

"I'd like to go upstairs and lie down," Genevieve said.

"May I ask your name?"

"Genevieve Richmond."

"Please wait here, Ms. Richmond." Simmonds's voice was low, her tone polite, but there could be no doubt that it was not a suggestion.

Barbara stood up. She was about my height, considerably shorter than Simmonds, but she did her best to stretch an inch or two. She put her hands on her hips. "And you are?" she asked.

"Detective Diane Simmonds. Rudolph PD."

"I'm Barbara Shaughnessy, and you can't detain us. We're guests here, in this house. We'll keep ourselves available for when we're needed, but in the meantime, I would also like to go to my room."

"Do you really want to get into a fight with me?" Simmonds asked. "Or do you want me to find out, as quickly and easily as possible, what happened to your friend?"

"I'm not talking about fighting," Barbara said. "Simply making sure we all know our rights."

"You do that, Counselor." Simmonds turned and continued on her way.

"How do you know Barbara's a lawyer?" I asked as I followed her into the kitchen.

"I can smell them a mile off," she growled.

I'd temporarily forgotten about Mattie. He must have

been highly agitated or at least very curious when the new arrivals began streaming through the front door, but he'd settled back down to enjoy a snooze on the warm floor beside the oven. He leapt to his feet the moment the kitchen door opened. He took one look at Diane Simmonds and dropped into a sit. If he could have grinned from ear to ear, he would have—instead, his big wet tongue lolled to one side.

"Matterhorn," she said. "Nice to see you." She walked over to him and held out a hand. He lifted his paw, and they shook.

Simmonds had told me her parents trained animals for TV and movies. She'd obviously learned a lot from them. She and Mattie seemed to have an almost mental bond. Sometimes I felt a twinge of unreasonable jealousy. All she had to do was cock an eyebrow and my dog immediately fell into sync with whatever she wanted.

She let go of his paw and glanced around the kitchen, taking in the empty pots, the chocolate cake and mince tarts sitting in the center of the island, waiting to be served. "If you think the food had been tampered with, Merry . . . And if the food was prepared in here . . ."

"I'll take Mattie outside," I said. If something had been in the food, the police would want to examine everything in the kitchen, and they didn't need the assistance of a slobbering, excessively friendly, eager-to-help Saint Bernard. "I can put him in the garage."

"I'll wait here."

I went to the back door and slapped my thigh. "Come on, boy. Let's go. Outside. Come on, Mattie. Mattie! I said, come here."

Simmonds was studying the contents of the trash bin under the sink. She didn't so much as turn around or raise her voice as she said, "Matterhorn, you will do what Merry tells you."

He jumped to his feet and ran toward me. He dashed past me, and then turned to look back over his shoulder as if saying, *What's taking you so long?*

I followed him outside. I pulled up one of the rolling doors of the converted carriage house that served as the garage. Mom had driven Dad to the airport for his flight to Fort Lauderdale, so both their cars were in the garage. The rest of the space was taken by the lawnmower, garden equipment, bags of mulch and potting soil, Eve's and Chris's hockey equipment, Carole's and my skates, boxes of Christmas decorations awaiting the official start of the season, a couple of broken lamps that for some reason had never been thrown away, the trash bins, and neatly stacked logs waiting their turn in the fireplace. All of which meant there wasn't much room left for a giant dog.

"Sorry about this," I said. "I'll try not to be too long." Fortunately, the night wasn't too cold, and he was a Saint Bernard, after all, bred to the icy mountain passes of Switzerland.

I tried to ignore his look of pained disappointment when he realized the garage door was shutting, leaving him alone inside, and went back into the house.

Chapter 7

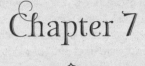

While I'd been seeing to Mattie, Simmonds had pulled on a pair of blue latex gloves, and she was sorting through my mom's trash. She straightened as I came in. "I want to talk to everyone who was here, but first, tell me why you think someone poisoned that woman deliberately. What's her name?"

"Karla. I don't know her last name, but the others will. She's from Minnesota, here for the weekend. She's highly allergic to peanuts, and that was no secret. She told everyone, several times. She told me she went through the shopping bags to make sure no one had forgotten."

"Accidents happen," Simmonds said.

"So they do. All I'm saying is I have my suspicions. You might want to examine the curried egg salad in particular. This was a potluck dinner, and everyone contributed something, even Vicky and me. At the beginning of the meal, we went around the table and each of the guests told us what she'd made or bought."

"Everything was prepared here? In this kitchen?"

"The guests are all from out of town, and they're staying here, so if they cooked, they did it here. Vicky brought the cheese and bread from her bakery as well as the mince tarts. The chocolate cake came from the bakery also, but no one ate the desserts yet, as you can see. I bought the salad ingredients at the supermarket and tossed it with the dressing, also store-bought, after I got here. But no one, I realized later, laid claim to the curried egg salad. It was delicious, so there should have been no reason the cook wouldn't tell us she'd made it."

"This dish was strongly seasoned?"

"Very strongly. Curry, mango chutney, maybe some paprika sprinkled on the top for extra color."

"Did you recognize the bowl in which it was served?"

"Yes, it's one of Mom's, as were all the other serving dishes." I felt a small shudder and glanced around me. We were in Mom and Dad's kitchen, the warm friendly place in which my three siblings and I had laughed and fought and grown up as good food was prepared and enjoyed. I shook my head, chasing the feeling of menace away.

Simmonds, of course, noticed. "Are you okay, Merry?"

"I'm fine. Terrible thing to have happen here. If it did happen, and I'm not simply imagining things."

"I don't think you are," she said. "You have good instincts. Did you see people preparing their contributions or adding the finishing touches?"

I shook my head. "No. It was ready when I arrived, and everyone had gathered in the living room. I was the last one here. We had cheese and bread and crackers in the living room for appetizers, and when the guests took seats at the table, Vicky and I volunteered to serve. Everything was ready to be brought out: either resting on the island or keeping warm in the oven. All we did was carry the bowls and dishes out."

"Anything else I should know?" she asked.

"After Karla collapsed, we tried to find her EpiPen. Her room and her purse were searched, but it couldn't be found. Karla must carry one, being as allergic as she is."

"That is interesting. Thank you, Merry. Let me talk to the women, see what they have to say. I'll save you for last."

"Okay."

My phone rang. At the same time Simmonds reached into her pocket and pulled her own out. We threw each other a glance before answering.

I turned away. "Mom? What's happening?"

A sob came down the line. My mother cleared her throat. "I'm sorry, dear. Karla has died."

"Oh my gosh, Mom. I am so sorry."

"Where are you, dear?"

"I'm still here. At the house. I'll stay until you get back. Do you want me to call Dad?"

"I'll do that. I have the number for Karla's house, so I'll call her husband also." She hung up.

Simmonds's face was grim. "That was the officer who went to the hospital with the ambulance. In light of what you told me, this is now a potential murder investigation." She punched buttons on her phone. "I'm calling in a forensic team."

She made the call, and then we went to join the others. The women had taken seats in the living room, under the stern and watchful eye of Officer Candice Campbell. They weren't talking, and they sat a bit straighter as we came in. Their faces were either pale or tear streaked, all of them questioning and expectant. I glanced at Vicky, and gave her a slight shake of my head. She nodded in acknowledgment.

"I'm sorry to have to tell you this," Simmonds said. "I received a call from the hospital. Karla died shortly after arrival."

Ruth's face turned even paler. Barbara gasped. Constance said, "That's not possible. We were having dinner less than half an hour ago." Genevieve began to cry.

"What was your friend's surname?" Simmonds asked.

"Vaughan," Constance said. "She was Karla Hennery in college, and she took her husband's name when they got married."

"Where does Mrs. Vaughan live?"

"Northfield, Minnesota," Barbara answered. "We're all from out of town. We're friends of Aline, here for the weekend."

Ruth stood up. "I'm going to get a glass of water. Would anyone else like one?"

"Sit down, please," Simmonds said. "That won't be possible at the moment. I'm ordering the kitchen to be sealed. A crime scene team is on the way."

Ruth dropped into her chair with a thud.

"Isn't that going a bit too far?" Barbara said. "It was an accident. It had to be. Karla was allergic to peanuts, we all knew that. I can assure you, none of us used peanuts in our cooking."

The other women muttered their agreement.

Constance lifted her hand and pointed one well-manicured finger directly at Vicky. "The peanuts must have been in something from her bakery. She said she didn't use peanuts, but how do we know that's true?"

"Hey!" Vicky said. "It's true because I said it's true. I run a respectable business. I don't lie about things like that."

"That's irrelevant," I said. "Constance, you said you bought the dessert at Vicky's, but the cake hasn't been touched yet."

"No, but she brought the cheese and crackers. Maybe something was in that."

"I do not—" Vicky began.

Simmonds held up a hand. "We will be analyzing all the food served here tonight and come to our own conclusions."

"No one would want to murder Karla," Ruth said. "The very idea's preposterous. I bet she ate something earlier that had peanuts in it. We weren't together all day."

"An attack like that comes on almost instantly," Constance said. "My son has a severe peanut allergy, too. I know all the signs."

"Did any of you notice Mrs. Vaughan behaving strangely before dinner?" Simmonds asked. "As if she was feeling unwell?"

We shook our heads.

"Nothing was wrong with her appetite," Genevieve said. "She ate most of that cheese platter single-handedly. 'Self-control' was not a word in Karla's vocabulary."

"Says the woman with one eye on the wine bottle all night," Barbara said.

Genevieve threw Barbara a vicious glare, but wisely she said no more.

Constance's face was streaked with tears, and she spoke sharply. "That's enough, ladies. Have some respect. Pay us no mind, Detective. We're simply devastated at what's happened. Genevieve's upset. She doesn't intend to sound mean. Karla simply . . . enjoyed life." She wept into a tattered tissue.

"I'd like to speak to each of you privately," Simmonds said. "Merry, do you have a room we can use?"

"Dad's study. Down the hall, on the left."

"Sounds like we're in a mystery novel," Ruth said. "But one I'm very sorry to be involved in. I'll help every way I can, Detective. But first, can I call my husband and ask him to come and pick me up?"

"I drove here." Barbara stood up. "I'm leaving tonight. Right now. If you still want to talk to me, you can call my office in the morning."

"I came on the train," Genevieve said. "And then a bus from Rochester. I'll never get home tonight. Can I have a lift with you, Barbara?"

"I hope none of you are deliberately misunderstanding me," Simmonds said. "I'm not asking anyone's permission. I will talk to you now, in turn, and then you can go to your rooms. None of you are to leave the town of Rudolph until I say you can. Do you understand?" She looked at each of the women, one after the other.

"You don't think this was an accident, do you?" Ruth said.

"I will not be jumping to any conclusions."

"That's ludicrous," Genevieve said. "Who on earth would want to kill Karla? Other than her husband, I mean. He might have wanted to kill her to stop her constant whining."

"I don't think that's at all funny," Barbara said.

Genevieve had the grace to duck her head.

"Tomorrow I'd like you all to come into the police station to be fingerprinted," Simmonds said.

Genevieve's head popped back up. "That's ridiculous," she said. "I have no intention of being treated like a common criminal."

"She needs them for elimination purposes," Ruth said. "You want to be eliminated, don't you?"

Genevieve sputtered.

"I could raise a legal challenge," Barbara said.

"You may," Simmonds replied. "If you want to delay finding out what happened to your friend."

"But," Barbara said, "in this case I won't."

"I'll speak to you first," Simmonds said. "Where do you practice law?"

"I'm a senior partner at Shaughnessy and Ferguson in New York City."

Simmonds gave Officer Campbell a nod, telling her to come with them. In turn, Candy glared at me, as though she expected me to run off into the night. I smiled at her sweetly. We had not been friends in high school. Nothing had changed on that front.

"You know where I live, Detective," Vicky said. "You also know I start work early. Can I go home now and give my statement in the morning?"

"No," Simmonds said. "I'll talk to you in turn. I don't want you all discussing what went on here while I'm not in the room. Can I trust you to do that?"

No one answered.

At that moment lights washed the front windows as a cruiser pulled up, followed by a white van. My mom got out of the police car. She walked up the path between Officer Reynolds and a short, overweight man in civilian clothes. As nothing exciting seemed to be happening, most of the neighbors had gone back to their houses and their beds.

I hurried to get the door. Mom's face was pale, her nose and eyes red. Most of her eye makeup had been rubbed off, leaving dark streaks behind. I wrapped her in my arms. "Did you get Dad?"

"He's trying to arrange a flight home. No one answered at Karla's house, so I left a message saying it was urgent. I didn't say why."

"Start in the dining room and then the kitchen," Simmonds said to the man who'd come in with Mom. "This was a dinner party, and I want all the cooked and prepared food analyzed."

"You got it, Detective," he said.

Simmonds then turned to Reynolds. "Stay here. I don't want any of these women talking about what went on tonight before I can interview them."

He grunted in acknowledgment and then he took a position in the center of the room, feet apart, arms crossed, scowl on his face. He was very young and looked, I thought, perfectly foolish, like he was playing the part of the village constable in a high school production of an Agatha Christie play.

I took a seat on the couch next to Vicky. Mom dropped beside me, and I put my arm around her. We sat in silence. It seemed as if the women had run out of things to say, or maybe shock was beginning to settle in.

Barbara and Candy were soon back. "Can I go upstairs now?" Barbara asked.

"The detective says you can each return to your room after she's spoken to you," Candy said. "But you have to stay out of the kitchen and the dining room. Vicky Casey, you're next."

Candy glared at me as though I'd done something more threatening than sit on the couch next to my mom. I gave the officer of the law a cheerful smile, and she turned so abruptly she was in danger of whiplash.

Vicky stood up and followed her to Dad's study.

Eventually, only Mom and I were left in the living room, but we remained sitting close together on the couch. Vicky had gone home, after giving us big hugs, and one by one the other women headed upstairs after their interviews. We listened to footsteps on the stairs, water running, and floorboards creaking. In the kitchen, cupboard doors slammed and people spoke to one another. The food from the potluck, dishes and all, along with serving platters and pots and pans, were dumped into bags, labeled, and carried away.

Simmonds dropped onto a damask-covered wingback chair next to the fireplace that now contained nothing but dying red embers. "Mrs. Wilkinson, Aline. Tell me what you know about the dead woman, Karla Vaughan."

Mom shook her head. "I hardly know what to say, Diane. I haven't seen her in almost forty years. We all roomed together our first year in college; we've kept in touch since, and I thought a reunion would be a great idea. Obviously, I was wrong." She took a deep breath, and I gave her hand a squeeze. "I was about to say they've changed so much, but now I realize they're exactly as they were then. Some of their bad points have only consolidated, strengthened over the years. We weren't getting on, Diane, not at all, and I was desperate for this weekend to end. But I didn't think anyone was angry enough at anyone to kill her. Surely you're wrong about that."

Simmonds said, "I won't know what was in the food until an analysis is done, but the missing EpiPen bothers me. It bothers me a lot."

"Maybe she misplaced it," Mom said. "Or she didn't bring one on this trip."

"Perhaps. I've had her room searched. No sign of it. All the other women say they didn't see one. Did you? Did she tell you she had one?"

Mom shook her head. "No."

"So it is possible she didn't bring one," Simmonds said, as much to herself as to us. "Or she lost it. Did she seem scatterbrained, forgetful to you?"

"No," Mom said.

"Even if she was," I said, "that's not something someone with such a serious allergy would forget."

"In what order did the women come downstairs tonight?" Simmonds asked. "Merry tells me she was last to arrive."

Mom closed her eyes and thought. "Karla was first down. We talked for several minutes. She talked, mostly, about how well her husband's construction company is doing. The doorbell rang, and I answered it. It was Vicky Casey, and she and I went into the kitchen to get a serving platter for her bread and cheese. We chatted for a few minutes, I asked her for news of her family, and when we came out, all the women had gathered in the living room."

Which meant, I thought, any one of them could have gone into Karla's room to steal her EpiPen before dinner.

It was possible she didn't carry one, but I didn't think that likely. Her allergy was, as it should be, at the top of her mind at all times.

"Was someone in the house all day?" Simmonds asked.

"The guests were in and out most of the day," Mom said. "Going for a walk, into town shopping. I can't account for their movements. I myself went for a walk before dinner, wanting to have some alone time. Things around here have been, I'll admit, a bit tense. Too many guests."

"Did you lock the house when you left?"

"No, I didn't. I don't usually, not during the day, and I don't have enough keys to give one to each of the women. You don't think someone came in, do you? Someone who shouldn't have been in my house?" Mom's eyes darted to the corners.

"I don't think anything," Simmonds said. "At this time, all I'm doing is asking questions. Merry, what was your impression of Karla?"

"She was sad," I said. "Bitter at life."

"Is that so? The other women said she was happily married, a loving mother and grandmother, who enjoyed the work she did for her husband's prosperous construction firm."

"Maybe she opened up to me more," I said. "She didn't know me, so she had nothing to prove. That's my impression of her anyway. I might be wrong."

"You say you haven't seen her in forty years?" Simmonds asked Mom. She kept her tone light, chatty, but my senses pricked up. "Yet you invited her to stay in your home?"

"I hadn't seen her since our college years, that's true, but we'd kept in touch. The entire group has. Letters at first, as well as Christmas cards, birth and wedding announcements, then e-mails."

"You've never been to her home, or she to yours, in all that time?"

Mom shook her head. "She lives in Minnesota, and I've never had cause to go there."

"Visiting your old college friend wasn't cause enough?"

Simmonds, I knew, was subtly digging for a reason Mom might want to kill Karla.

"What can I say," Mom said. "Life takes over. We have our families, our careers, time passes so fast. Perhaps that's why I wanted us to get together this weekend. A way of slowing time down, if only for a few days."

The detective's eyes flicked toward me before settling on Mom once again. I breathed. If that had been a test, Mom had passed. "What about the others? Have they visited Karla since college, or she, them?"

"I don't know for sure, but I don't remember anyone saying anything to that effect. Of course, they might not have told the rest of us about it. If that happened."

"Merry," Simmonds asked. "What do you mean they weren't getting on?"

"They bickered," I said. "All of them, all the time. I can hardly sort out who was fighting with whom. Except for Mom, she tried to make nice, but they didn't seem to be able to help themselves."

"Bickered about what?" Simmonds asked.

"Everything," Mom said. "Status, money, family. Even looks. Karla was overweight, and Genevieve kept making digs at her. She couldn't even stop after the woman had died, for heaven's sake. I suspect Genevieve has her own issues with food, and she took those out on Karla. Ruth doesn't have much money, and Constance kept offering to pay for things, but she didn't do it in a nice way."

"What does that mean?" Simmonds asked.

"Constance was showing off, using the offer of money to put Ruth down, not being generous or thoughtful. As I recall, she did that in college, too."

"Anything else that caused tension in the group?"

"Karla has grandchildren, and the rest of us, except for Ruth, don't, so Karla talked continually about how important grandchildren are. Barbara and Genevieve are divorced, although Barbara has remarried. Karla pointedly talked about her happy marriage. Barbara's an environmental law-yer, and Karla thinks—thought—laws to protect the envi-ronment are damaging to businesses like hers. And on and on it went. It was, frankly, a horrible weekend. I couldn't wait for it to be over. But I didn't want it to end this way."

"Thank you, Aline, Merry. I'm sorry to have to keep your guests in town a while longer. It would be perfectly understandable if you asked them to go to a hotel tomor-row."

"I got a text from Noel a few minutes ago," Mom said. "He's booked on a flight getting into Rochester at ten to-morrow morning. It'll be expensive, but he'll catch a cab home. He should be here before noon. I'll talk it over with him."

"Don't go into Mrs. Vaughan's room," Simmonds said. "I've sealed that off. I left a message at the number you gave me for her house, but if you hear from her husband before I do, let me know."

"I will." Mom shook her head sadly. "The poor man. They've been together since high school. It's going to be hard on him."

"I'll stay the night, Mom," I said.

"You don't have to do that, dear," she said.

"I know I don't. But I will. As all your guest rooms are full, I'll sleep here, on the couch." Not that I expected to get much sleep, as the police were still at work, talking in loud voices, slamming doors.

Mom smiled at me. "I've a new toothbrush I haven't opened yet. I'll lay that and a clean towel out for you."

"Thanks, Mom." I kissed her good night, and she went upstairs, her tread unnaturally heavy on the staircase.

"Any reason you're staying here tonight you didn't want

to share with your mother?" Simmonds said once my mom had gone.

"If one of these women killed Karla, we don't know why and thus we don't know if they might be after someone else next. I'm not leaving Mom alone. Not until Dad gets here, anyway."

"I'll be back first thing in the morning to talk to everyone in more detail."

"Did you learn anything?" I asked. "Aside from the fact that my mom had no reason to kill Karla."

Simmonds smiled but didn't acknowledge my point. "None of them confessed, and none of them pointed the finger of suspicion at any of the others. They all said they were shocked and are convinced it was an accident: peanuts had somehow gotten into a food item in the store or factory. I didn't want to tell them I'm particularly interested in the curried egg salad, but it was hard not to. They all say, including your mother, that everyone was in and out of the kitchen this morning and afternoon at different times preparing their contribution. Some dishes went in the oven and some in the fridge. No one confessed to making the curried egg salad, and no one noticed it being made or being placed into the fridge or onto the kitchen island."

"That bowl has a matching lid," I said. "If it was put in the fridge with the lid on, no reason anyone would pay any attention to it. It was on the island waiting to be served, along with all the other food, when I arrived. When it was time to serve, I took the lid off and brought it out. Same for the EpiPen, if Karla had one. This isn't a B&B. The bedroom doors don't lock, so any of the women had access to Karla's suitcase or purse if she wasn't in her room."

Diane Simmonds sat quietly, her hands folded in her lap.

She was looking at nothing. I said nothing and watched her think. Finally, she stirred and said, "Do you know whose idea it was to have this potluck?"

I thought back. "Mom said Ruth suggested it, and Mom was quick to agree. Ruth doesn't appear to have a lot of money, and Mom wanted to avoid going to a restaurant again. I don't think anyone objected to that."

"When you got here, all the guests were in the living room?"

"Yes, including Mom and Vicky."

Simmonds pushed herself to her feet. "We're almost finished here. My people will be out of your hair soon."

"Take your time. I don't see myself getting much sleep." I patted the beige leather couch. "This isn't the most comfortable bed in the world. I'd better go out and check on Mattie and take him for a short walk before turning in. He will not be happy spending the night in the garage. I don't suppose I can bring him in?"

"He's fine outside for one night, but you can leave him in your dad's study if you want. Your mom said none of the women had reason to go in there, and she doesn't think they ever did." She turned as though to leave, hesitated, and then swung back to face me. "One more thing. You've helped with cases in the past, and I appreciated it, although you put yourself in danger."

"I . . ."

She lifted one finger. "Not this time. Stay out of this, Merry. I want no unofficial investigating. No questioning of those who you consider suspects. No placing yourself in danger. Do you understand?"

"Yes," I said. And I meant it.

Chapter 8

'd left my coat over a chair in the kitchen and didn't want to ask one of the forensic officers to get it for me, so I grabbed one of Mom's, a nice calf-length brown suede number, out of the front closet. Mattie's leash was in my coat pocket, so I'd have to manage without, but that shouldn't be a problem as it was late, the streets were quiet, and we weren't going far. Saint Bernards are not rambunctious dogs, and he could usually be counted on to stay by my side and enjoy the walk, with only an occasional detour to sniff under a bush. Saint Bernards are not at all aggressive, either, and Mattie would never start a fight with another animal. Any passing dog would take one look at his bulk and, failing to see the timid pussycat inside, run for the hills.

I left the house by the side door, the one closest to the garage. Before freeing Mattie, I stopped in the soft light under the portico and checked my phone. I'd put it on "vibrate" when the emergency personnel arrived, and while

I'd been sitting on the couch it had been shaking as though it were lost in a hurricane. I scrolled through the texts and voice mail messages. I ignored my landlady, Mrs. D'Angelo, the fastest gossip in the East, not at all surprised she was up to date on the news. Jackie breathlessly reported that "everyone" was talking about police cars outside the Wilkinson home, and Sue-Anne Morrow, mayor of Rudolph, complained that my dad wasn't answering her calls demanding to know what was going on. Russ Durham, editor in chief and head bottle-washer at the *Rudolph Gazette*, asked me for an off-the-record statement. I deleted his message along with the rest.

I called my father, who answered before the first ring died away. "Merry! What's happening there?"

"We're okay, Dad. Mom's upset, but that's all. She's gone up to bed. I'll spend the night at the house and keep an eye on things. Detective Simmonds told Mom's friends they can't leave town, and they're going to be mighty mad about that in the morning, but we can deal with it."

"Diane's calling this a murder? Your mother said her friend died from an allergic reaction."

"The police haven't come to any conclusions yet, but they have their suspicions. As do I. We can talk about it when you get here."

"Okay. I'll be home around noon."

"I'll ask Jackie to come in early and open the store so I can stay until you get here."

"You don't have to do that, honeybunch."

"I think I do, Dad. The visit with Mom's friends was not going well even before this, and tensions are going to be sky-high around here tomorrow. Oh, Sue-Anne's trying to get in touch with you."

"So she is. As a town councilor, not to mention responsible citizen, I should call her back, but I need to save all my battery power in case Aline calls."

I chuckled. "Don't they have landlines in Florida?"

"Landlines? What are those? See you tomorrow, honeybunch. Take care."

"I will, Dad. Good night." I felt a smile on my face. Just talking to my dad went a long way toward making me feel better.

Mattie had recognized my voice, and he let out a loud bark from inside the garage. "Be right there," I called. First, I needed to reply to one more call.

I texted Alan: *One of Mom's guests has died. Mom Vicky and I are fine, just upset. Talk tomorrow.* I added a line of *X*'s, then decided that looked silly and deleted them before pressing "send."

I put my phone into the coat pocket and stepped out of the light of the portico.

"Hey, Merry," came a voice from the darkness.

I yelped and must have jumped about a foot into the air.

Russ Durham came into the circle of light. "Sorry. Did I scare you?"

"No. Not at all. Nothing like a voice looming out of the night to make a girl feel all warm and fuzzy."

"Sorry," he said again, not sounding sorry in the least. He had a big black camera strung around his neck and was dressed against the night's chill. He nodded to the house. "Can you tell me what's going on in there?"

"No."

"Come on, Merry. Cruisers are parked outside, state police forensic vans are at the back, people are coming and going in white suits carrying evidence bags. Something's happened. No one's been dragged out in handcuffs, at least not while I've been watching. You can tell me." He spoke in a soft, slow, liquid Louisiana accent and gave me a crooked grin.

I tried not to grin in response. He was a darn good-looking man, Russell Durham. When I came back to Rudolph a little over a year ago, having quit my job as a style editor at a national lifestyle magazine to buy Mrs. Claus's Treasures, Russ and I had casually dated. Nothing came of it—I realized in time that the Southern charm I'd started to fall for came as naturally to him as pointing his camera at a crime scene. I also realized, again just in time, that Alan Anderson was the man for me.

Russ and I had remained friends, although at the moment he was a newspaper reporter, not my friend. And I'd better remember that.

"I'm not telling you anything, Russ," I said. "You'll have to speak to Diane Simmonds."

"Who, for some reason, isn't taking my calls and shut her car door firmly in my face. She almost took a finger off while she was at it. I might sue."

"You do that," I said. I headed for the garage. Mattie had tired of waiting for me and set up a series of increasingly frantic barks.

Russ fell into step beside me. "Cops all over the house. Simmonds slamming doors. Mattie confined to the garage. Something's up, all right." He opened the people door and was almost knocked over as Mattie ran out, heedless of who might be in his way. "Whoa! I keep forgetting to stand aside when I open any door when you're around. How you doing, boy?" Russ gave the dog a hearty pat, and Mattie wagged his tail and bounced on his toes.

Any friend of my dog is a friend of mine.

"I'm taking him for a short walk," I said. "You can come with us if you like, but I won't talk about anything that happened here tonight."

"In that case, I'll decline. I'll head back to the sidewalk and resume my post. Who knows, Simmonds might return and decide to tell me all." He glanced up into the night sky.

I followed his gaze. It was a cold, clear night, and this side of the house faced away from town. The stars above us glittered like diamonds on a bed of black velvet. The lights of an airplane crossed the sky heading north to Canada. "What are you looking at?"

"Searching for flying pigs." He shook his head. "Nope, not a one. I think I'll call it a night and try to get a statement from our determined detective first thing in the morning. Maybe I'll call Sue-Anne. See if she knows something, unlikely as that is. The cops have learned not to tell her anything they don't have to. Nothing our mayor loves more than to get her name in the papers."

I laughed. "Good night, Russ. I'll switch off the garage light, and we'll walk with you to the road." I stepped into the garage and groaned.

Mattie had knocked over the garbage can and ripped open the thick green bag, leaving trash spread across the garage floor.

Russ joined me. "Bored, was he?"

"Obviously," I said to the man. "That was very naughty, Matterhorn. You know better," I said to the dog.

Mattie smiled up at me.

"I hope he didn't eat anything he shouldn't."

"He looks okay to me," Russ said.

Earlier, when Simmonds had poked through the kitchen

garbage, the can had been almost full. Most of what Mattie had disturbed, I was glad to see, were old bath towels and faded kitchen linens Mom had thrown out as she prepared for a house full of guests. Among the debris, I recognized one of Dad's favorite Christmas sweaters, the one he refused to admit was too full of holes to salvage for another year.

"Have you got a broom in here?" Russ asked.

"Against the wall behind Dad's car." I reached for a fresh bag on the shelf while Mattie sniffed through the trash.

"Get away from there," I said, giving him a mighty shove.

He looked up at me, and I saw something in his mouth. "What have you got there? Give me that." I held out my hand and snapped my fingers. "I said, drop that."

Reluctantly, he opened his mouth. A tube fell into my palm. At first I thought it was a marker, white and yellow with a blunt orange top, the type used for children's drawings or to print signs. Then I noticed the illustration on it and the word "EpiPen" clearly printed across the top.

I squealed and dropped it. Mattie moved to pick it up again, and I shoved at his big head. "No!"

"What's the matter?" Russ stood beside me, holding the broom. "What's that?"

"Nothing!" I grabbed Mattie's collar. "We have to get out of here."

Russ bent over and stretched out his hand.

"Don't touch that," I said sharply.

He gave me a quizzical look and then he straightened. "Okay. I get it. Evidence, right?"

"I'm afraid so. Let's go." I pulled Mattie out of the garage. Russ followed and shut the door behind him.

"I'm going to call Detective Simmonds." I let go of the

dog and found my cell phone in the pocket of Mom's coat. Mattie wandered off to check on recent squirrel activity in the yard. It was late, and Simmonds had a young daughter. But this was her case, and she'd not thank me for not disturbing her.

Due to past events, I have Diane Simmonds's cell phone number in my contact list. I made the call. She didn't sound sleepy when she answered. "What's happened, Merry?"

"I found an EpiPen in the trash in the garage."

"On my way," she said. "Don't touch anything. Are any of the forensic people still in the house?"

"Yes."

"I'll call them, but I don't want them going in until I've had a look. Wait there." She hung up.

"We're to wait here," I said to Russ.

He fingered his camera, looking as pleased as Mattie did when he flushed a squirrel up a tree.

Apparently no squirrels were on the prowl tonight, and Mattie soon gave up his inspection of the yard and came back to me.

The short, chubby man who'd arrived when Mom returned from the hospital came around the side of the house. "Detective says you've found something."

"In the garage."

"She says we're to wait for her." He eyed the man with me suspiciously. "Who are you?"

"Russ Durham," Russ said. "*Rudolph Gazette.*"

"You can't be taking any pictures."

Russ just smiled.

Mattie sniffed at the newcomer. He ignored the dog completely. Mattie, all one hundred and seventy pounds of him, might as well not have been there. Mattie wasn't used to being ignored. He touched the man's leg with a front paw and got no reaction. I grabbed his collar and pulled him away.

We didn't have to wait long before headlights washed the driveway as Simmonds drove up. We watched her walk up the path, wrapping a woolen scarf around her neck and pulling on gloves. "What are you doing here?" she said to Russ.

"I was having a friendly chat with Merry, enjoying the evening, when we found what I suspect you're looking for. I guess that means I'm a witness."

"Did you find it yourself?"

"I was with Merry when she did."

"Mattie found it," I said. "And I found it in Mattie's mouth." This important piece of evidence would now be covered in dog slobber.

"Then you can leave, Mr. Durham," Simmonds said. "If I need to talk to you, I know where to find you."

"I'm sure you do," he said.

Chapter 9

Leather couches do not make comfortable beds. For one thing, they're narrow and slippery.

The temperature in my parents' house is set to automatically go down at midnight. The fire had gone out, the readily available supply of wood was used up, and I wasn't allowed to venture out to the garage to get more firewood. With all the guest rooms occupied, the only covering remaining in the linen closet was a thin summer-weight comforter that wasn't up to the task of keeping me warm. The living room faces the street, and a streetlight stands at the bottom of the property. I'd left the curtains open, in case of further police activity outside, and the light shone on my face all night. Mattie, who can spend the entire day in the back of the shop without making a sound, didn't like being alone in the study while people were moving about the house, and at regular intervals he let me know he was displeased.

All in all, it had not been a good night.

"Can we go into the kitchen?" a low voice said. "I'd kill for a coffee. Sorry, bad choice of words."

I opened one eye to see Barbara standing over me. She wore red flannel pajamas decorated with cupids and hearts, and her cropped gray hair stuck out in all directions.

I groaned.

"Oh, sorry, were you asleep?"

"No." I pushed the cover aside and swung my legs off the couch. Not having come here expecting to spend the night, I hadn't brought pajamas and had gone to bed wearing my T-shirt and underwear.

I glanced out the window. It was still full dark, the streetlight shining on a quiet neighborhood. "What time is it?"

"Five thirty."

"Nothing will be open yet. Even the bakery doesn't open until seven."

"I'm an early riser," she said. "Not that I slept much last night."

"I doubt any of us did." I got off the couch and fumbled for my clothes. "The police have gone, but Detective Simmonds said we're to stay out of the kitchen until she gives us the okay."

"I'm not the sort to do anything just because she tells me not to."

I gave her a look.

"Don't worry, I know better than to interfere with a crime scene."

I pulled on my jeans and ran my fingers through my hair. "I have to let the dog out."

Barbara followed me down the hall to the study. She greeted Mattie almost as enthusiastically as he greeted her.

Surely this woman couldn't be a killer.

Barbara followed us to the closet, and we got our coats. Before I'd gone to bed, I asked Simmonds if I could have my coat, and she sent an underling into the kitchen to get it. I took Mattie's leash out of the pocket, snapped it onto his collar, and we left the house. A thin layer of ice covered the pavement, and we walked carefully. I took a lungful of the crisp cold air, hoping we'd get some snow soon. In Rudolph we love winter, the snowier, the better. There's nothing better for building Christmas spirit than a fresh snowfall.

"Sometimes," Barbara said, falling into step beside us, "I think Constance has the right idea. Southern California. Los Angeles. Sunshine and heat. Must be marvelous." She rubbed her hands together against the cold.

"Um," I said. I had a lot to process, and I wasn't in the mood for a friendly chat. I hadn't invited Barbara to walk with us, but she'd put her coat on over her pajamas, slipped bare feet into her sneakers, and followed. The police had been almost finished in the kitchen when I found the EpiPen. They then spent a lot of time crawling around inside my parents' garage. I watched them for a long time: they took away only that single bag of garbage. My dad keeps a spotlessly clean garage. Mom says it compensates for the way he cooks: he uses every pot and pan, every spoon and knife, spreads splatter everywhere, and leaves the trash can overflowing and soapy water spreading across the countertops and dripping onto the floor. Most of my childhood fights with my siblings were, as I remember, over whose job it was to clean the kitchen after Dad made dinner.

A thin red band began to grow in the sky to the east, and the stars overhead slowly faded. A car drove down the road as someone headed to work. It put its turn indicator on and took the next corner.

"When was the last time you saw Karla?" I asked Barbara. "Before this weekend, I mean?"

"College. A lifetime ago."

"Really? Not since then?"

"Karla was the one who kept the group together all these years, but only through letters and then e-mails and social media. I wouldn't have bothered myself, and I suspect the others felt much the same, but when someone writes you a letter, you have to reply. That's the way I was brought up, anyway. She talked a lot over the years about having a reunion, but I don't think she ever seriously tried to organize anything. Maybe she hoped someone else would. I don't know that any of us saw Karla after college. I mean, not many people go to Minnesota for a vacation, right? Even I, who love nothing more than a week of hiking, camping, and canoeing, have never been there, although I've heard it's beautiful. I saw your mom now and again when she was in New York, and Genevieve sometimes. I visited Constance a couple of times when I was in California on business, and she came to New York once or twice. I went out to L.A. for her husband's funeral. Your mom was there, too, but not Karla, who'd been the one who let us know he'd died. I think the only reason we bothered to still be friends was because Karla kept us all in touch."

"Karla mentioned she came on this weekend because Constance told her she was planning to come. Did you ever meet up with Ruth? She lives in Rochester, not so far. Mom would have lunch with her sometimes, when she was in town."

Barbara sighed. "Maybe I should have made the effort, but Ruth, well, she hasn't done so well in life. She had talent, real talent. She and your mom were the ones our teachers expected to go somewhere. Your mom did. Ruth—" Barbara's voice faded away.

"Ruth what?" I asked.

"She went to college on a full scholarship. When she graduated, she waited tables for a while, like all the other wannabe young actresses, but then her mother got sick so she had to go home and look after her. I guess she just never left again."

"Going home's not so bad. I lived in New York for a while. I worked at my dream job, and I loved it. But . . . things change, and now I'm glad to be back in Rudolph."

"Because that's what makes you happy," Barbara said. "Losing her dream didn't make Ruth happy."

"And you?" I asked.

She opened her mouth and sang a scale. The notes rang through the morning, pure and clear. A starling settled in the branch of a nearby maple tree, as though to listen. Mattie stopped sniffing under a bush and lifted his head.

Barbara smiled. "I used to sing. I intended to be the next big thing in pop music. Karen Carpenter had nothing on me, or so I thought. Yes, I had the talent, if I may be so immodest, but I eventually realized I didn't have the ambition, or the ruthlessness, to make it. Maybe not the luck or the patience, either, so I went to law school instead."

"And that worked out okay?" It was a bold, personal question to ask a virtual stranger, but somehow, on this pleasant morning, we had fallen into deep conversation.

"More than okay. I love it. I care passionately about the environment and I'm making a difference, in my own small way." She sighed. "Which is why I can't spend any more time here. I have to get back to work. My husband and I are partners in the firm. I spoke to him last night. I have a court date tomorrow, and he can't take it for me. I have to be there."

"Speak to Detective Simmonds. I'm sure she'll understand."

"Ha," was Barbara's reply. Then she changed the subject. "What about you, Merry? Do you sing?"

"I inherited all my musical talent from my father. Meaning absolutely none. My sister Carole's an opera singer, like Mom, and doing fairly well. Eve is acting in Hollywood, and our brother, Chris, although he inherited no more talent than I did, got the performance bug. He's a stage designer. Carole and Chris are planning to come home for Thanksgiving this year."

If we even have a Thanksgiving.

Chapter 10

"I cannot believe you're gotten yourself involved in another murder, Merry." Jackie stood in front of my desk with an accusing expression on her face.

I groaned. "Neither can I. But it might not be a murder case. The police still have tests to run."

Mattie walked in circles, deciding how best to settle himself in exactly the right position on the big dog bed that took up about half the available floor space in my office.

"Poison's what I heard." She narrowed her eyes and studied me. "Are you feeling okay?"

"I'm tired."

"You don't look so good."

"I didn't sleep much last night, that's all."

"Did you eat what the dead woman ate? Or did she have something special?"

"Jackie, I'm not talking about it. I appreciate you coming in early and opening the shop, but right now you have to get back to work. We have customers."

"They'll be fine for a few minutes."

"They will not!"

"Okay," she said with a martyred sigh. I swear she must practice that sigh at home in front of the mirror. Along with her world-weary expression. "We'll talk about it later. Kyle has a theory. He heard the mob followed one of them here and got the wrong woman."

"Gosh, that might be important. Kyle had better take that information to the police right away."

Jackie failed to notice my sarcasm. "Do you think so, Merry? Kyle doesn't like to have contact with the police, not if he can help it."

I didn't like to ponder what that meant. Kyle was Jackie's boyfriend. I thought he was lazy and not too bright. He didn't have a regular job, just picked up the odd piece of work around town now and again in the busy season. He claimed to be an artist, but as far as I knew he'd never produced any actual art.

"Go to work, Jackie," I said. "I'll come out in a few minutes and let you have your break."

"Going," she said. And she did.

I dropped into the chair behind my desk with a groan.

When Barbara and I got back to Mom's house from our walk, she went upstairs to get dressed and I checked the kitchen. No police tape was wrapped across the door, and no signs had been posted warning us to keep out, so I'd gone in.

The trash can was empty, all the pots and pans that had been in the sink or left on the counter, gone. The police had taken away the leftover food from the potluck, the bowls the meal had been served in, the dishes we'd eaten off, the bottles of wine—whether empty or not—and the used drinking glasses. They'd even carried away the untouched desserts. I wondered if they'd dig in to the chocolate cake and mince tarts down at the police station. The kitchen had been left perfectly neat and tidy except for the thin layer of black dust over all the surfaces. Fingerprint powder.

I hoped word wouldn't spread that having an unexplained death during a dinner party was a cheap way of getting someone else to clean up your mess. Although Mom wouldn't be at all pleased at the thought of them packing her good china and crystal into boxes and lugging it all down to a lab somewhere.

The day-to-day dishes remained untouched, so we wouldn't be reduced to eating our Thanksgiving dinner off paper plates.

I could only hope the pack of visitors would be gone and Karla's death solved by Thursday, so we could enjoy a nice, peaceful family Thanksgiving.

I made a big pot of coffee and found bagels and cream cheese in the fridge. I laid the breakfast things out in the dining room for guests to help themselves when they came down.

Mom was first to arrive. She'd pulled a silk wrap over her nightgown and scrubbed her face. In the absence of the makeup she never appeared in public without, including in front of her own children, the lines on her face were deep and the circles under her eyes dark. I suspected she hadn't slept much, if at all. I wrapped her in my arms and felt her body quiver.

"You okay, Mom?" I asked when we separated.

"I will be when your father gets here. I see the police have left. Thank you for making the coffee, dear."

I poured her a cup without asking. Black, no sugar.

"Did they discover anything of significance after I went to bed?" she asked after she took the cup from me and enjoyed her first sip.

"I found an EpiPen in the garbage can in the garage."

Her perfectly sculpted eyebrows rose. "What do you suppose it was doing there?"

"I don't know, but it's highly unlikely Karla went into the garage herself to throw it away."

"Was it empty?"

"I don't know. I didn't hold it for more than a fraction of a second before I realized what it was and dropped it."

"This is a nightmare," Mom said. "This morning I have to drive them all into town to the police station to have their fingerprints taken. Do you think Diane expects you to come also?"

"My prints should be on file. They were taken after Max . . ."

"Oh yes. That." Mom left the sentence hanging. *After Max was murdered in my office.*

"So I know from experience," I said, "that it's not pleasant, even when one knows one is completely innocent."

"They're not going to be happy about it. Except for Ruth. I suspect she'll be delighted at being a suspect."

"Why? Do you think she had something to do with Karla's death and deep inside she wants to be caught?"

"I mean nothing of the sort, dear. It will be like living in one of those books she reads all the time. She'll get a kick out of it." Mom's face softened. "Although that might be a bit harsh of me. None of us are getting any sort of kick out of this."

Footsteps clattered on the stairs. I touched my finger to

my lips. Mom nodded and took another sip of her coffee as Constance and Ruth came in. They were both dressed, Constance in a dark red dress with a white belt and Ruth in the same jeans and T-shirt she'd worn yesterday. Constance's makeup and hair were perfect. Ruth's hair was still wet from the shower.

"I called my father before turning in," Constance said. "His lawyers will ensure I'll be allowed to go home when I want to."

"If the police need us here," Ruth said, "we should respect that."

"Nonsense," Constance replied. "I know nothing about what happened to Karla, and I'm not going to stay here a moment longer than I intended to at the whim of some small-town cop who wants to make a name for herself."

Mom and I exchanged glances. Diane Simmonds had been a homicide detective in Chicago. She came to Rudolph after a difficult divorce from another Chicago cop, seeking a quieter life with her young daughter. The last thing she wanted was any attention.

Constance caught our look. "Sorry. I don't mean to sound heartless. Poor Karla, it's hard to accept that she's dead."

I had no wish to be in the company of Mom's friends any longer than I had to. Fortunately, I had an excellent excuse to get out of there without seeming rude. "I have to take Mattie for a walk."

I walked the dog for a long time. When we got back to the house, it was empty. Mom had left a note on the table by the door saying they'd gone to the police station.

They returned a few minutes after me. Constance immediately marched upstairs, yelling into her phone as she went. She slammed her bedroom door behind her.

"That was interesting," Ruth said to me. "It was all over in no time. I wanted to stay and watch them run the results through the computer, but they wouldn't let me."

"You're a ghoul," Genevieve said.

"I call it wanting to be informed," Ruth said with a huff.

Genevieve snorted. "I need a smoke." She headed for the back door.

"Wouldn't mind one myself," Ruth said, following her.

"I'm going for a walk," Barbara said. "Get the scent of the police station off me."

"You okay, Mom?" I asked when the women had gone their separate ways.

"I'm fine, dear, but I cannot wait to see the backs of them. All of them. And I'd thought this visit wasn't going well before."

"Why don't you have a sit, and I'll make you a cup of tea."

She smiled at me. "I'd like that."

I waited with Mom until Dad, still dressed in his orange and pink Bermuda shorts, got home. I'd given him a quick hug, then left him and Mom to talk over what was happening and headed for Mrs. Claus's Treasures.

As soon as Jackie left the office, I checked my phone once again. More messages from Mrs. D'Angelo, pretending she was worried about me; from Sue-Anne, wondering why my father wasn't returning her calls; from Russ Durham, hoping for a statement. I deleted them all.

"In the back," I heard Jackie say.

A footstep sounded on the floorboards. Mattie's ears pricked up. I straightened in my chair.

The office door wasn't closed, and Alan Anderson's unruly blond mop peeked around the corner. "Are you receiving guests?"

"Meaning you? Anytime."

He walked in and gave me a kiss. It was only a light one, as he had to lean across the desk, as well as Mattie, who was begging for attention, but it was welcome nonetheless. He then gave Mattie a rub on the top of his head as he said, "You okay, Merry?"

"Tired, but I'm fine. I was worried about Mom, but Dad cut his fishing trip short and he's home now."

"That's good."

"What brings you into town today?" I asked.

"You do, Merry. I called the store at opening this morning and asked Jackie to give me a call when you got here. I've been sitting next door at Cranberries, waiting."

"In that case, I'm guessing you don't want to go for a coffee?"

"You guess right. But if you want to, we can."

I shook my head. "No, I had a coffee at Mom's."

"Do you want to talk about what happened last night?"

I explained briefly. I told him about the curried egg salad, the missing EpiPen, and my suspicions.

"You think someone killed her deliberately?"

"I do. From what I've heard, people who are highly allergic can detect the presence of the forbidden substance from the slightest taste and they immediately stop eating it. Karla dug into the curried egg salad without hesitation and had several spoonfuls. Because no one claimed to have made it, even before we started to eat, I have to think that dish had been made specifically to disguise the taste of peanuts. If the EpiPen turns out to be full, which I suspect it will, that has to mean someone deliberately hid it so we couldn't find it to help Karla when we needed to."

"You have a limited pool of suspects," he said. "The women at dinner. Not including you, your mom, and Vicky."

I'd been thinking about that while walking Mattie. "Not necessarily. The kitchen door was unlocked when I arrived at the house. It usually is during the day."

He nodded. Rudolph was generally a safe town.

"Which means just about anyone could have come in and left the salad," I said. "Granted, they would have had to be mighty cool about it. To walk into someone's house, rifle through the cupboards looking for a serving bowl, dump the salad in the bowl, put it in the fridge, and walk out again."

"To poison someone's food and sit there and watch them eat it, you'd have to be mighty cool also," Alan said. "Cool, and totally heartless."

I felt a shudder run through me. Alan touched my hand and gave me a gentle smile. I tried to smile back. "You didn't see anyone creeping around the outside of the house, I suppose," he said.

I mentally slapped my forehead. "I did, Alan, I did. I forgot all about it until now. When I arrived, a car was backing out of the driveway. I assumed it was one of Mom's or Dad's friends who'd dropped in and then left when they realized Mom had guests. I never thought about it again, and I didn't ask Mom who it had been. My gosh, it might have been the killer."

His face tightened. "It might. You say you forgot about it until now. Meaning you didn't tell Simmonds?"

"I didn't, but I will."

"Do you have any idea why someone would want to kill the woman? What was her name?"

"Karla Vaughan. I know nothing about her except that she's a bookkeeper at her family's construction company in Minnesota, and she's married with children and grandchildren. I didn't get the feeling she was a particularly happy person, but nothing stood out about her. That's a thought. Construction. Doesn't the mob have a lot of ties in construction?" I didn't mention I'd first heard that suggestion from Kyle, via Jackie.

"So they say, but I wouldn't know. I'm glad I'm a small-scale, simple woodworker."

"Your business might be small," I said, giving him a smile, "but it's anything but simple." In Alan's workshop, next to his house in the woods outside Rudolph, he crafted everything from solid, practical, beautiful furniture, to works of whimsy and charm that were guaranteed to delight children on Christmas morning. He even made jewelry, which was popular in the store: bracelets of polished wood and necklaces of interlocking rings in different colors of wood.

"Speaking of my business, we need to talk about what extra stock you need for the holidays," he said. "But right now, you should call Simmonds and tell her what you just told me about that car you saw. How about dinner at my place tonight?"

"I'd like that. I'd like it a lot."

"I'll see you later then." He leaned over the desk, and I stood up and leaned toward him. We kissed across a stack of design magazines, craftspeople's catalogs, a pile of accounts addressed to me, a smaller pile of bills *from* me waiting to be put in the mail, and a tattered and well-chewed dog rope that had somehow not made it back onto the floor.

I called Diane Simmonds to tell her about the car I'd seen last night backing out of my parents' driveway. Unfortunately, I couldn't say anything about the make, the model, the identity of the driver, or the number of people inside. All I could describe was a small compact. Maybe gray. Maybe black. Maybe dark blue or even deep red. I realized that covered about half the cars in North America. Simmonds thanked me for my help, but didn't offer any information. Not that I expected her to.

Once I was off the phone, I went to the shop floor to relieve Jackie. I'd had a quick shower at Mom's but I felt dirty and grubby in the clothes I'd been wearing yesterday and had slept in last night. Monday is never a busy day in the shop, other than in December, so I hoped to be able to get home when Jackie finished lunch, shower again, change, and come back to relieve her. I'd drive so I could lock up at six and head straight to Alan's. I was so looking forward to a relaxing evening with a glass of wine by the fire.

Last night, even before Karla had died, had been anything but relaxing.

Jackie left for her lunch break, and I tidied the shelves while keeping an eye out for anyone who needed my help. A woman took the last of the turkey brooches off the display and showed it to her friend. "Look at this, Gale. Perfect for Thanksgiving dinner, don't you think?"

"I love it," Gale said. "But not as much as I love this wreath brooch." She helped herself to one of Crystal's pieces. "We're starting our Christmas shopping," she said to me, "but we both believe in the principle of one for them and one for me."

Her friend laughed heartily. "Do you think Vivienne would like that set?" She pointed to the train winding around the outside of the toy display. The engine, bright red caboose, boxcars, and interlocking tracks had been hand-carved by Alan.

"I think she'd love it," Gale said. "I certainly do."

The first woman peered at the price tag. "It's pretty expensive."

"Hand-made by a local artisan from wood he gathered on his own property," I said. "You don't have to buy the entire set, if it's too much. The pieces can be purchased separately."

"What the heck. It's my granddaughter's first Christmas. I'll take the full set. She's only two weeks old, as of tomorrow, but she can play with it next year."

"This year, her father will be the one playing with it," Gale said, and both women laughed once again.

I grinned at them. I love owning a Christmas store. No matter the time of year, there's something about the atmosphere in here that simply makes people happy.

Most people, that is. The door hadn't shut behind the two women, laden with their purchases, before Margie Thatcher, owner of Rudolph's Gift Nook, the shop next door, was through it. "Merry Wilkinson," she said in a voice stiff with disapproval. Then again, disapproval is her normal style of speech; I've never heard any other. "I cannot believe your family's caught up in another scandal."

"What scandal might that be, Margie?" I asked politely.

She peered at me through her small black eyes. The look wasn't friendly. Margie didn't do friendly. When she arrived in Rudolph last Christmas to take over running the Nook from her twin sister, Betty, she introduced herself to me by saying, "Don't you dare call me Margaret. I am not the former prime minister of England." Now she said, "The scandal that's all anyone's talking about in the take-out line at Cranberry Coffee Bar. Someone was murdered at Noel Wilkinson's house."

"A woman died, that's true," I said. "Out of respect, we're not discussing it pending the results of the autopsy and forensic report."

Margie sniffled. I don't think she knows what "respect" means. She certainly had none for me, my family, or my store. Rudolph's Gift Nook specialized in mass-produced, cheap, imported goods. I believe there's room for every sort of business in Rudolph, and I believe in catering to all tastes and all pocketbooks. Not everyone can afford hand-made twenty-piece train sets or intricately crafted silver jewelry. Margie believed Mrs. Claus's Treasures was stealing customers that would otherwise be pouring through the door of the Nook, ready to engage in a shopping frenzy for made-in-China trinkets.

"Your father's supposed to be our Santa Claus," she said. "A murder in his house is not a good image for the town."

"My father was at the other end of the country at the time. He was fishing in Florida. He had nothing to do with anything that happened."

"We will see. Have you met Mr. and Mrs. Fitzroy?"

I wondered at the sudden change of topic. "I met them yesterday. They seem nice."

"Changes are coming around here, Merry Wilkinson, and not a moment too soon." She slammed the door on her way out.

I didn't much care what Margie thought—of me or my store. But I cared a great deal about the rest of the town, and my father's position in it. As Margie had said, Dad was the town's official Santa Claus. Even out of costume he looked the part, with his twinkling blue eyes under heavy white eyebrows, round belly, full white beard, and prominent red nose. He liked playing the role, and he was good at it, but his identity wasn't tied up in it. He'd been mayor of Rudolph for a long time and was still a town councilor. Sue-Anne was worried he'd run for mayor again, knowing that if he did, he'd win. Dad had no intention of doing that; he insisted that part of his life was over, but the ambitious Sue-Anne didn't believe him.

"Oh dear." A customer peered out from the alcove, clutching a plush reindeer doll to her chest. "Did she say a woman was murdered in this town? Is it safe here?" She glanced around the store, as if expecting to see armed assassins leaping over the display tables at any moment.

I couldn't help but sneak a peek at the row of angels, complete with wings, song sheets, and trumpets, made by Alan, lining the shelf next to the curtained doorway leading to the back rooms. One of those angels had saved my life over the summer. "Sadly, a woman died last night," I said. "But you know how fast rumors can spread. Some people like to make themselves sound important by repeating idle gossip, the more lurid, the better." I smiled at her. "Can I wrap that doll for you? It's so charming, isn't it?"

"Doll? Oh, this doll, right. Yes, please. I'll take it. I have a collection of stuffed Santas I bring out every year. My grandchildren love them."

Once she left, several groups of customers came in and I was kept on the hop greeting them, answering questions, ringing up their purchases, and waving them a cheery good-bye. When I next got a few moments of downtime, my thoughts returned to my mother. I wondered what was happening at my parents' house, what Mom and her friends were up to, and if Simmonds was making any progress. I totally forgot to wonder what Margie had meant when she told me changes were coming, and why she'd linked that comment with the Fitzroys.

Chapter 11

"Merry Wilkinson! I've been calling you and calling you! Stop right there!"

I considered making a run for it, but unfortunately Mrs. D'Angelo knew where I lived. Which is on the second floor of her house. She'd have no hesitation in following me there. I might as well talk to her on the front porch rather than upstairs in my apartment.

"Good afternoon, Mrs. D'Angelo," I said. "It's cold, but not cold enough to snow yet, I don't think. Do you agree?"

"One of your mother's guests killed another of the guests, and the entire house is in lockdown. How did you get out?"

"Because the house wasn't locked down," I said.

Mrs. D'Angelo was dressed in her fall gardening clothes: baggy track pants, a heavy sweater under a purple raincoat, pink and purple rubber boots. The garden was put away for the winter, perennials and wild grasses trimmed back, bushes wrapped in burlap, annuals dug up, and the soil turned over. We had the nicest garden on the street in spring and summer, the tidiest in fall, and the best-shoveled paths in winter. Not so much because Mrs. D'Angelo was a keen gardener, but because time spent outdoors enabled her to keep an eye on the comings and goings in the neighborhood. In order to keep her up to date on events she couldn't personally witness, she carried her ever-present iPhone in a pouch around her waist and had the earphones permanently attached to her ears.

"Janice Reid called me first thing this morning. She heard sirens last night and hurried over to see if she could help. She saw an ambulance and police cars outside your parents' house. And then forensics officers coming and going all night. She wanted to call on your mother, to check if she was all right, of course, but that silly Candy Campbell said it was a crime scene and ordered her to go away."

Whenever I got annoyed at Candy, when she tried to intimidate me or shove her weight around, I reminded myself that it can't be easy being a police officer in a town in which half the residents remember you peeing your pants on the school stage while performing as the second shepherd in the first-grade Christmas pageant.

There was no point in trying to shame Mrs. D'Angelo into stopping gossiping, the way I had with the customer earlier. Mrs. D'Angelo lived on gossip the way normal people lived on air. And if she didn't know the latest dirt, she simply made something up.

"One of my mother's visiting friends died, yes," I said. "It was sudden and unexpected so the police came out, as they do in such cases. Nothing has been determined yet about the cause of death. She had some health issues."

"I hope that's the case, Merry," Mrs. D'Angelo said

sternly. "Noel makes a good Santa Claus. Everyone says so."

"What's that got to do with anything?" I asked, but my landlady was already speaking into her phone. "Noreen, I've just spoken to Merry Wilkinson. She confirms that . . ."

Mattie and I let ourselves into the backyard (not nearly as nicely maintained as the front, as it doesn't overlook the street) and climbed the stairs. I share the second floor with another apartment, so mine is small, but it's perfect for Mattie and me. I tore off my clothes and hopped into the shower. When I got out, hair washed, body tingling, I felt like a new woman.

The thought of seeing Alan tonight had lifted my spirits considerably.

I dressed for a casual dinner at his place in a short red and black striped tunic over black leggings and ankle-high black boots. The moment I took the car keys down from the hook by the door, Mattie's ears popped up and his tail began to wag. Mattie loves to ride in the car.

"Back to work we go," I said. "But we're going to have a nice treat later." He dashed for the door.

When we got back to the shop, I told Jackie she could have the rest of the day off. She went home after making sure I knew what a giant favor she had done for me by coming into work early (not acknowledging that I was paying her for that and also not acknowledging the giant favor I had done for her by letting her leave early without docking her pay). We were busy for the rest of the afternoon, but the last of the customers left at quarter to six.

At five minutes to six, when I was contemplating risking Margie's disapproval and closing early, the bells above the door tinkled cheerfully and Dad came in. The bells may have been cheerful, but that was not the word I'd have chosen to describe his expression. "What's happened? Is Mom okay?"

"Your mother's fine," he said. "If you're asking if there have been any developments around the death of her friend, nothing has happened. Nothing of significance, anyway. Diane talked to them all again. They protested their innocence and expressed their shock at the death of their friend."

"Did she ask them about the EpiPen?"

"I believe so. They all claimed never to have seen it and had no idea how it ended up in our garage."

"Are they going to be allowed to go home?"

He shook his head so vehemently his beard shook. "No. Diane said quite plainly that until she knows the cause of death for sure, no one leaves Rudolph. A couple of the women, the rich one from California and the New York lawyer, tried to argue, but Diane doesn't argue with anyone. She walked out and left them sputtering."

"You mean Constance and Barbara."

"I get them mixed up," Dad said. "It's natural enough that they want to go home for Thanksgiving, but it's also natural enough that Diane needs them here in town. Looks like we're stuck with them for the duration."

"You can ask them to go to a hotel," I said.

"Your mother and I huddled in the backyard earlier discussing precisely that. One of her friends can't afford a hotel."

"Ruth."

"I'd be happy to offer to pay, but your mother thinks Ruth would take offense at that. I suggested Ruth stay in our house and the other three be shown the door, but Aline doesn't want to embarrass Ruth by singling her out."

"What a mess."

"That it is. I escaped to come into town. After I retired, your mother suggested we turn my study into a TV room. Thank heavens I put my foot down against that. At least I have someplace to flee to, but your poor mother doesn't. Were those women so nasty to each other before their friend died?"

"Yup. Mom was seriously regretting extending the invitation."

"If this isn't cleared up by tomorrow," Dad said, "Aline's going to call Chris and Carole and tell them Thanksgiving's off."

"Oh no! I was looking forward to it. I haven't seen Chris since last Christmas."

"There is, as the old story goes, no room at the inn. I don't feel in a festive mood anyway."

"Speaking of unwelcome guests, Dad, I saw a car leaving the house last night when I arrived. I told Simmonds about it, and that I couldn't see who was in it. Did she ask Mom who it might have been?"

"Aline didn't know. No one came to the door last night other than you and Vicky."

"No one she knows about, anyway," I said.

Dad nodded. "Bad business all around."

I studied my father's face, all rosy red cheeks, soft blue eyes, deep crags, and white whiskers. At the moment, those blue eyes were not twinkling, and the crags were deeper than usual. "What else has happened that you're not telling me, Dad?"

"You know me too well, honeybunch. Gunpowder, treason, and plot."

"What on earth does that mean?"

"I called Ralph Dickerson a short while ago on another matter."

"And?" Ralph was our town's chief financial officer.

"Ralph informed me that my unexpected return to town has interrupted a plot to unseat me."

"Dad, you're making no sense."

"Have you met a man named Wayne Fitzroy?"

"Yes, I have. He and his wife came in on Sunday on their way home from church. She bought several things, as I recall."

"Sounds like him. A twofer: buying locally and being seen in church. They bought Ed and Jean Fernhaugh's house over the summer."

The Fernhaughs were longtime Rudolph residents. They were getting on in life, and their children had moved away and rarely came home, so they decided, reluctantly, to sell. Their house, a large early-twentieth-century mansion on a beautiful property on the lake, had been for sale in the two-million-dollar range. A heck of a lot for a small, rural town in Upstate New York. "Nothing wrong with trying to fit into a new community, is there?" I asked.

"Not unless he has ulterior motives, which I believe he does. He wants to be Santa."

"Is that a problem, Dad? You're always saying you'd be happy to quit and let someone else take it on if the right person wanted to."

My father stroked his beard. His eyes were dark and serious. "The right person, yes. Fitzroy isn't the right person. I've had a couple of encounters with him. He's come to town council meetings a few times, introducing himself to everyone, glad-handing all the councilors, saying he wants to—and I quote—'get up to speed on what's important in

Rudolph.' He wants to be a big man in this town, but I can't figure out why. I didn't get the slightest impression he was in any way nice. Frankly, I find it hard to believe he even wants to be Santa."

I nodded. "Not nice." Nice, as everyone knows, is the prime requirement for playing Santa Claus. Like my dad, I'd detected something false beneath Fitzroy's getting-to-know-you charm. "Margie Thatcher was in here earlier, saying that having a murder take place at your house disqualifies you from being Santa." She'd also mentioned Wayne Fitzroy and muttered about changes coming. I didn't tell Dad that.

His face twisted. "I normally wouldn't give a fig for anything Margie has to say about anything. Her community spirit, like that of her sister before her, is known to be non-existent. But if she's saying that, you can be sure others are, too."

"Does Ralph think Fitzroy has a chance? If you don't offer to step down, the council will have to fire you, won't they? Not many, if any, of them will do that."

"It isn't up to the council. The mayor has sole responsibility. Ralph thinks Fitzroy and Sue-Anne are becoming very chummy."

"Chummy? What does that mean?"

"I don't know. But I intend to find out. This is a bad time for this to come up, with what happened yesterday."

"Except that you wouldn't have even known about this plot if you hadn't had to cut your vacation short. How was it, anyway?"

"Too short. Keep your ears open, honeybunch."

"I will," I said.

The chimes sounded again and the door opened. I began

to tell the customer we were closed but snapped my mouth shut when I recognized Diane Simmonds.

"Noel," she said.

"Diane."

"How was your vacation?"

"Altogether far too short."

"I was driving past, and I saw your car out front. I figured I might as well give you the news in person."

"I assume," Dad said, "it's not good news."

"I got the results of the toxicology report on the food served at your house last night."

"That was quick."

"Not really. It's easy when they're looking for a specific substance. Finely ground peanuts had been mixed into the dressing on the curried egg salad."

I let out a long breath. I'd expected that, but it still came as a shock to hear it. "I assume no one's come forward to say they made that salad."

"No. And that means I'm treating this as a murder. Someone might have thought they were playing a mean joke; they might have thought Karla was pretending to be sensitive to get attention and sympathy, but as no one has confessed to doctoring the curried eggs, as far as I'm concerned, it's premeditated murder."

My dad and I looked at each other. We didn't say anything.

"You can let Matterhorn out of the office," Simmonds said. "He knows I'm here and he wants to say hello. It's after six, so you're closed for the day."

"How do you know that?"

"The sign on the door says so."

That wasn't exactly what I meant, but I went in the back

anyway as Dad said, "I suppose that means Aline's friends can't go home."

"Not yet," Simmonds said. "I still have more tests to do, and a lot of questions have to be answered. You can send them to a hotel if you want them out of the house."

I had to shove, hard, at the office door to get it open. Mattie was sitting there, his tongue drooling, his tail thumping on the floor, his eyes round with excitement.

"You can come out," I said, "but behave yourself."

He trotted politely at my heels into the shop. Yes, having a fully grown Saint Bernard loose in a china shop isn't usually a good idea. But he was so well behaved around Diane I wasn't worried. He trotted straight up to her. She touched the top of his head lightly, pointed to the floor, and said, "You will remain there, Matterhorn."

"I've never . . ." My dad shook his head.

Mattie sat.

"What did the fingerprint analysis show?" I asked.

"Nothing conclusive," Simmonds said. "Your prints were found on the EpiPen, which we expected, as you picked it up before you realized what it was. Beneath those, and evidence of it being in Matterhorn's mouth, the pen appears to have been wiped completely clean, as had the bottle of mango chutney we found in the kitchen trash. The bowls, including the one used to serve the curried egg salad, were covered in a variety of prints."

"We passed the plates around the table," I said. "Everyone tried pretty much everything. It would be more suspicious if someone's prints *weren't* there." I had a sudden thought. "What about the peanuts? They had to have been carried in something."

"We found a small plastic bag, of the sort you get for

using with the bulk bins at a supermarket, in the garage trash with the EpiPen. It had been washed thoroughly, inside and out, with water and the same brand of detergent as found in the kitchen."

"Meaning, no prints," Dad said.

Simmonds nodded. "I have officers going to every supermarket in the area, asking about anyone purchasing those ingredients, but as you can imagine, that's a big job."

"Harried and overworked clerks in big stores aren't likely to remember individuals and what they bought," I said.

"Exactly. But we have to try. Sometimes we get lucky. Unfortunately, the houseguests were left largely to their own devices yesterday. No one can account for all of anyone else's time between breakfast and gathering in the living room before dinner, and they all say they didn't notice anyone making the curried eggs or going out to the garage. We found no prints on the garage door or the trash can that don't belong to either of you or Aline. Other than Russell Durham's, but Merry told me he'd shut the door after I'd been called."

"If someone had gone outside with gloves on, in this weather that wouldn't be commented on," I said.

"So you have nothing," Dad said.

"Give me time, Noel," Simmonds said.

"When's Mr. Vaughan arriving?" I asked her.

"That's turning out to be a problem. I can't get hold of him. I've called the house number repeatedly and left messages, but I get no reply. I have Karla's cell phone, but it's a good one and password protected. We haven't been able to get into it, not yet anyway, to search her contact list, and she doesn't have any stored numbers in the medical ID part of her emergency option."

"He owns a construction company," I said. "Have you tried finding it? Maybe it has his name in the title."

"I thought of that, but nothing called Vaughan comes up locally."

"He has to be told," Dad said. "Maybe with her on holiday he went away, too."

"I've been in touch with their town's police department," Simmonds said. "They're trying to locate him."

At that moment, the detective's phone buzzed. She checked the display and said, "Speak of the devil." She glanced between Dad and me. "Might as well let you two listen in." She put the call on speakerphone.

"Detective Simmonds?" a man's deep voice asked.

"This is she. Good evening."

"Hi. I'm Officer Montgomery from Northfield, Minnesota. Sorry this has taken so long. We had a bunch of drunk teenagers running through town throwing rocks at windows and I've been out on that."

"Not a problem."

"I've found the man you're looking for."

"Thank you. Give me his number and I'll arrange to meet him when he arrives in Rudolph."

"Yeah, I can do that, Detective. But first, there's something you should know."

"What?"

"The reason Eric Vaughan hasn't been answering the number you've been calling is because he doesn't live there. He hasn't lived there for a long time."

"Do you know why?" Simmonds asked.

"Soon as I got the request to look into this, I recognized the name. Eric and Karla Vaughan have been fighting over their divorce for a couple years, and in a town as small as this one, it's been mighty big news. I called his office, and they told me he was traveling at the moment but gave me his cell number, and I got him on that. Fact is, Detective, Eric sounded darn pleased when I told him his wife had died. I believe his words were, 'Free at last.'"

Chapter 12

"That is interesting," Simmonds said. "Can you send me details about what you know about the divorce situation?"

"Happy to, Detective. Vaughan's construction company is in a bad way. I'd look into his insurance situation if I were you. His wife worked in the business for a long time, and she was claiming she's entitled to be treated as a full partner, and—"

His voice died as Simmonds cut the speakerphone and held the phone up to her ear.

Drat! I wanted to hear that.

"I'm out right now, Officer," Simmonds said. "I want to talk to Mr. Vaughan myself. Send me his number, and I'll call him when I'm back in my office. Thank you for your help." She hung up.

"That was interesting," Dad said.

"It sure was," I said. "Karla never said anything, not when I was around, anyway, about getting divorced. Quite the opposite, she prattled on about how successful her family business was and how happy she and her loving husband were. At one time she said she was lucky that she found the right man when she was young."

"Ashamed of it, maybe," Simmonds said.

"Divorce is nothing to be ashamed of these days," Dad said.

"Not usually," I said. "But it might be if your self-image depends on being part of a stable, happy marriage. A couple of Mom's friends were dismissive of Karla because she spent the rest of her life after college in a small town in Minnesota, working as a bookkeeper. In return, she made digs at them for being divorced or not part of a happy family."

"I'm going to have a talk with Mr. Vaughan," Simmonds said.

"You might ask him if he was in Rudolph yesterday evening," I suggested.

"That I intend to do. 'Traveling' can mean a lot of things."

Dad and Detective Simmonds left, and Mattie and I locked up the shop. Deep in thought, I drove to Alan's. This might all be over soon. If Karla was a threat to Eric's company, maybe he did sneak into Rudolph and plant the curried egg salad. Her husband, of all people, would know about her allergy.

Alan lives in a nineteenth-century stone farmhouse deep in the woods outside Rudolph. I drove up the long dirt driveway, my headlights illuminating the bare trees on either side of the trail. At this time in late November, it was already fully dark when we arrived. The lights were off in the detached workshop and the garage, but lamps in the house and over the front door shone brightly in welcome. By the time I parked my car and opened the back door and Mattie had leapt out, Alan was waiting on the porch to greet us, dressed in a rough oatmeal hand-knitted sweater and brown cords. I allowed Mattie a few minutes to check out the exciting scents in Alan's yard, and climbed the steps. I stepped into Alan's arms and we kissed. He smelled of freshly applied aftershave, clean wool, and woodsmoke.

We were still kissing when Mattie ran past us and into the house. He barked, telling us to hurry up.

We separated, laughing, and went inside, Alan's arm draped across my shoulders.

Logs in the big stone fireplace in the main room were blazing, and I slipped off my coat. A delicious smell wafted in from the open kitchen.

"Get you a glass of wine?" Alan asked.

"I'm driving, so I'll save it to have with dinner," I said. "A hot tea would be nice though. It's cold out there."

I followed him into the kitchen. It was a real country kitchen, with a big wood island, plenty of open cabinets displaying a mishmash of assorted dishes in bright colors, copper pots hanging from hooks in the ceiling, a large range tucked into its own nook, a farmhouse sink, and big windows overlooking the dark woods. A small breakfast table was tucked under a bay window. The bones of the old house had been good when Alan bought it, although the house had needed some renovations and modern improvements. He'd made most of the furniture and cabinetry himself.

He put the kettle on the gas stovetop, switched it on, and set about laying out tea things. Two pots bubbled on the stove.

"What's for dinner?" I asked.

"Beef stew and mashed potatoes with green beans. Hope that's okay?"

"Yum," I said. "Sounds absolutely perfect." Alan was a good cook, and comfort food was exactly what I was in the mood for tonight.

When the kettle whistled, he poured hot water into a brown pot and took a bottle of beer out of the fridge for himself while the tea steeped.

We carried our drinks into the living room. Mattie had already claimed the warmest spot on the rug in front of the fire. I curled up on the sofa while Alan lit a few candles on the mantel and then called an Adele album up on his iPad.

"Any developments in the case?" He joined me on the couch as the music played.

"Oh yeah. A mighty big one." I told him what Simmonds had learned about the state of Karla's marriage.

"Why would she lie about something like that?" he asked me.

"She didn't want to seem like a failure in life, I guess. As she saw it, anyway."

"Makes me wonder what else she lied about."

"Makes me wonder what else all of them were lying about. Do you know a newcomer to town named Wayne Fitzroy?"

"I've met him a couple of times," Alan said. "Why are you asking?"

"Ralph told Dad Fitzroy wants the Santa Claus job."

Alan laughed. "That's nonsense."

"Why?"

"I can't imagine anyone more un-Santa-like than him. He used to be some big shot in a property-development company, I think. Tough business type. He's new to town, retired, and looking for something to do, so he's been making friends—contacts, anyway—around town."

"Ralph thinks he and Sue-Anne are becoming chummy."

"What does he mean by 'chummy'?"

"That's what I asked Dad. He didn't know, either."

"I wouldn't be surprised if Fitzroy's planning to run for town council. Sue-Anne doesn't have many allies, as you know, so a new councilor in her court would be good for her. But Santa? He doesn't seem the type to me."

"How do you know him?" I asked.

"He wanted some work done on that house they bought. He asked me to quote him on putting custom-made, built-in bookshelves in the den. I went out to have a look in September."

"You didn't get the job?"

"He didn't like my price. He wanted to haggle and offered half my quote. I don't bargain. My price is my price, and I don't cut corners, either, which I would have had to do to get it in for what he was willing to pay. I might have told him for that price he needed to go to a MegaMart. He didn't like that and threatened to ruin my reputation."

We were curled up together on the deep, soft couch, my legs tucked into his lap. I leaned back and looked at him. "What did you say to that?"

Alan shrugged. "I didn't say anything. I left. My reputation around here's pretty solid. No big deal."

"Did he follow up on that threat?"

"Not that I ever heard. And I would have."

"Would you mind, personally, I mean, if he did become Santa?"

"I won't be toymaker for him, if that's what you're asking." Alan played the role of head toymaker whenever

Santa made a public appearance. He put on a cute costume of woolen jacket and britches and stockings, and shoes with a big metal buckle. He stuck a fake mustache and sideburns to his face and stood behind Santa, writing the kids' wishes down on a long paper scroll with a pen with a white ostrich feather stuck on the end. The children loved it, as did their parents, and occasionally they tried to circumvent Santa to talk to the toymaker directly. Alan was slightly shy and never wanted to be in the spotlight, and the role suited him perfectly. "I like doing it for Noel," he said, "but it wouldn't be the end of the world if I gave it up. It's starting to cut into my work time." He plucked my legs off him. "Dinner's ready, and I'm starving."

Mattie heard the magic word "dinner" and leapt to his feet with a bark.

My mom called me as the lights of Rudolph came into view. I answered with Bluetooth and kept my hands on the wheel. While Alan and I had been enjoying his fabulous stew—thick hunks of seared beef, plump mushrooms, caramelized onions in a rich gravy—a light, wet snow had begun to fall, and the road was slick. "Hi, Mom. Is everything okay there?"

"We managed to get through dinner with no more high drama," she said. "Which was perhaps helped by the fact that Ruth said she wanted to finish the book she's reading and would have a sandwich in her room, and Constance and Barbara went to a restaurant."

"So you only had Genevieve."

"Your father opened one bottle of wine as we sat down, and despite her numerous, increasingly desperate hints, he didn't bring out another. She went outside for a smoke after dinner and then went straight upstairs and all's quiet. For once. But I fear it won't be quiet for much longer."

"Why's that?"

"Your father told me what he learned about the state of Karla and Eric's marriage. To our considerable surprise, considering how acrimonious their separation was, Eric is coming to town tomorrow."

"He is? Why?"

"Diane gave him our number, and he called earlier. He wants, he said, to bring Karla's body home himself. He said it's time to let old bitterness die."

"That sounds nice . . . I suppose."

"In other news, I am considering divorcing your father."

That set me back. She didn't sound like she was kidding. "Are you serious, Mom?"

"The police removed the keep-out tape from what had been Karla's room, and your father happened to mention to Eric that we now have a free guest room in this house."

I groaned.

"And he told Eric he was welcome to use it."

"Eric didn't actually agree to that, did he? Did you tell him it had been Karla's room?"

"He agreed, very quickly, and we did not tell him. What could I say after Noel made the offer?"

"Maybe it'll be okay. He's probably trying to be nice for the sake of their children."

"Perhaps," Mom said. She didn't sound entirely convinced.

"Talk to you tomorrow, Mom," I said, and we hung up. I mulled over what I'd just heard. "Free at last," Eric Vaughan had said when told of Karla's death. Had he killed his bothersome wife and was now planning to return to the scene of the crime? Supposedly killers did that. Did he know he'd be a suspect in the killing? If he did, you'd think he'd want to stay as far away as possible.

Then again, maybe he was trying a double bluff.

Or he might be innocent.

No point in speculating. I turned into my driveway.

I try hard not to ever go into my landlady's part of the house. I fear that if I get in there, I'll be trapped forever under an endless barrage of innuendo, gossip, and accusations. Sort of like Rapunzel in the tower, but without long-enough hair to make a rope and climb out the window.

I'd have to take the risk. When I turned on the tap in the bathroom sink on Tuesday morning, I was greeted by . . . nothing.

Not a drop of water.

I padded down the hallway and knocked on Steve and Wendy's door.

Wendy opened it and greeted me warmly. She was ready for work in a gray skirt, teal blouse, stockings, patent leather pumps, and sedate gold jewelry. The only thing spoiling the image of the perfectly put-together office worker was the patch of fresh porridge dripping down the sleeve of her silk blouse. The sound of someone being torn limb from limb erupted from a back room, and a man swore.

"Sorry to disturb you," I said. "Problems?"

"Tina has decided she doesn't want to go to day care anymore. Steve has decided he wants to run away to sea. She's in her bedroom having a tantrum, and he's hiding in the bathroom." She gave me a strained smile. "Life with a toddler. What's up?"

"Do you have any water?"

"Last I checked, we did. Hold on." She ran into the kitchen, and I heard the sound of running water.

"Just me then," I said. "I'll go down and tell Mrs. D'Angelo."

"Good luck. If you're not back when we get home from work, I'll send a rescue party."

I returned to my apartment and pulled on jeans and an old sweater. Mattie and I went down the back stairs, and I let him romp in the enclosed yard while I went around to the front. Last night's snow was rapidly melting, leaving everything wet and mushy.

I climbed the steps to the veranda. The front door opened before I'd so much as raised my hand to knock. Mrs. D'Angelo stood before me, dressed in a white satin robe with some sort of fluffy pink furlike substance at the ends of the sleeves, the fuzzy, backless slippers called "mules" now rarely seen outside of '50s-era movies on her feet, and her ever-present iPhone stuffed into the belt around her waist. "Merry Wilkinson. You'd best come in. I was about to call around and see if there were any more developments in your parents' case."

"My parents don't have a case," I said. "They were unfortunate enough to have someone pass away in their house."

Mrs. D'Angelo dismissed that trifle with a wave of her hand. The pink furry substance fluttered.

"But that's not why I'm here," I said. "My . . ."

Her hand shot out, too fast for me to dodge it. She grabbed my arm in a surprisingly powerful grip and dragged me into her house. Behind me, the door slammed shut. Trapped!

"I've put the coffee on," she said. "I'm normally a much

earlier riser than this, but I was up late talking to Ruth Johnson. You know Ruth, don't you, Merry?"

I'd never heard of her before. I'd never heard of most of Mrs. D'Angelo's contacts. I wondered if there was a secret network of spies lurking underground in Rudolph. And if so, did the FBI and CIA know about it? They might be able to use the help.

A cup of thin black coffee was poured and placed on the kitchen table. Mrs. D'Angelo gestured to me to sit down. Reluctantly, I did so. "I don't have time to visit," I said. "I have to get to work."

"Nonsense. It's only eight o'clock. Your store doesn't open until ten."

"I . . . uh . . . wanted to get in early today."

"Toast?"

"What? No, thank you."

I might as well not have spoken. Into the toaster went two pieces of squishy white bread and out of the fridge came store-bought raspberry jam and a budget-sized tub of margarine.

Mrs. D'Angelo's kitchen overlooked the backyard. I guessed she didn't spend a lot of time in here (as she spent most of her time peering out the front window hoping to find her neighbors doing something gossip-alert-worthy). The room was neat and clean but hadn't been updated in a long time. The floor was covered in brown linoleum, curling at the edges; the fridge was the color known as harvest gold, hugely popular, so I'd been told, around the time I'd been born; and the Formica kitchen table had matching steel-rimmed chairs with cracked cushioning.

The toast popped out of the toaster. Mrs. D'Angelo

slapped the slices on a chipped plate and put it on the table in front of me. "Eat up," she ordered.

"I have no wa—" I began.

"Unfortunately," she said, "none of my friends know anything about your mother's visitors, so it's difficult to come to conclusions. What are the police saying?"

"Nothing they're sharing with me. I came down because—"

"The family of the deceased is in construction, I've heard. That often means organized crime, doesn't it?"

Kyle Lambert, Jackie's boyfriend, had said the same thing. I wondered if he was tied into Mrs. D'Angelo's network. "They're a small family company. I don't think the mob had anything to do with anything."

"It's a working theory." She stirred a huge spoonful of sugar into her own coffee and then dumped in another.

"Do you have water this morning?" I asked.

"Unfortunate timing for Noel, of course."

"Because I don't . . . What do you mean by that?"

"Wayne Fitzroy's making noises about taking on the role of Santa, and Sue-Anne seems to be going along with him. Some think he wants to use the Santa position as a stepping-stone to a seat on the town council, and eventually mayor, but I disagree. All he's doing is making trouble, mark my words. I've known men like that before. The late Mr. D'Angelo comes to mind."

Despite myself, I said, "Really?"

"Always out to make trouble. Wayne tells everyone he retired, but that's not the case. He was kicked out of his company for embezzlement and told if he left quietly charges would not be laid."

"Really?"

"To pay his substantial legal fees, he had to sell the apartment in Manhattan and the vacation home in Sag Harbor and flee to what he dismissively calls 'the boonies.'" She sniffed in disapproval.

"How do you know all that?" I asked, truly impressed.

"His wife." My landlady gave me a sly grin. "She's lonely here. Her fancy society friends dropped her like a hot stone when he got into financial trouble, and she blames her husband for her reduced circumstances. She's trying to fit into Rudolph in her own way."

"Ah," I said. "I get it. Strange that Sue-Anne would be friends with him if he's after the top job. Which is currently her job."

"Friends? What on earth makes you think he and Sue-Anne are *friends*?"

"Isn't that what you said? Someone else told my dad they were 'chummy.'"

She snorted. "Really, Merry, you shouldn't listen to idle gossip. So easy for things to be misinterpreted. Sue-Anne and Wayne Fitzroy are not chummy in the least. If they seem to be close, it's only because Wayne's blackmailing her."

"Blackmail?"

"If she supports him as Santa Claus this year, then in next year's elections for town council, he'll hold off running for mayor for one more term."

"What on earth has he got to blackmail her with?" I asked. Sue-Anne Morrow wasn't the brightest bulb on our town's Christmas tree, but no one ever suggested she wasn't honest or didn't have the best interests of Rudolph at heart.

Mrs. D'Angelo looked very smug indeed. "It wouldn't be proper for me to make insinuations about anyone else's marriage. But seeing as to how your father's position as Santa Claus is threatened, I'll make an exception in this case. Sue-Anne's husband, Jim, is known to be *carrying on* with a woman on the Muddle Harbor town council."

"I get it," I said. Jim Morrow was scarcely ever seen in Rudolph. He wasn't a typical politician's spouse: standing by his wife's side at events, holding hands and exchanging not-so-secret smiles, nodding enthusiastically at her speeches. Mr. Morrow was a good-looking man for his age, semiretired from a successful career in the city. He was full of charm, or so he thought, and no doubt some women thought also. To me, his charm was severely undermined by the creep factor. The first time I'd met him, out walking Mattie one snowy evening, he'd asked me out.

No, thank you.

I wasn't surprised to hear that the mayor's husband was cheating on her. It couldn't have come to much of a surprise to Sue-Anne, either. But maybe it did. And maybe her pride made her vulnerable to blackmail.

I thought of Karla, trying so hard to make her friends believe she was in a loving marriage; meanwhile, she and her husband were fighting to the bitter end in court, and everyone in their town knew every salacious detail.

"If you and your friends know about this," I asked my landlady, "what makes it blackmail-worthy?"

"We," she said proudly, "will not be talking to the press."

"Fair enough."

"I'm not saying Sue-Anne has ambitions at the state level, nothing she's declared at any rate, but a wandering husband won't help her if she does, now, will it, Merry?"

"No, it certainly won't."

Mrs. D'Angelo's phone rang. "You don't mind if I get this, do you, Merry? It might be important." She pushed buttons. "Mary Beth, what have you learned? No! I can't say I'm surprised."

I got up from the table, leaving my coffee and toast untouched. I didn't know if Dad was aware of any of this, but in case he wasn't, I needed to tell him right away.

Mrs. D'Angelo walked with me to the front door, talking all the while. Someone, I didn't catch a name, had caught her teenage son rummaging through her purse late one night.

I opened the door and stepped onto the veranda. Only then did I remember why I'd come, and I turned around. "I don't have any wa—"

The door shut in my face.

Chapter 13

M rs. D'Angelo finally answered the door in answer to my repeated hammering, and I blurted out that I had no water in my apartment. "One, moment, Jenny," she said into the phone.

Jenny? I thought she was talking to Mary Beth.

"I'll call my nephew Keith to come over soon as I'm off the phone," she said to me.

"Is Keith a licensed plumber?" I shouted at the closing door.

I decided not to wait for Keith to come. If Mrs. D'Angelo needed to be off the phone to give him a call, that might be quite a while. Particularly if there were nefarious activities going on in Rudolph.

I needed to talk to Dad.

I left Mattie in the yard—covered from head to toe (and that was a vast distance) in mud—telling him I'd be right down, and ran upstairs for a change of clothes, my purse, and the leash.

Mattie and I walked the short distance to my parents' house. The sun had come out in a clear blue sky, and the last of yesterday's snow was nothing but muddy puddles. In the park, municipal workers were stringing even more lights and hanging decorations on the town's Christmas tree.

A lit tree stood on the bandstand twelve months of the year to remind everyone we were a year-round Christmas destination. The tree was replaced once a month, but the December one was always the biggest and the brightest and the most heavily decorated. The Sunday after Thanksgiving, the mayor would preside over the official lighting of the holiday tree. The Santa Claus parade was the following Saturday, and then it would be all Christmas, all the time, until the shops closed at three P.M. on Christmas Eve.

The Santa Claus parade was less than two weeks away. If Sue-Anne was thinking of replacing my dad, she didn't have a lot of time.

I arrived at my parents' house and rang the doorbell. I waited for someone to answer while Mattie scratched at the door. My mom didn't normally get up until noon—still living on a performer's schedule, she said. But Dad was always up with the birds. I rang the bell again and put my ear closer to the door to check that it was still working. Mattie whined. I thought I could hear the distant peal.

I knocked. I knocked again, harder this time. I had my own key, but I didn't normally use it when I wasn't expected.

Slowly, the door opened. My dad peered out. "Oh, it's you, Merry."

"Of course it's me. Who were you expecting?" I unhooked the leash from Mattie's collar, and he dashed into the house, almost knocking my father to one side.

"I'm not expecting anyone. I didn't hear the bell over the noise in the kitchen. We're having breakfast."

"Who's 'we'?"

"All our houseguests. Your mother's still upstairs."

"Are you feeling okay? You don't look too well." His face was drawn and pale under the traces of his holiday tan.

"I'm fine, honeybunch. I didn't sleep all that well last night. Being confined to the couch in my den as I was."

"That bad, eh?"

"Aline's not pleased that I invited Karla's husband to stay with us. What else was I to do when the man asked outright?"

I refrained from telling him he could have said no.

The sound of women's laughter came from the kitchen.

"Everything going okay?" I asked.

"They're in good moods this morning. I doubt that will last. What brings you here?"

I lifted the overnight bag into which I'd put my work clothes. "I have no water in my apartment, so I need a shower, and Mattie could use a hosing down."

"So he could." Dad's eyes followed the trail of giant dog prints crossing the formerly clean floors of the hall, heading for the kitchen. "I'd better get that mopped up before your mother comes down, or I won't even get a bed in the study."

"I have some news for you that I picked up when I was asking Mrs. D'Angelo about my water situation. Let me see to Mattie and then we can talk."

I followed the trail of paw prints down the hall. By the time I entered the kitchen, Barbara was crouched on the floor with a kitchen towel in hand, wiping off Mattie's feet.

"Good morning," I said. "Thanks for doing that, Barbara."

"It's my pleasure." She ruffled the fur around his neck. "Such a gorgeous boy." Mattie's entire body wiggled with pleasure.

The women sat around the kitchen table, sipping coffee and eating toast and eggs or cereal. Ruth had her nose buried in a book. She didn't look at me, but lifted one hand in greeting. Constance's and Genevieve's heads were down as they typed on their phones.

"I hope you've come to tell us we can go home," Constance said without bothering to look at me.

"No such luck. You won't hear that news from me in any event. Detective Simmonds will tell you herself."

"If she bothers," Genevieve said. "I'm expecting a callback for a second audition for a major TV production. When it comes, and if she still says I can't leave, I'm going anyway. She can arrest me after I've got the part."

"I don't know why you bother," Constance said. "You've had hundreds of callbacks over the years. Nothing comes of them. Remind me, what was the last role you landed?"

Genevieve punched keys on her phone.

"Detective Simmonds is wasting everyone's time," Ruth said. "I still say the food that killed Karla was a mistaken delivery. Someone ordered takeout, the delivery person went to the wrong address, and no one's willing to confess."

Barbara wiped the last of the mud off Mattie, gave him a hearty pat, and got to her feet. "Ruth and her mystery novels," she said to me. "She's absolutely determined to play detective in her head. As if anyone ever orders one curried egg salad to be delivered."

"It might have been part of a larger order that got

overlooked," Ruth said. "I saw a sign at the place where I went for lunch on Saturday saying they deliver full meals. Merry, have you seen those curried eggs served anywhere?"

"No," I said. "But even I haven't eaten at every restaurant in town."

"Stupidest idea I've ever heard," Genevieve said without looking up from the screen in front of her.

Ruth put down her book. She stared at each of the women, one after the other. In the silence, Genevieve and Constance tore their eyes away from their phones.

"The alternative," Ruth said, once she had everyone's attention, "is that one of us deliberately added peanuts to the food, knowing Karla would eat it."

"One of us? Remind me what Karla said to you, Ruth," Genevieve said. "Something about working for others, unlike her."

Ruth didn't rise to the bait. "I know I didn't kill her. That leaves the three of you—four, counting Aline."

"Hey," I said.

"I haven't forgotten you and your bakery friend, Merry," Ruth said. "Although, I'll admit neither of you had a motive, not as far as we know. Must I remind you all that one of us has been close to a murder before?"

Genevieve laughed.

"You'd better not be repeating that," Constance said. "Not to the police or anyone else."

"Or what, Constance? What would you do then?" Ruth glared at her.

"Let's not be making threats," Barbara said. "Not to each other. That doesn't help anyone."

Ruth tapped the tattered paperback in front of her.

Whose Body? by Dorothy L. Sayers. "What would Lord Peter Wimsey do, is what I say."

Barbara groaned and Constance rolled her eyes. "What on earth that means, I do not care enough to ask."

"Lord Peter Wimsey," Ruth said, "was . . ."

"I said," Constance snapped, "I do not care."

"Can I give Mattie the last piece of my bacon?" Barbara asked me.

"Sure. He'll like that." I left the bickering women and went in search of my dad. I found him putting the mop back in the broom closet. "When does Karla's husband arrive?"

"Midafternoon."

"That's going to add to the festivities."

"Oh yeah."

"Did you know that Wayne Fitzroy is threatening to tell everyone Jim Morrow is having an affair with a town councilor from Muddle Harbor if Sue-Anne doesn't back his attempt to become town Santa?"

Dad threw up his hands. "That's all I need. Where on earth did you hear that? Wait, let me guess. Mable D'Angelo. Not the most reliable of sources."

"No, but even a stopped clock is right twice a day. Mrs. D'Angelo thinks Sue-Anne has state ambitions, so she doesn't need the scandal."

"The only scandal is why Sue-Anne stayed with Jim all these years, and he with her, but that's not my business or anyone else's. Thanks for telling me, honeybunch. I'm planning to go into the town offices this morning, let everyone know I'm back, and try to get a sense of what's going on." That, I thought, explained his clothes. My dad liked to dress in what he considered seasonally appropriate attire. Today he wore brown pants and a brown and orange checked shirt, the collar of which peeked above his knitted sweater. The orange and brown sweater featuring a turkey with a tail spread out behind it like a fan. "Let's hope this is nothing but a misplaced rumor. Speaking of Santa Claus, how's your float coming on?"

"It's not. Not only have I not started on it, I don't have much of an idea for this year."

"Do the one you had last year. The stores aren't supposed to repeat, but seeing as how yours was disqualified, you can make the case that it didn't get the attention it deserved."

"I consider that idea to be cursed."

He gave me a warm Santa smile that went a long way toward reducing the tension on his face. "You'll think of something. Your mother's classes are rehearsing hard for the big day. She told her friends they have to be out of the house by four today and stay away for two hours while her students are here."

I had my shower and got ready for work. When I went into the kitchen for Mattie, the only woman still there was Ruth. Her book was closed and she was on the phone.

"I love you, too," she said. "Tell the kids not to worry. I'll think of this as an extension to my holiday."

I got Mattie and we left through the back without seeing anyone else.

Chapter 14

We arrived at the shop fifteen minutes before opening, giving me enough time to run one quick errand. I unlocked the door off the alley behind Mrs. Claus's Treasures and took Mattie into the office. "Now you be a good boy," I said, as I did every day. "And stay here."

He was used to the routine and immediately settled onto his bed with the usual performance involved in finding the exact right spot. I filled his water bowl, once again reminded him to be good, and left the office. Today was Jackie's day off, and Crystal wasn't back in town yet, so I'd be working on my own.

I hurried down Jingle Bell Lane. The sign on the door of Candy Cane Sweets said "Closed," but I could see Rachel McIntosh moving around inside, getting ready for the day. Rachel looked like a human candy cane: with her pale skin and hair dyed a brilliant scarlet. She wore a long white apron, decorated with a bold pattern of traditional red and white striped candy canes, over a red T-shirt and black slacks, plus a necklace of real candy balls, strung together with red string, around her neck.

I knocked on the glass. She turned, recognized me, and unlocked the door.

"Good morning, Merry. What brings you here?"

"Something I've been thinking about and I'd like to get your impression, if you have a minute."

"Sure. I'm about to open, but I have some time. Terrible what happened at your parents' place. Do the police have a suspect yet?"

"Not that I know of. This is about something else. Have you met a man named Wayne Fitzroy?"

"Oh yes. Such a lovely man, isn't he?"

"He seems to be making an impression wherever he goes."

"He's new to town and he's trying to get to know everyone. I find him so refreshing, don't you? He has some great ideas."

"What sort of ideas?"

Rachel shrugged. "Nothing specific—he's still learning, he says. He thinks Rudolph can do better with more forward-thinking leadership." Her eyes narrowed. "Oh dear. Noel's not planning to run for mayor again, is he?"

"Why do you ask?"

"I wouldn't want to see Noel running against Wayne. Noel's done marvelous things for this town, and we're all so grateful, but Wayne represents new and modern. He ran a very important multinational corporation, you know. He retired to take up the simple life."

"Dad doesn't want to be mayor."

"I'm glad to hear it."

"Rudolph has a mayor," I said. "Sue-Anne hasn't even

been in the job a year yet." She'd taken over from the previous mayor in midterm. "What about her?"

"Sue-Anne will work well with Wayne. The old and the new. Then, when she's ready to go on to bigger things, he'll be in a position to step into the job. It's a win-win for everyone, Merry."

I didn't like the sound of that. Rachel was a sharp businesswoman, not the sort, I'd have thought, to be influenced by a bit of false charm. Margie Thatcher had also seemed to be impressed by Wayne Fitzroy. Why, if people liked him, did he think it necessary to blackmail Sue-Anne? (If he was, and if Mrs. D'Angelo and her network hadn't made up something out of thin air.)

The only answer to that question would be that he was intending to cause trouble for the sake of it.

"Thanks, Rachel," I said. I wanted to ask her what she'd think if Wayne took over as Santa, but the first customer of the day came in, and Rachel turned to him with a welcoming smile.

The scents drifting from Cranberry Coffee Bar, two doors down from my shop, reminded me I hadn't had breakfast. Not even Mrs. D'Angelo's toast and jam. Before going back to open the store, I went for a coffee and a muffin. Cranberries was busy, as the shops on Jingle Bell Lane were about to open and store clerks filled up. People nodded at me and exchanged greetings. No one asked what had happened at Mom's, for which I was grateful.

I ordered an extra-large latte and a cranberry muffin and went to stand at the end of the counter while waiting for my drink to be prepared. Conversation buzzed all around me.

"I reported it to the police," the owner of Diva Accessories was telling Jayne from Jayne's Ladies Wear. "They said they'd look into it, but didn't seem terribly keen. I mean, what can they do now? I'm telling everyone to be on extra lookout this season."

"Lookout for what?" I asked.

"Morning, Merry. We're talking about shoplifters. I had one of my ribbon scarfs stolen on the weekend. I might not have noticed except there were only two left, and I made a point that morning of reordering more stock for the holidays."

"I had something snatched, too," I said. "On Friday before lunchtime. What time was yours?"

"Saturday, but I can't say what time of day for sure. Shortly before closing a customer asked if I had it in another color, and when I went to look—gone."

"We try so hard," Jayne said, "to keep our prices reasonable, and then things like this happen."

"Let's hope they were weekend visitors and have left," I said.

The barista called my name as she put my drink on the counter. I took it with thanks, said good-bye to the others, went back to my shop, and flipped the sign to "Open."

A rush of eager customers did not knock me over in their hurry to get in.

I should spend this quiet time planning what to do about my float. Vicky and the bakery would be eager to win the trophy again, and I imagined her and her legion of bakery staff, most of whom were her relatives, working hard on it. Whereas I hadn't even asked old George Mann if he and his equally old tractor would pull my float again this year.

Instead of looking up ideas for a showstopping Santa

Claus parade theme—maybe something around the story of the dogs of the Great Saint Bernard Pass rescuing snow-trapped travelers in the Swiss Alps—I pulled a stool up to the sales counter and opened my iPad.

Ruth had said something this morning about one of the friends being previously connected to a suspicious death. Judging by the way Constance reacted, Ruth had been talking about her. Now I remembered something else: at the fateful dinner party, Karla had said that the death of Constance's husband had been "suspicious." I'd been so uninterested in their petty squabbles and this morning anxious to talk to Dad, the comments had gone straight over my head, but I was thinking about it now. If it was true, Diane Simmonds should know all about it. She hadn't exactly wanted me to help with the investigation, but it wouldn't hurt to check into the story and, if she hadn't heard about it, give her the tip.

I found it easily. The case had gotten a lot of press, particularly on the West Coast.

Five years ago, Frank Westerton, head of Stewart Industries and son-in-law of company founder Phillip Stewart, had died in an apparent home invasion. He'd been at home alone while his wife, Constance, was at the theater with friends. Constance had left the theater during the first intermission, telling her friends she had a headache, and arrived home to find the back door broken and her husband lying on the floor, stabbed in the back. Constance called 911, but Mr. Westerton was dead by the time help arrived.

What made the story interesting, from my point of view, was that no one was ever arrested. The respectable newspapers reported that Mrs. Westerton was found kneeling by her husband's body when the police and ambulance arrived. The less respectable online gossip sites said she was covered in his blood. Which, I thought, was natural enough if he'd been stabbed and she had tried to help him.

The couple were, the gossip sites reported, "going through a difficult patch in their marriage," according to friends.

Some friends, blabbing to the press.

Reading between the lines, it was implied that the police suspected Constance of the murder. Constance's father, Phillip Stewart, described as "ailing" and having earlier "handed the reins of his company to his son-in-law," whisked his daughter away to his vacation home in Bermuda for "rest," and referred all press inquiries to his lawyers. That didn't quell interest in the case, but over time, attention began to drop off. The police made no arrests and appeared to have no suspects. Occasionally someone suggested the cops had been bought off, and the implication was that Constance would have been charged had her father not been wealthy and influential.

It seemed to me that the press had been trying to make something out of nothing. Some crimes were never solved, and robberies-gone-wrong did happen. Then again, wives did kill their husbands, and vice versa.

Frank and Constance had one son, Edward, aged thirty-two at the time of his father's death. That day, Edward had been in Washington, D.C., conducting business for Stewart Industries. He flew back to California immediately to be with his mother and grandfather, but he did not accompany his mother to Bermuda. Edward, so the gossip sites told me, had political ambitions, but on the premature death of his father, he took over running Stewart Industries.

The chimes over the door tinkled, announcing the first

customer of the day. I put my professional smile on and my iPad away and went to work.

Shortly after four o'clock my dad's car pulled up outside Mrs. Claus's Treasures. Barbara, Ruth, Constance, and Genevieve got out, all looking various degrees of grumpy. Dad drove away at a speed that wasn't entirely appropriate for midtown in the afternoon, and the quarrelsome quartet came into my shop.

"We have been told," Genevieve announced, "we are persona non grata at Aline's house for the remainder of the afternoon."

"That's because she has singing classes," I said. "She can't have people making noise in the house while her students are trying to concentrate."

"I know how to be quiet," Constance snapped.

I didn't reply. If Mom could have locked them in their rooms, maybe that would have worked, but other than that, nothing seemed to be able to stop their constant bickering. I hid a grin at a mental image of them tying their sheets together and climbing down the drainpipes, shouting insults at one another as they descended.

"What else is there to do in this town but shop?" Constance flicked through the rack of cocktail napkins.

"This is the end of the shoulder season," I said, "so it's quiet, but there's plenty to do when the snow falls: skating, cross-country skiing, enjoying a mug of hot chocolate or a glass of mulled wine by the fireplace. In the summer, we have a wonderful beach with good swimming and a harbor and hiking trails through the woods."

"So dreadfully exciting," drawled Genevieve.

"I think it sounds delightful," Barbara said.

"You would," Genevieve replied.

Barbara ignored her. "Nothing better than an invigorating ski through the winter woods."

"Perish the thought," Constance said. "Is there a half-decent women's clothing store in town? If I'm going to be stuck here any longer, I need to get some new things."

"You could try washing what you brought," Ruth suggested.

Constance didn't bother to reply. Ruth went to the toy display and picked up the engine of Alan's train set.

"You have a grandson about the right age for that train, don't you?" Constance said to her. "Would you like to get it for him? I bet it's expensive. Let me treat you."

Color rose into Ruth's cheeks. "No. Thank you."

Constance gave me an exaggerated roll of her eyes, which I pretended not to notice. "Only trying to be helpful."

The four women spread through the store. I tried to watch them all, but more customers came in. Someone wanted a closer look at the jewelry display; another needed suggestions for napkins to match her new table runners (which were red and green, or were they red and gold?). One woman knocked the bracelet display over and jumped out of the way, crashing into the table containing the tree ornaments. I managed to catch the vase of glass balls an instant before it spilled its contents, and then I had to crawl across the floor on my hands and knees for the bracelets before someone stepped on them. All the while the panicked woman tried to help me but ended up unbalancing more delicate items.

Finally, I had everything back in place. I let out a sigh of relief as the clumsy customer went on to examine the selection of plush reindeer and elf dolls.

Genevieve bought a set of paper cocktail napkins for $4.99. Constance got earrings, and Barbara chose one of Alan's necklaces of interlocking rings. "Now, you're sure," she said, "this is locally made from non-imported wood?"

"I've been to the woodworker's house myself," I said, "and toured his workshop."

As they left with their purchases, Barbara said, "I'm thinking a nice brisk walk beside the lake would be nice. Noel said the path goes a long way. The rest of you don't have to come if you don't want to."

"Thank heavens for that," Constance said. "I'm thinking that bar across the street looks inviting."

"I'm in," Genevieve said.

"My treat," Constance said. "That way you can come, too, Ruth."

Ruth—who'd bought nothing—pulled the door closed behind her with more force than was necessary.

I stock a lot of goods in my shop and many of them are small. I ran my eyes over the tables and shelves, piled high with items in preparation for the approaching holiday season. I couldn't see anything missing at a glance, but if one of the women had stolen something, I might not know about it until I ran an inventory.

On Saturday, Vicky and I had both thought one of Mom's friends had stolen from us. The death of Karla had pushed that to the back of my mind, but my conversation with the other shop owners in Cranberries, followed by the visit of the quarrelsome quartet, brought it back.

In the scheme of things, one necklace and one jar of

red-pepper jelly, plus a ribbon scarf, wasn't much when a killer was out there. But . . . might the same person be responsible for both acts?

I debated calling Detective Simmonds, but not only did I have absolutely no proof, it was entirely possible the necklace had been stolen by someone not part of Mom's group, and I didn't want to make unfounded accusations. There was nothing Simmonds could do.

The police might not be able to do anything, but I could.

Simmonds had ordered me not to get involved in the murder investigation. She hadn't said anything about investigating other crimes.

The minute no one needed my attention, I pulled out my phone and called Dad. "Take Mom and her friends out to dinner tonight."

"Why on earth would I want to do that? I'm planning on spending the evening cowering in the study, eating dry bread and water if I have to."

"Because I asked you to. You don't need an excuse; they must all be dying of boredom. Has Mr. Vaughan arrived yet?"

"I told him not to come to the house before six because of Aline's classes. I'm at the town offices now."

"Invite him, too. Leave for dinner at seven."

"Are you going to tell me why?"

"I'll fill you in later."

"Merry . . ."

I hung up before he could ask any more questions and called Vicky. "Are you free tonight?"

"As it happens, I have a space in my busy social schedule, yes."

"Good. I'll pick you up at quarter after seven. We're walking. Don't bother to dress up."

"Where are we walking to?"

"No place exciting." I hung up and turned to the customer standing at the counter. "Would you like a gift box for that?"

Chapter 15

We'd been so busy I hadn't had time for a lunch break, but by the time the shop closed, Cranberry Coffee Bar and Victoria's Bake Shoppe were also closed. I considered going home for a quick bite, but decided to stay and work on some accounts and order a pizza when I got home.

I let out a long groan and mentally slapped my forehead. I'd forgotten to check on the water situation at my apartment. Mrs. D'Angelo said she'd call her nephew when she got off the phone. The problem was, Mrs. D'Angelo *never* got off the phone.

Mattie cocked one ear at me, and I rubbed the top of his head. I'm normally a highly organized person. I have to be with the job I had at *Jennifer's Lifestyle* and then owning my own shop. But too much was happening: Mom's visitors and all their drama, the death of Karla, the shoplifting, Wayne Fitzroy and the plot to unseat Dad, the upcoming Santa Claus parade, and the arrival of the holiday season.

Plus business accounts waiting for my attention. I sat down at my desk and got to it.

At five after seven, I closed the computer. Mattie leapt to attention as I got my coat and his leash from the hook at the back of the door.

We walked the short distance to Vicky's house. Sandbanks met us at the door. Mattie wanted to play, but no amount of refusal could convince him that the old dog didn't want to engage in an excited romp around the house.

I crouched down and gave Sandbanks a hearty rub. "How's the old guy doing?" I asked Vicky.

"Getting older," she said. "But he's still hanging in there."

Sandbanks rubbed his head into my chest. Mattie tried to push him away, as if saying, *My human!*

When Vicky's aunt, who bred Saint Bernards, had one of her top dogs fall under the spell of a non-purebred with a wandering eye, and the resulting puppies-without-papers needed homes, Vicky had leapt into the task of placing them. But she couldn't take one herself: having an enthusiastic puppy around the place wouldn't be a good match for Sandbanks.

About the last thing I wanted or needed at the time was a puppy to care for and to train. But it turned out Vicky knew me better than I knew myself, and now I couldn't imagine life without Matterhorn.

"Guard the house, Sandbanks," Vicky said as she pulled on her coat. He curled into a ball and happily settled down on the floor for a nap to await our return.

Vicky shut and locked the door, and we stepped off the porch. "Now are you going to tell me where we're going?"

"Mom and Dad's house."

"Why didn't you just say so? You were being so secretive, I was expecting we were going to rob a bank or break into Diane Simmonds's office or something similarly nefarious."

"It's sort of along those lines," I said. "I'll tell you the plan when we get there."

We hurried through the busy streets of Rudolph. People walked dogs or drove home after work. Lights shone from most of the houses as parents helped their kids with homework and families ate dinner. At my parents' house, the lights over the front porch and the garage were on.

I marched down the driveway, my steps firm. Mattie ran eagerly ahead of me. He knew where we were, and he was hoping something delicious waited in the kitchen.

I unlocked the kitchen door with my key and let us in. "Hello!" I called in a good loud voice. "It's Merry, anyone here?"

I held my finger to my lips, asking Vicky to be quiet. A blanket of silence lay over everything, but more than that the house felt unoccupied. These grand old Victorians seem to almost change their aura when they're empty.

"Sounds like no one's home," Vicky said.

"As arranged by yours truly," I said. "They've all gone out for dinner."

"Meaning what exactly?"

"Meaning there's a shoplifter loose on Jingle Bell Lane. Something was taken from the accessories store on Saturday."

"The day after you and I had items stolen."

"Which we noticed after Mom's friends paid us a visit. I suspect one of them is our thief, so I'm here to search their rooms."

"I think they call that breaking and entering," Vicky said. "Or something along those lines."

I held up the key I'd used to enter the house. "It can't be breaking and entering, as I haven't broken anything, and I have my own key, which was given to me by the homeowners in case I need to come in when they're not here." More like the key had never been taken back when I moved out, but that was irrelevant right now.

"Okay," Vicky said, "but I bet that doesn't give you permission to rifle through guests' things."

"Probably not. You can guard the back door if you don't want to go upstairs."

"And miss the action? Are you kidding? Do you know who has which room?"

"No, but we should be able to tell which is which by their clothes and things."

"You're thinking the shoplifting has something to do with Karla's death?"

"It might. If Karla knew about it . . . If she threatened to expose the thief . . . Mattie, stay." I pointed to the spot in front of the stove, and he lay down.

To ensure he didn't follow, I closed the kitchen door behind us. It would be hard to make the guest rooms look as though someone hadn't been in them if Mattie got into the women's things.

I went first. I found myself creeping up the staircase as Vicky tiptoed behind, and then gave my head a shake. This was the house I'd been raised in, in which I'd lived for the first eighteen years of my life, where I was welcome anytime I wanted to come. I'd slid down that wide oak banister more than a few times. On one memorable occasion I'd come off the end too fast and had to be taken to the hospital to have my head stitched up.

It's a large house, built in the days when the affluent of Rudolph had big families and plenty of servants to care for them. The servants' quarters on the third floor are closed up now and used for storage, but the six bedrooms on the second level are all still in use. Even with four children in the family, we'd each had our own room as well as a guest room for visitors.

Upstairs, all the doors were closed, and the big old house remained silent. My room, the one I'd had when I was a child, was first on the right. I knocked hard and called out once again, "It's Merry here. Anyone home?"

No one answered, so I slowly pushed the door open. "You start at the far end of the hall," I said to Vicky. "I'll take this one. The room in the middle on the left is Mom and Dad's. Don't go in there. Mom uses the closet in the one to the right of theirs for her off-season clothes, so you don't need to search them."

"What if the thief decided to hide the things in Aline's pockets or something?"

"I'm hoping she—whoever she is—won't think anyone would search her room, so she didn't bother to hide them. We don't have time to check all Mom's clothes or pry up the floorboards."

"My uncle Doug lifted my floorboards when I had the new floor laid. He found a trapdoor. I was hoping for a skeleton, but the only bodies we found were from mice and spiders."

"We don't need to be finding any more bodies around here." I went into the room, and Vicky slipped down the hallway.

I'm the oldest child, and I was the first to leave home, so most of my things were moved out of here to make another guest room. An open suitcase containing men's items lay on the bed. Eric Vaughan must have arrived. This room had originally been given to Karla, and no one had yet packed up her things. I went through the closet and the drawers quickly. Simmonds and her officers had searched here, but they wouldn't have been looking for the items I was after.

No men's clothes hung in the closet. Either Eric didn't mind living out of a suitcase, or he hadn't had time to unpack. Or, more likely, Mom had strongly hinted he wasn't entirely welcome here, and he'd gotten the hint. My mother was very good at saying one thing while expressing something completely different. Karla's clothes were plain, shades of brown and gray mostly. I slipped my hand into her single pair of shoes and felt nothing. Nothing of interest was in her pockets, either. Her purse, big enough to contain the stolen items, lay on the top of the dresser. I rifled through it, finding the usual debris, but nothing of interest.

A pair of earrings sat on the dresser, next to a phone charger, a pen, and a couple of sheets of paper. I flipped through the papers. Printouts of her flight details and a letter from Mom providing her visitors with her address and phone number. A photograph lay next to it, facedown. I flipped it over, expecting to see Karla and her family. Instead, Constance was posing at what was probably her house in California—swimming pool, palm trees—with a young man. The man was in his early thirties, a touch shorter than Constance but very handsome. They had their arms around each other and were smiling at the camera. Constance's hair was different—longer and blonder, and she had fewer lines on her face. I guessed the photo was about five years old.

Wasn't that just like Constance? I thought. Send all her friends pictures of herself, expecting them to display it as if they were close relatives or something. I went to the next room. My brother's hockey team and heavy-metal band posters still hung on the wall. Mom had replaced the hockey-themed comforter with something with pink flowers. It clashed horribly with the dark red walls, chosen by Chris in his rebellious years, but I guess it was hard to find a pretty comforter that matched. The bed was unmade, a towel had been tossed onto the floor, and several dirty glasses and a half-empty coffee mug sat on the side table next to a small stack of threadbare paperbacks, almost certainly from a used bookstore. I read the spines of the books. All mysteries from the so-called Golden Age. This had to be Ruth's room. Two pairs of jeans hung in the closet, and a couple of T-shirts and sweaters were in the dresser. I saw no shoes, meaning she'd brought only the one pair.

I found nothing interesting among her possessions.

I met Vicky in the hallway. "Wow, that Constance doesn't pack light," she said. "Why she thought she'd need a sequined cocktail gown and matching shoes in Rudolph in November, I have no idea."

"Is that the only room you searched?"

"As I said, she has a lot of things. Her makeup bag alone must count as extra baggage on the plane."

"Two left. You take that one, and I'll take the other. We won't bother with the bathrooms, as they're shared."

The next room I went in had been Eve's. The year before she went to Hollywood to pursue an acting career, she'd done the decorating herself, proclaiming that she was no longer a child so she needed an adult room. Down came the movie posters and pictures of famous actresses and out went the stuffed bears and My Little Ponies. She replaced it all with so much pink you might have been standing inside a giant Pepto-Bismol bottle.

The room was neat, the bed made, the pink quilt smoothed, the pink cushions propped up against the headboard, the pink curtains pulled closed. I recognized the high-heeled shoes as ones Genevieve had been wearing the night of the potluck dinner.

I opened the closet and sucked in a breath. Bingo. A blue and turquoise ribbon scarf was draped over a blue sweater. I quickly went through the drawers. Tucked in among Genevieve's underthings and T-shirts, I found my necklace and the jar of red-pepper jelly from Vicky's bakery. I also found a small wooden decoration of a reindeer on skis that I hadn't missed, and a couple of plastic tree ornaments with the price tag ($2.99) from Rudolph's Gift Nook still on them. Genevieve might have bought the ornaments from the Nook, but I didn't think so. Two small paper bags from Mrs. Claus's, one containing the tree ornament purchased on Friday, and the other with the cocktail napkins she'd paid for this afternoon, had been tossed onto the armchair under the window. The other things were in the drawer because they hadn't come home in bags. They were all small enough to slip into a coat pocket or a purse.

Margie probably hadn't even realized she'd been robbed.

The door opened, and I yelped.

"Only me," Vicky said. "Nothing in there, but a lot of reading that would put anyone to sleep. Legal stuff, so I guess it's Barbara's room. That, plus her hiking shoes. What about you?"

I held up the necklace. "Your jelly's here, too, as are a few other things that I doubt came with shop receipts."

"Whose room's this?"

"Genevieve."

"Which one's that again?"

"The actress."

"What are you going to do?" Vicky asked.

"I don't know. To be honest, I didn't expect to find anything. The shoplifting was a box I wanted to tick off because it was bothering me. I don't know if this has anything to do with the death of Karla."

"Stealing is a crime in itself," Vicky said.

"So is searching someone's possessions without a warrant. And, as we are not police officers, we obviously do not have a warrant and will never get one."

"Are you going to tell Simmonds?"

I dropped onto the bed. "I don't know."

"What's with all the pink?" It's making me feel queasy. Your mom has better taste than this."

"Eve was going through a stage. Something about helping an actor focus on their emotions when not interrupted by breaks in color."

"Or breaks in taste," Vicky said.

I pushed myself to my feet and smoothed the cover. I wasn't sure if I should put the things back, so Genevieve wouldn't know someone had been in here, or take them with me, so she'd know someone was onto her. "I'll talk to Dad. See what he says I should do."

"Do you think Karla might have been blackmailing Genevieve over this?"

"It's entirely possible." For now, I decided, I'd leave everything as I found it. If the petty thieving had some relation to the death of Karla, the stolen goods were evidence. "Maybe Karla threatened to expose Genevieve."

Vicky nodded, making her lock of orange hair bounce, a sharp contrast to the seriousness of her expression. "And Genevieve decided she had to eliminate the threat."

Chapter 16

held out my begging bowl.

"Still no water?" Wendy said.

"Not a drop."

"Come on in," she said.

When I'd arrived home from my search of Mom's guests' rooms—after taking care to ensure no evidence of our presence remained and locking the door behind us—I'd turned on the kitchen tap to fill Mattie's bowl. Nothing came out.

Lights were still on in Steve and Wendy's apartment, so I gathered up a stockpot and a towel and toothbrush and went begging.

"If you need a shower in the morning," Wendy said, "you're welcome to use ours."

"Thanks. I'll have to venture back down and ask if Mrs. D'Angelo remembered to call the plumber. Which she probably didn't. This time I'll get his number myself." I'd also stand well out of snatching range on the porch and not allow myself to be dragged inside.

I filled my stockpot, brushed my teeth and washed my face, stayed for a few minutes so Tina could show me her new dance moves, and staggered the four steps down the hallway under the weight of the water.

I then gathered my courage around me and ventured downstairs to face my landlady. I knew from past experience there was no point in phoning Mrs. D'Angelo. If I got her on the line, she'd not let me get a word in edgewise, and if I reached voice mail, she'd never reply.

To my considerable surprise, and relief, I was back in my apartment in a matter of minutes with a piece of paper containing the plumber's phone number clenched in my fist. Apparently my parents and their guests had been spotted at the Yuletide Inn, and because I was not with them, I obviously had nothing to contribute to the gossip mill.

Even better, it turned out that Mrs. D'Angelo's nephew was indeed a licensed plumber, and he promised to come around in the morning.

I rummaged in the fridge for ingredients to make a sandwich and then called Alan. "Are you busy?" I asked.

"Never too busy to talk to you, Merry. I'm in the workshop, about to paint the newest batch of train sets, but I can take a break."

"I need some advice."

"If I can help, I will."

"What would you do," I said, "if you knew someone had committed a crime, but the reason you know verged on the slightly illegal? I'm asking for a friend."

He chuckled. "I won't ask what you and Vicky have

been up to this time. I guess it depends on how serious the crime is and how slightly illegal your activities have been."

"Not serious and only slightly."

"Does this have anything to do with the death of that woman at your parents' house on Sunday?"

"I'm not sure."

"If you're not sure, Merry, but you think it might, then my advice is to tell Detective Simmonds anything you know."

"I was afraid you'd say that. Not that I'm talking about me, you understand."

"Right. Has your dad said anything about next Saturday?"

"What's happening next Saturday?"

"The Santa Claus parade. Don't tell me you forgot."

I sighed. "So much is happening, I can't work up any enthusiasm for it. I'm thinking of skipping the parade this year."

"That'll have you run out of town. How about I come around on Sunday and we put something together? It doesn't have to be fancy, but it does have to be something. You have arranged for a flatbed and someone to pull it, haven't you?"

"Must have slipped my mind."

"I'll take care of it."

"You don't have to do that, Alan. You have your own role to play."

"Which brings us back to my original question. Did Noel find anything out about the attempt to unseat him as Santa?"

"Not that he's told me."

"I might not have a role to play after all. Not if Noel's

not going to be Santa. If it comes to that, I can make a few minor tweaks to my costume and sit on your float."

"I did give it some thought, before all this with Mom and her guests took over. Maybe we can take advantage of Mattie and do something around the mountain rescue origins of Saint Bernard dogs?"

"Great idea. I'll paint some black lines on a hollow piece of wood to make it look like a barrel and tie it under Mattie's chin. That, plus a few pine branches and some birch stumps, maybe a painted backdrop to look like high mountains, will be all you'll need. You can wear your Mrs. Claus costume, and Jackie her elf getup. Christmas in the Swiss Alps."

"Alan Anderson, I think you might be the perfect man."

"Goes without saying," he said modestly.

I spent a restless night. Alan's advice, about both my float and my break-and-enter confession, was practical and sensible. As was he.

But I still wasn't sure. In the past, Diane Simmonds had seemed to value my help, but this time she'd ordered me to stay out of it.

Mattie snorted and rolled over. His legs moved as he slept as though he dreamt he was chasing squirrels. Or maybe his dreams were of cold-blooded killers.

It was possible Genevieve killed Karla because Karla either was blackmailing her or threatened to expose her.

I decided I had to tell Simmonds what I'd discovered, and then I drifted off to sleep. If I dreamt I was also chasing killers, I don't remember.

Chapter 17

I let Mattie into the backyard first thing in the morning, showered at Wendy and Steve's, filled my pot, and took time to admire Tina's new outfit.

As I was leaving, I caught a glance between Steve and Wendy.

"What?" I said.

Wendy sighed. "I guess you need to know. There's going to be a piece in the paper this morning about the Santa Claus situation." Wendy was the receptionist at town hall. Which means she was the first—and sometimes the only—person to know what was going on.

"What Santa Claus situation?"

"Russ came in yesterday afternoon, asking councilors for comments for a story he's putting together. The rush for the doors was then on. Only Sue-Anne agreed to talk to him. She shut the door to her office, so I don't know what was said."

"Thanks," I said. "I'll check it out."

I fed Mattie and put the coffee on. Then I settled at the

kitchen table with my iPad while waiting for the plumber. I didn't want to, but I had to. I called up the page for the *Rudolph Gazette*.

FITZROY CALLS ON "SANTA" WILKINSON TO STEP DOWN, screamed the headline.

The byline was Russell Durham. Wayne Fitzroy had given an interview to the paper yesterday.

With the Christmas season only a few days away, Rudolph resident Wayne Fitzroy is questioning the ability of former mayor Noel Wilkinson to continue in his role of Santa Claus.

Fitzroy, who with his wife, Norma, moved to Rudolph over the summer and instantly fell in love with the town, expressed his concerns to this newspaper.

"Noel Wilkinson's loyalty to Rudolph is beyond question and it's with much regret that I am calling upon him to remove himself from his central role in the forthcoming Christmas season. A woman died in suspicious circumstances at the Wilkinson home only a few days ago, and as of yet, despite the best efforts of the Rudolph police, the case remains open. For the good of the town and its reputation as a family-friendly place to spend the season of goodwill, it would be a mistake to have a man involved in a police investigation playing such a prominent role."

Fitzroy has called upon the mayor and town council to "show some courage and do the right thing."

When contacted by this newspaper, interim mayor Sue-Anne Morrow had no comment other than to express her confidence in the success of the forthcoming holiday season. Other councilors were unavailable for comment.

I swore so heartily, Mattie looked up from where he was demolishing a stuffed Santa, a damaged castoff from the store.

Two pictures accompanied the article. One showed Wayne and his wife smiling broadly, standing arm in arm next to the Christmas tree at the bandstand. They looked very Christmassy and community-minded. The other was of Dad coming out of the house with a scowl on his face and his hand in the air, as though shooing away the pesky photographer. The photo did not scream "Christmas spirit."

The story repeated what precious little it knew about the death of Karla Vaughan. It mentioned that the police had not ruled her death a murder, but I knew everyone reading this article would take it that way. Dad had refused to comment on Fitzroy's statement. Sue-Anne Morrow, mayor of Rudolph, had made some mealymouthed comment to the effect that no one wanted scandal to reflect on the town. She made no attempt to support Dad or even to point out that he hadn't even been in Rudolph at the time of the death.

Other councilors had, as Wendy said, scurried for their rat holes when asked to comment. They'd wait until they knew who was winning before declaring their loyalty to one side or the other.

I shouldn't have, but I sent a text to Russ anyway: *Mean article.*

He replied almost immediately: *Asked Noel to defend himself. He wouldn't*

Me: *You coulda found a better pic*

Russ: *Sent junior photog. Noel refused to smile*

Russ: *Still friends?*

Me: *No*

Russ: *I'll make it up. Dinner tonite?*

Me: *No*

Despite myself, I found myself smiling. Russ knew I was with Alan now, but he just couldn't help himself. I did feel a bit better toward him after our brief exchange. He'd given Dad a heads-up about Fitzroy's statement. If Dad chose not to respond, that was his business.

A link on the page led to a statement from the police. They weren't yet calling Karla's death a homicide, but they were asking anyone who'd been on Mom and Dad's street on Sunday night between five thirty and six fifteen to get in touch with them.

That would have town tongues wagging.

Mattie leapt to his feet a second before the doorbell buzzed, and we went downstairs to greet the plumber.

Today was Wednesday, the day before Thanksgiving, but there would be no Thanksgiving for the Wilkinsons this year. Mom had called Chris and Carole to tell them not to come and told me to uninvite Alan to dinner.

I wondered if I should ask Mom and Dad to my place to have the holiday meal with Alan and me. Not that I'd ordered a turkey or done any grocery shopping. We could always have pizza.

Might the quarrelsome quartet tag along?

I couldn't think of a worse way to celebrate Thanksgiving.

While Keith the plumber banged on walls, ran up and down the stairs, and talked to himself in deep serious tones, all while being supervised by Mattie, I called Jackie. Today would be a busy day in town. Locals who'd moved away were arriving to spend the holiday with their families, and the shop-owner grapevine said the hotels and inns were fully booked with Thanksgiving vacationers.

"What's up?" Jackie groaned into the phone.

"How'd you like to open the store again this morning?"

"What's it worth to me?"

"Time and a half."

"I don't know, Merry. I was out late last night. I need my beauty sleep." She yawned loudly.

"You can sleep tomorrow when we're closed for the holiday. Double time."

"I feel energy returning even as we speak."

"I hope not to be too late, but I have a plumber here, and then I want to go around to my dad's."

"Did you like the picture in the paper? I haven't seen it yet. Is it good?"

"What picture?"

"Of your dad. Kyle got a job as an on-call photographer for the *Gazette*. Isn't that cool?"

"Kyle took that picture?"

"Yeah. He's thinking he'll spend a year at the *Gazette*, make his reputation, and then maybe move to New York City or Los Angeles."

"Kyle's working for the *Gazette*? Russ Durham hired him?" *What had Russ been thinking?*

"That guy who was working there quit and went back to college. He told Kyle about it and Kyle applied for the job."

I could only assume Kyle had been the sole applicant.

"He's wanting to be a fashion photographer. You should see some of the pictures he's taken of me, Merry. They're so good." She giggled. "Then again, maybe you shouldn't see them."

I rolled my eyes.

From under the stairs, Keith the plumber yelled, "Gotcha," and I was rewarded by the sound of rushing water.

* * *

Keith told me far more about pipes and corrosion and intake valves and outlet valves and other assorted thingamajigs than I ever wanted to know. When he finally paused for breath, I reminded him to send the bill to Mrs. D'Angelo, not to me, and waved him out the door.

As soon as he was gone, Mattie and I headed to Mom and Dad's house. I called Diane Simmonds on the way. "I know you're going to tell me it's none of my business," I said, "but what's happening with the Karla Vaughan case?"

"It's none of your business, Merry," she said. "If you want an update, you can read it in the paper like everyone else."

"All the paper ever says is that you have no comment, and the chief says the investigation is still ongoing. You can at least tell me when you're going to allow Mom's guests to go home. The situation there is not good."

"I never said they had to stay at your parents' house, only that they aren't to leave the town of Rudolph without my permission. Mrs. Westerton's lawyers have been on to the chief, as has Barbara Shaughnessy's law partner. I can't keep them in Rudolph forever, so they do have a point. Obviously I can't allow the two who have lawyers at their beck and call to leave and detain the others. I called your parents' house this morning to tell them they can leave tomorrow if I don't come up with any further reason to detain them."

"They must have been pleased to hear that."

"Not so as you'd notice. Constance Westerton intends to send the Rudolph police department the bill for the extra airfare and a night in an airport hotel if she can't get a flight at the last minute on Thanksgiving Day."

"Thanks for telling me. Karla's husband arrived yesterday. Did you know that?"

"I did. I've met with him."

"What did you think?"

"Nothing I'm going to share with you, Merry. I can tell you that he is not under arrest, nor is he a suspect. At this time."

The tone of her voice loaded the last sentence with significance.

"Did anything come of trying to find who bought the peanuts and other egg salad ingredients?"

"Not yet. We have people still to talk to. Many clerks work part-time or on a casual basis at grocery stores and have other jobs, so they can be hard to track down. We never give up, Merry."

I took a deep breath. "I have to tell you something. It might not mean much, and if possible I'd prefer not to tell you how I know, but—"

A man's voice in the background yelled, and in reply Simmonds shouted, "Be right there. I told you not to interfere in this, Merry," she said to me. "That order stands. Gotta go."

"Hello? Are you there? Detective? I have something to confess. Detective Simmonds? Diane?"

Silence came down the line. She'd hung up on me.

I put my phone away. "I tried," I said to Mattie.

I hadn't planned on confronting Genevieve; I hadn't planned on anything, but when I let myself in through the back door of my parents' house, she was the only person in the kitchen, hunched over a mug of coffee while flipping through a fashion magazine.

"Hi," I said.

She glanced up. "Hello." She looked down and turned a page of her magazine.

Mattie trotted over to sniff at her legs. Genevieve was still in her nightwear, a peach satin nightgown with a stain on the right sleeve and a rip in the bottom hem. The nightgown was low cut, showing the sharp collarbones and folds of skin on her neck. Her hair was mussed and she hadn't put on any makeup. Sunlight streamed in through the wide kitchen windows, and she looked about twenty years older—her real age—than she did in soft light and full makeup.

"Where is everyone this morning?" I asked.

"Barbara has gone on yet another of her tedious hikes. Ruth is upstairs reading. She's determined to get to the bottom of Karla's murder by uncovering a clue in one of her dratted books. Constance is probably still on the phone to her father's lawyers, demanding that everyone in the Rudolph police department, from the chief down to the janitor, be fired. Eric's no doubt watching some dreary sports program on TV. Your mother's not yet up, and I haven't seen your father. I suspect he's hiding." She sipped her coffee.

"How was dinner last night? I heard you went out."

"It was passable. The restaurant was good, the food excellent. But I'm getting dreadfully weary of the company. As for the newcomer, that husband of Karla's . . ." She let out a bark of laughter. "He's as dull as I'd have expected a husband of hers to be. Soon-to-be-ex-husband, I should say. Imagine that, Karla with her perfect little family and her perfect little life had been dumped for another woman. They aren't even divorced yet, and he and his new girlfriend already have another baby on the way."

"Really?"

"Oh yes. The new woman is half Karla's age, but so ugly

Eric must have been the only man she could catch. He passed around a picture of her. Totally tasteless thing to do, if you ask me."

About as tasteless as Genevieve's conversation.

"Considering," Genevieve said, "that we're Karla's friends."

"Did he seem sad?"

"You mean about Karla's death? He put on a show of wiping his eyes now and again and blew into his handkerchief. But then he blathered on and on about how he was looking forward to being a father again." She snorted. "What a fool. He's forgotten about midnight feedings and temper tantrums, not to mention driver's license arguments and college tuition." She might have been talking to me, but her attention had returned to her magazine. She continued flipping pages. Upside down, I saw lean, pouting models, excessive amounts of alabaster skin, ridiculous clothes, brilliant jewelry. And that was the men. The women wore even more jewelry and showed even more skin.

I wondered how best to approach the subject most on my mind, then I decided nothing would suit but full speed ahead. "Some items were stolen from my shop on Friday and again yesterday afternoon. Other stores along Jingle Bell Lane report the same thing."

That got Genevieve's attention. Her head snapped up. "Is that so?"

"Yeah. We're a tight-knit community here, the shop owners in particular. When I heard what times the other stores had been hit, it occurred to me that the pattern followed your path through town."

Her right eye began to twitch. "That's too bad, but you can't possibly be thinking one of us—"

"Actually, Genevieve, I think you shoplifted from my

store, twice; from Victoria's Bake Shoppe; from Rudolph's Gift Nook; and from Diva Accessories."

Another twitch.

"Because the Nook is next door to me, I'm good friends with the owner." Okay, so I lied. It was all in the pursuit of justice, and I wasn't under oath. "When she realized what had happened, she came to talk to me. She described a tall, thin woman, sophisticated, very pretty. That could only be you." It never hurt to pile on a layer of flattery when forcing a confession.

"Rubbish." She shut her magazine. "I might have been in those stores, there's nothing else to do in this miserable town, but I didn't steal anything. If you'll excuse me, I have calls to make. I'm supposed to be getting a callback for a role, and if I don't hear today, everything'll be shut down until next week."

"We—the shop owners, I mean—intend to tell the police and ask them to investigate. Only a few small insignificant items have been taken, but it's important to nip this sort of thing in the bud, don't you agree?" I glanced at my watch. "My friend should be dropping into the police station anytime now. They'll be here soon with a warrant to search the guests' rooms."

"In that case"—Genevieve stood up and gave me a bright smile that did nothing to eliminate the fear in her eyes. Judging by her acting today, I wasn't surprised she wasn't getting any roles—"I'll run upstairs and get dressed."

"I'll go with you and stand outside your door. We wouldn't want any items being moved about, now, would we?"

She glared at me, the expression on her face alternating between anger and fear. Fear won out, and she dropped into her chair with a groan. "I'm sorry, Merry, really I am. I'll give everything back. There's time still, isn't there? You can take the things so the police don't find them. Please. I don't need any more shoplifting charges on my record."

More charges?

I attempted to look stern. Sensing Genevieve's distress and wanting to comfort her, Mattie put his head in her lap. She shoved him away. He wasn't used to being rebuffed, so he came to me instead. I scratched behind his ears.

"Why did you do it?" I said. "The ornaments from the Nook cost less than three dollars. They'll be discounted after Christmas to ninety-nine cents."

Genevieve's shoulders slumped, and she began to cry. I got up and pulled a sheet off a roll of paper towels, handed it to her, and sat down. I waited for her to cry it out and hoped no one would come in. Mattie nuzzled his face into my lap, and I stroked his soft fur.

She cried for a long time. Eventually, she let out a deep breath, and her whole body shuddered. She lifted her head and stared at me through puffy red eyes. She looked far older than her years. "I can't really say. I see pretty things, and I want them, but I can't afford them. Sometimes I don't even realize I've taken something until I'm out on the street and my bag feels heavy. I can't land roles anymore. Work's dried up, and I don't know what I'm going to do. Last week, I was turned down for a detergent commercial because they said I was too old. Can you imagine how I felt, being told I'm too old to play a middle-American housewife? I need a smoke."

"Not in the house." The slightest whiff of a cigarette would have Mom charging in here though the place were on fire.

"There's no callback coming, like I told the others. I haven't gotten my foot in a door for months." She sobbed. "I'm washed up. Finished. And I never even began. What else have I got in life? I deserve a few nice trinkets now and again."

"Not if they belong to me," I said, but she didn't hear.

"Look at Constance. She has everything she wants. Anything she asks for, her father gives it to her. Look at Barbara with her law office and her fancy airs about the perils of consumerism."

"Your friends aren't all well-off. Ruth isn't. Karla wasn't."

"Even your mother." Genevieve waved her arms to take in the modern kitchen, the big house. "She was a major star. She made it, and she didn't even try to keep it. She gave it up and buried herself here. It could have been me. It should have been me!"

"My mother didn't exactly bury herself. She simply chose a new path. She worked hard for everything she got."

"So did I! I can't help getting old. It's all so unfair."

All of this had nothing whatsoever to do with shoplifting—except that it seemed to be Genevieve's excuse—or with the more important matter on my mind. "Did you kill Karla," I asked, "because she threatened to expose you to the others?"

She looked genuinely startled. "What? Kill Karla? No."

"This group wouldn't have been at all understanding of your situation, would they? Petty thieving. A police record. Constance would have laughed at you. Ruth and Karla would have pitied you. You couldn't have that, could you? Particularly not pity from Karla, whose husband left her for a woman half her age. So you killed her."

"That's ridiculous."

"Is it?"

She stood up. "I didn't know Karla's husband dumped her until last night. Okay, I've confessed to taking your cheap junk. I've said I'll give it back, and I will. I didn't kill Karla, and you can't make me say I did."

I believed her. Maybe she was a better actress than I gave her credit for. Maybe she'd pretended to be a bad actor at the shoplifting accusation to deflect questions about the murder, but I didn't think so. I got up and rummaged under the kitchen sink. I pulled out a shopping bag and handed it to her. "Put the things you stole in here, and I'll return them to the owners, telling them to ask no questions. But don't take anything else. Like I said, this is a close town. I'll hear about it, and then I *will* call the police."

"Meaning you haven't called them yet."

No need to say I did call, but Detective Simmonds didn't have time to hear me out. I shook my head. "You need help, Genevieve. When you get home, why don't you talk to someone?"

"Talk isn't going to take away these wrinkles on my face or tighten up the sagging skin under my arms."

"No, but it might make you not so bitter about it."

She left the kitchen.

I spoke to Mattie. "I think that went well, don't you? One problem down, now on to the next."

Chapter 18

The door to Dad's study was open, but he wasn't there. I followed the sound of the TV down the hall to what Mom grandly called the conservatory. This room overlooked the backyard, facing south, and is where Mom kept outdoor plants too fragile for a New York winter: dwarf palm trees, flowering hibiscus, geraniums, and begonias, and a myriad of tumbling ivy and stretching branches. Dad was sitting in an armchair, the wide leaves of a palm looming over his head, reading the *New York Times*. A man I didn't recognize had taken ownership of the La-Z-Boy that offered the best view of the TV. A golf game was playing, the announcer speaking in hushed tones, the player lining up his shot.

Dad put his paper away when I came in. "Good morning, honeybunch. This is early for a visit, isn't it?"

I bent over and kissed his fuzzy cheek. "Never too early to see you, Dad."

The La-Z-Boy straightened with a clunk, and its occupant politely got to his feet.

"Eric," Dad said, "this is my daughter Merry."

Eric was a short, round man, at about five foot eight and well over two hundred and fifty pounds, most of the excess weight trapped in his basketball-sized belly. His nose was a network of thin red lines, and lengths of gray hair had been allowed to grow too long, in a failed attempt to cover the shiny bare patch at the top of his head.

Not yet ten o'clock, but a beer bottle sat on the table beside him.

He took a step toward me and held out his hand. "Pleased to meet you."

I shook. His grip was firm, but not too strong.

"I'm sorry for your loss," I said.

"Yeah. Thanks. Karla and I were . . . well, we weren't getting on so well this last little while, but it's still a shock. Despite it all, we had been married for a long time."

I turned to my dad. "Have you got a minute?"

He put the paper aside. "Shall I assume you saw this morning's *Gazette*?"

"Yes."

"Let's talk in the study."

Eric dropped back into his seat as Dad and I left the room.

"How's it going?" I jerked my head toward the sound of polite clapping coming from the TV. "With him, I mean?"

"Aside from the fact that I have better things to do than watch golf and drink beer at ten in the morning, fine. Actually, come to think of it, I have nothing better to do this morning than watch golf and drink beer." The mug next to Dad's seat, I'd noticed, had contained coffee.

"Which is why I'm here," I said. "What's our defense against Wayne Fitzroy? Russ said he asked you to comment and you declined. Is that part of your strategy?"

"My strategy? Our defense? We have none, honeybunch. Everything the man said was true. A woman did die, under suspicious circumstances, here in our house. It's up to Sue-Anne and the town council to decide if they want to make something out of it."

"You can't be serious, Dad. Never mind the personal insinuations against you and Mom, the job of Rudolph's Santa Claus is far too important to leave to some jumped-up outsider wanting to make trouble."

"We don't know that he is wanting to make trouble."

"Yes, we do."

"Never forget, Merry, 'it is a capital mistake to theorize in advance of the facts.'" My dad could always be counted on to have a Sherlock Holmes quote at the ready.

"I'm not theorizing; I'm telling you what I've heard."

"What you've heard are not facts. All I know, and all you know, is what Mable D'Angelo and her cohort of busybodies have to say about him. They are not a reliable source."

"I'll agree with that," I said, "but the way he's gone about this is underhanded, don't you think? Talking to the newspaper first?"

"Your mother and I discussed it last night. We decided not to fight it. It's not worth the effort."

I was stunned. "Not worth the effort! For Santa Claus in Rudolph! The parade is not much more than a week away."

"I called Sue-Anne and left a message, saying if she wanted to talk, I'm available. I'm leaving it at that. The ball is in her court."

"You could have at least smiled for the newspaper. You look like the Ghost of Christmas Yet to Come in that picture. No one's going to want to put their child on that knee."

"I wasn't aware Kyle Lambert had started working for the paper."

"He didn't identify himself?"

"No. He popped out from behind a bush and asked me if it was true Aline had murdered her friend. Next thing I knew, a bulb had gone off in my face."

"No wonder you were scowling."

"A reaction which, I assume, was his intent," Dad said.

"I might have a word with Russ Durham about proper journalistic ethics and behavior."

"You do that, honeybunch. Otherwise, the subject is closed. I have a house full of unwanted guests, a wife getting angrier by the minute, the police popping around at all hours of the day and night." He shook his head. "And now I'm expected to talk sports over dinner."

I decided this wouldn't be a good time to tell him about Genevieve and the shoplifting.

"By the way, Eric's new lover has left him," Dad said. "He told her that at his age he couldn't be expected to change diapers or babysit. He mentioned that to me last night after dinner, when he was into his third glass of my brandy, expecting me to be on his side. Which, I'll assure you, I am not. I'm not supposed to share that information with Karla's friends."

I shook my head. "Everyone in this house is keeping secrets."

Dad grinned at me. "Not me. I'm an open book."

"And I'm glad of it."

"Speaking of last night's dinner. Why did you want me to take them out?"

"No reason."

He gave me *that* look. The Dad look.

"It's probably better you don't know," I said.

"Better I don't know you searched the guest rooms?"

"How'd you—" Too late, I snapped my mouth shut. I'd stepped neatly into the trap.

"I can think of no other reason you'd want us all out of the house at a particular time. I considered advising you against it. If you're searching for clues—almost certainly with the assistance of Vicky—like some sort of adult Nancy Drew and her friends, you'd be advised to leave that to Diane rather than risk interfering with evidence that can be used in court."

"What we were after had nothing to do with the killing of Karla," I said.

"Everything in this house, right now, has to do with the killing of Karla."

"Why didn't you stop us . . . I mean me . . . then?"

My dad smiled at me. "Because I trust you to keep your head on your shoulders and do the right thing."

I swallowed around a substantial lump in my throat. "Thanks, Dad."

"But," he continued, "as for the Santa Claus business, I do not trust you one bit. I don't want you getting involved. And for goodness' sake, don't talk it over with Vicky. The two of you will then come up with some plan to save Christmas in Rudolph."

"Would we do that?"

He did not bother to reply.

The doorbell sounded. Dad groaned. "It's early for visitors. This can't be anything good."

I followed him to the front door. As he'd said: nothing good. Detective Simmonds stood there. She was not smiling. At least she'd come alone, in her own car. No need to attract more attention from the neighbors or get Mrs. D'Angelo's network buzzing. "Good morning, Noel, Merry," she said.

"Morning, Diane," Dad said.

"I thought you'd want to know that moments ago the chief announced to the press that the death of Karla Vaughan is now an official murder investigation."

Dad's face tightened. We knew Karla had been murdered. It was still a shock to hear it expressed so plainly.

"I would like to speak to Mr. Vaughan," she said. "Is he in?"

Dad stepped back and waved her inside. "Merry, would you tell Eric someone is here to see him?"

"Sure." I headed down the hall as Simmonds said, "Snow's in the air."

"That'll help people get in the mood for the Christmas season," Dad replied.

Eric Vaughan was comfortably reclined in the La-Z-Boy, finishing the last of the beer. The players and their caddies were carefully studying the grass, while the announcer continued to speak in hushed tones.

"Detective Simmonds is here," I said. "She wants to talk to you."

With a groan Eric straightened the chair and put the bottle onto the table. "One more time."

When we arrived in the front hall, Mom had joined Dad. Constance and Ruth stood on the stairs, watching.

Mom was dressed in cream wool pants and a chocolate brown cashmere sweater, her hair washed and styled, her casual at-home makeup applied. She had not been in bed, as Genevieve had thought; she just hadn't wanted to come down.

I didn't blame her.

"A word, Mr. Vaughan," Simmonds said.

"You can use my study," Dad said.

"Do you know how difficult it's going to be to get a flight tonight or on Thanksgiving Day itself?" Constance said. "Anything available at the last minute is going to cost a fortune. I'm going to send the bill to your boss and tell him to take it out of your pay."

Simmonds looked at her. "You are welcome to stay in Rudolph until next week, Mrs. Westerton, if that would be more convenient for your travel arrangements."

I thought Mom might choke.

"I have no intention of remaining here one minute longer than I have to," Constance said.

"Your decision," Simmonds replied. She led the way to the study, and Eric followed along behind. Dad followed, because it's his study, and I followed because I'm the curious sort.

I expected Dad and I would be asked to leave, but Simmonds said nothing. So Dad shut the door, with us inside.

"Have a seat, Mr. Vaughan," the detective said.

Eric settled himself slowly into a chair. Dad and I stood against the wall, trying to look like part of the furniture. Simmonds took the chair behind the desk. She studied Eric's face for a long time. No one said anything. "I had a look at your divorce papers," she said at last.

"That must have made for interesting reading." The room wasn't warm, but beads of sweat began to appear on Eric's forehead.

"Very interesting. You and Karla have been battling it out for more than two years now. Your lawyers' fees must be exorbitant."

"It's ruining me," he said.

Simmonds looked at Dad and me. "Karla wanted one half of the worth of the business as part of the divorce settlement, on the grounds that she had been a full partner in the company since its founding."

"She was a part-time bookkeeper," Eric said. "I brought her in to give her something to do when the kids were young."

"So you claim. But employees and former employees have stated that she not only worked there full-time, she often seemed to be the one in charge. Most noticeably when you were, as they say, unavailable."

"I traveled a lot. It's what businessmen do. Making contacts, sourcing suppliers." He glanced over his shoulder at Dad. "You were in business, Noel. Tell this woman what it's like."

Dad shook his head.

"Mr. Vaughan," Simmonds said, "I have no interest whatsoever in the details of your divorce battle or what might or might not be your case. What I am interested in, is that Karla wanted money equal to one half of the value of the business, and you've been fighting her over that for two years. Two years in which the value of your company has steadily declined, which some say is because Mrs. Vaughan was no longer around to run it."

"Some say. You can't take the word of that miserable bunch in the back office. They were always on Karla's side. She paid them off, I bet."

"Not my concern," Simmonds said. "What is my concern is that the legal action was destroying you and your company. Not to mention you appear to have thought it a good idea to start a new family, with all the expense that entails."

"That wasn't my idea." Eric's head dropped. "Besides, that . . . relationship's over."

Simmonds raised one eyebrow. "Is it? Meaning more legal fees, I presume."

She let his silence fill the room.

"The death of Karla Vaughan has worked out rather well for you, hasn't it, Eric?" Simmonds said at last.

"I don't look at it that way," he said.

"Why did you come here? To Rudolph? Why did you tell Karla's friends you wanted to be the one to bring her body home?"

He dropped back into his chair. "My son asked me to come. He said it was the least I could do for his mother. His wife's expecting any day now, and he didn't want to leave her. My daughter started a new job a couple of weeks ago and can't get away." He stared intently at his hands. "My children and I are . . . not close. I thought it the least I could do for them."

"Where were you on Sunday evening?"

"I told you that yesterday."

"I'm asking again. You must be aware that airlines keep passenger data these days."

I glanced at Dad. He lifted his bushy white eyebrows. Wherever Eric was on Sunday, the day of the fateful pot-luck, Simmonds knew. And she knew it wasn't what he'd originally told her.

Eric twisted his hands together. "Vegas," he mumbled.

"Where?"

He lifted his head and spat out the words. "Las Vegas. It's in Nevada."

"So I've heard," Simmonds said. "Are you a regular visitor to Las Vegas?"

"A man needs some relaxation," Eric muttered.

"The primary activity, I've also heard, in Las Vegas is gambling. Do you gamble when you're there, Mr. Vaughan?"

He mumbled something.

"I'll take that as a 'yes,' shall I?" she said. "And I'll venture to guess—"

Diane Simmonds, I knew, never guessed.

"—you've been going there a great deal for a long time. Probably when you've been on your numerous business trips, leaving your wife in charge of the company. But, as I said, that's not my concern. Gambling is a dangerous pastime for a person in severe financial difficulties—collapsing company, expensive divorce, new family to support—to engage in."

"It helps me relax," he mumbled.

"I'm sure it does," Simmonds said. "Another thing I've heard about Las Vegas is that members of organized crime circles have been known to gather there."

Eric said nothing.

"When you were in Vegas, did you hire someone to come to Rudolph and kill your wife on your behalf, Mr. Vaughan?"

He let out a bark of strangled laughter. "Detective, if I had that sort of money, I might have considered it. But I don't. And I didn't."

"Don't treat me like a fool, Mr. Vaughan." Simmonds bit off the words. "We might be a small town with a small police department, but I do have access to other law enforcement databases, you know. Plus, I have my share of personal contacts in the outside world. You'd be wise to remember that. If you didn't hire someone to take care of it for you, did you kill Karla Vaughan yourself?"

He lifted his head and stuck out his chin. "I did not kill Karla, and I did not hire anyone to do it for me."

"As tomorrow's the holiday, and the morgue staff will be working reduced hours over the weekend, I'll order the body to be released on Monday. Thank you for your time, Mr. Vaughan."

"What?"

"You can go now."

"Oh." He slowly got to his feet.

Simmonds nodded at Dad, and he opened the door. Eric left.

"Merry, a word, please," the detective said.

Dad shut the door again.

"I put out a request for anyone who'd been on this street around six o'clock on Sunday evening, the time you said you saw someone in the driveway, to get in touch with us."

"I read that in the paper," I said. "Did anyone call?"

"Aside from the usual citizens wanting to be helpful, yet having absolutely nothing to contribute, yes. A man dropped into the station to tell me he and his wife were going to dinner at the house of friends. They hadn't been there before, and he got confused in the streets. He couldn't say for sure, but he thought he might have turned around in your parents' driveway. He described this house, as seen from the driveway, fairly accurately. Can you tell me again what sort of vehicle you saw?"

I shook my head. "It was nothing but an impression. I saw headlights, a shape backing out. It was a car, I'm pretty sure, meaning not a truck or an SUV or something like that. Dark colored, not big, not excessively tiny. A car."

"As vague as it is, that description does match the vehicle this man drives."

"Did you believe him? If he'd been leaving after dropping off poisoned egg salad, he isn't exactly going to tell you that."

"I believe no one, so I had officers follow up. He's lived in Rudolph for many years, has no criminal record, and appears to have never met either of your parents, other than at the usual community events. I can find no connection between him and the Vaughans."

I had to admit, that didn't sound like a hired hitman to me. *Then again, what does a hired hitman sound like?* "Do you think Eric hired a contract killer to get rid of his wife?" I asked.

"No," she said. "The manner of Karla's death wouldn't be their style. Sneaking into a house full of people to plant a bowl of tainted curried eggs?"

"Maybe they wanted it to look like an accident?"

Simmonds smiled at me. "The thing is, Merry, in no way does this look like an accident. You'd have to be a total fool not to know we'd immediately find the ground peanuts in the food and in Karla's stomach. This wasn't done by any professional killer. It was a crime of opportunity, by someone who either didn't think things through or was prepared to take a heck of a chance. A total amateur, in other words."

I didn't ask Detective Simmonds why she was telling me this. She'd ordered me not to get involved in the investigation. Was it possible she'd changed her mind and didn't want to come right out and say so? I tried to look thoughtful and intelligent. The sort of person the police would come to when they were stumped.

"Meaning it was done by someone who is in this house right now," Dad said.

Simmonds said nothing.

"Not Eric," I said, "if he was in Vegas."

"I'm not eliminating him yet," Simmonds said. "Despite Homeland Security's best efforts, it is possible to travel, even by air, under the radar."

"What about insurance?" Dad said. "Does he stand to get a payoff for Karla's death?"

"No. The company had a big policy on her when she worked there, but he canceled it when the divorce action began and she left the company."

"Some people in town are saying it was a mob hit to get at Eric," I said.

"You're not saying that, I hope," Simmonds said.

"Just repeating the gossip, and only to you. In case you didn't know."

"I know, but thank you for telling me anyway. The police in Northfield tell me they've never had reason to suspect anything in that business was not aboveboard. Eric's gambling debts are far more than a man in his precarious financial position should have, but nothing the mob would consider more than peanuts." She smiled. "Even if it was, and they wanted to send him a message, they would have known that bumping off a troublesome wife was doing the man a favor."

We showed Simmonds to the door and then went into the living room, where we found Mom and the quarrelsome quartet. Strained silence filled the air. They all looked up when we entered.

"It seems as though Eric isn't under arrest," Ruth said. "He went upstairs without saying a word."

"He's not," Dad said.

"You have porous walls," Ruth said. "I couldn't help but overhear some of what was said."

"It helped that you almost had your ear pressed up against the door," Constance said.

"Nothing wrong with wanting to know what's going on," Ruth said.

Constance stood up. "Thanksgiving or not, I've had enough. I can't get a commercial flight tomorrow, so I'm going to ask my father to arrange a private plane. I can't bear to spend another day here."

"A private plane," Genevieve said, "must be nice. I don't suppose you'll drop me in New York on the way."

"New York City is not on the way to Los Angeles," Constance said.

"So, make a small detour," Genevieve said.

"You can drive back with me," Barbara said. "That's assuming Detective Simmonds gives us permission to leave tomorrow."

"You're all scurrying off home, are you?" Ruth said. "Taking your secrets with you?"

"What does that mean?" Barbara asked.

"Secrets. Secrets. We all have secrets. Don't we?" Ruth glanced around the circle. Barbara, Constance, Genevieve, even Mom, shifted uncomfortably. "Some new, some old. Some serious, some not so. What do we do to protect our secrets? How far would we go? How far *did* one of us go?"

"You're talking absolute nonsense," my mother said.

"Secrets," Ruth said, "are at the heart of any murder. Particularly one as personal as this one."

"Did you read that in one of your books, Ruth?" Constance sneered.

A smile tugged at the edges of Ruth's mouth. "As a matter of fact, Constance dear, I did. Uncover the secret, and you've found the killer."

"Spare me," Barbara said.

"Detective Simmonds might not have grounds to arrest Eric for killing Karla," Mom said, "but as far as I'm concerned, he's still a suspect. And a good one. Not to mention a cheating rat of a husband." She turned to Dad. "I want him out of my house, Noel. Today."

"The hotels are full for the weekend," he said.

"Then he can sleep in a ditch for all I care," Mom replied. "The rest of you can stay tonight, and then I don't ever want to see any of you again." She stood up and headed for the stairs.

Chapter 19

Mattie and I headed back into town. Simmonds had been right about one thing: the scent of snow was in the air. A snowfall at Thanksgiving was early but not unprecedented. I was looking forward to it. I enjoyed snow: the sheer beauty of it, the silence it laid over everything, the cold clear air against my face. In that, I was still like a small child.

It helped that I didn't have a driveway to shovel and I walked to work.

I gave Alan a call. "Mom's canceled Thanksgiving dinner because of all the trouble. Do you want to come to my place? You can take the day off, can't you?" His siblings were going to their parents' place in Florida for the holiday this year, but Alan had stayed behind, claiming the pressure of work.

"I have a big job to finish for a particularly demanding customer," he said.

"I assume that means me. Come for dinner anyway. I

have no idea what I'm going to make, but I'll think of something."

"I'd like that," he said. "Anyone joining us?"

"I'll ask Mom and Dad. If Simmonds doesn't turn up anything new today, their guests are going to be allowed to leave town tomorrow. Which is just in time, before we have another murder on our hands. I can't imagine either of my parents is in the mood to celebrate Thanksgiving, but we should try to mark the day."

"Sounds good to me," he said. "I have a lasagna in the freezer—want me to bring that?"

"Did your mom make it?"

"She's worried I'll starve over the winter, and last time she visited she left me with a full freezer."

Mrs. Anderson loved to cook. She didn't have much of a chance these days to make huge family meals, now that her children had grown and her husband had to watch his weight. So she enjoyed making casseroles and baking up a storm at her son's house. Not that Alan needed to be supplied. Mrs. Anderson had ensured that all her children, not just her daughters, could cook as well as she could. But no one, not even Alan, could make lasagna like she did.

"That would be great," I said. "I'll head to the market after checking in at the shop to get salad things, and I'll ask Vicky to put a couple of baguettes and something for dessert aside for me."

"Sounds good," he said. "Uh . . . I love you, Merry."

"I love you, too," I said.

It was the first time the L-word had been said between us, and when I hung up, I felt positively giddy. Before I could forget what I said I'd do, I called Vicky. "Want to come for Thanksgiving dinner at my place? We're having Mrs. Anderson's lasagna."

"I never say no to lasagna. Thanks. Mark and I are going to my mom's for brunch because he's working dinner shift, and we'll be having our festive meal on Friday, when he's off."

"Great. Drinks at six. Dinner around seven."

"Can I bring anything?" she said, as I knew she would. Unlike Alan's mother, my mom isn't particularly fond of cooking, and she hadn't been around much when I was growing up to teach me what little she knew. My dad's idea of cooking was a step up from frozen TV dinners, but not by much—although he was good with a grill and a can opener.

So as to contribute *something* to my own holiday feast, as well as a salad, I'd stock up at the wine store on my way home tonight.

"Now that you mention it," I said, "if you don't mind. A couple of baguettes and a dessert would be nice."

"Sometimes I think you only invite me so I'll bring food."

"That, and for the charm of your company."

"Thanks, sweetie. See you tomorrow."

I arrived at Mrs. Claus's Treasures shortly before noon with a spring in my step. I liked the L-word. I liked hearing it, and I liked using it. Along with all the shops on Jingle Bell Lane, we were due to close at three, so people could get away to visit their families or prepare for guests.

"It's been a madhouse, Merry." Jackie wiped invisible sweat from her brow when I came in after settling Mattie in the office for the afternoon. "An absolute madhouse. Good thing I can manage in here on my own."

The shop was busy, and plenty of stock had been

removed from the shelves, but "madhouse" wasn't the word I'd have chosen. Particularly not as when I came in, I'd found my assistant chatting to Kyle.

"Hey, Merry," Kyle said. "Didja hear 'bout my new job?"

"I heard."

"I'm on my way now," he said. "Next stop, the big time. I was telling Jackie all about it. Did you know they pay hundreds of thousands for pictures of famous people?"

"Not just for pictures, Kyle. They have to be pictures of famous people doing something . . . uh . . . newsworthy."

He brushed off that triviality.

"Did you buy yourself a camera?" I indicated the solid black Nikon hanging around his neck and the camera bag slung over his shoulder.

"Belongs to the paper. I get to use it when I'm on assignment. I'm saving for one of my own."

"Are you on assignment now?"

His eyes shifted toward the door. "Lots happening in Rudolph this weekend, Merry."

"It's the start of the holiday season," Jackie explained to me.

"Speaking of the holiday season," I said, "I'll need you to wear your elf costume for the parade again this year. You might want to do up some of the . . . uh . . . more exposed bits." Jackie had made a few unauthorized alterations to her costume. "It's supposed to be cold next weekend."

Jackie and Kyle exchanged glances.

"What?" I said.

"You're going to have a float?" she asked.

"Of course I'm going to have a float. Why wouldn't I? I'm going to dress Mattie as a mountain rescue dog, and that will be our theme this year."

"Kyle thought . . ."

I looked at Kyle. "What did Kyle think?"

"Nothing." He glanced at his watch.

"What's going on here?" I said.

He was saved from answering when a customer brought a selection of red and silver glass balls to the counter. "Can you wrap these carefully, please?" she said.

"I'd be happy to." Jackie reached under the shelf and pulled out a stack of tissue paper.

Kyle checked his watch once again and then wandered off to have a look at the Santa and his reindeer dolls.

The bells over the door tinkled cheerfully and none other than Wayne Fitzroy came in. He threw me a huge smile and crossed the floor in confident strides. "Merry! So nice to see you again." He thrust out his hand, and I took it in mine. His grip was firm, not too strong, not too light, and not clammy. He smiled into my eyes and held my hand a moment too long. I pulled it away.

"I'm pleased to find you here, Merry. I've been hearing good things about Mrs. Claus's Treasures. A Rudolph institution, folks say."

"I've only had the shop for a year. This will be my second holiday season."

"Doesn't take long to create an institution, does it?" he said. He then turned the force of his charm onto my assistant. "And the lovely Jackie O'Reilly."

Jackie beamed. "Hi, Mr. Fitzroy."

"Call me Wayne, please. 'Mr. Fitzroy' makes me sound so old." He winked at her.

Jackie giggled. I struggled hard not to roll my eyes.

Wayne took in my shop in a single glance. "Lookin' good, Merry. Lookin' good. And I don't mean just you and your assistant." Another giggle from Jackie. Another effort not to eye roll from me. I've worked in fashion and design in New York City: I know false charm when I see it.

"It's easy to see you're pumped and ready for the holiday season," Wayne said. "Here, allow me to get that for you, madam." He rushed to the door and held it for the customer. He gave her a little bow, and she favored him with a big smile.

Kyle took the lens cap off his camera. "Kyle Lambert, *Rudolph Gazette*. Can I take a picture, Mr. Fitzroy? I'm with the *Gazette*. That's a newspaper."

"A picture. What would you want a picture of an old man like me for?" Fitzroy flashed a mouthful of white teeth.

"We like to feature pictures of people enjoying all that our town has to offer at Christmastime," Kyle said as if by rote. In fact, it was by rote. I'd heard Sue-Anne Morrow say those exact words to Russ Durham many times.

"Perhaps a shot with Merry and Jackie? In front of the Christmas tree?" Kyle suggested.

Jackie almost leapt over the sales counter in her eagerness to get to the tree. She was wearing an unusually short skirt today, and she'd undone the top two buttons of her blouse. I'd never seen those ankle boots with the four-inch heels before. They were not shoes in which a shop clerk would normally want to spend her day.

This whole thing was a total setup.

"I'm not . . ." I protested, but to no avail. Jackie grabbed my arm and pulled me after her. The customers stood back, smiling, and watched.

"You don't want me in the picture," Wayne said. "Why not have one of these lovely ladies enjoying a day of shopping?" He gestured to two women clutching their laden store bags.

"Oh, I couldn't," one of them said as she practically knocked her friend out of the way to be first.

"Please, Wayne," Jackie said. "It'll be great." She playfully plucked at his sleeve.

"I can do both," Kyle said. "And the paper can choose which one to use."

The picture of the two customers with Jackie and me was taken quickly. Pose, snap, done.

It would be deleted the minute they were out the door.

Wayne arranged Jackie and me on either side of him and put his arms loosely around our shoulders. Kyle lifted his camera and said, "Say cheese."

I ducked as a light flashed.

"Hey, Merry," Kyle said. "That wasn't a good shot. Let's try again."

"No, thanks. We're done here. Jackie, we have customers. Mr. Fitzroy, it's nice to see you again, but Jackie and I have work to do. See you around sometime, Kyle."

Something moved behind Wayne's eyes. He dropped the big smile and studied my face. A grin touched the edges of his mouth. "Not as dumb as you look," he said.

"If that's supposed to be a compliment," I said, "it's not a good one."

Kyle was holding his camera at chest height. He threw a glance at Jackie, clearly waiting for instructions.

I provided them. "Kyle, get lost."

"Okay. Call me, Wayne, when you want to try again." Kyle threw a "Catch you later, babe," to Jackie and sauntered off.

A pout crossed Jackie's overly lipsticked mouth, but then

a customer called her, and she turned with a smile. Jackie had a lot of faults, her attitude toward me—her boss—high among them, but she was an excellent salesclerk.

"All I'm trying to do here," Wayne Fitzroy said in a low voice, "is to make the point that there shouldn't be any hard feelings. Noel's your dad, and I'm sure he has your loyalty, as he should, but some people think his time as the big man around town is over."

"My dad has never been the big man, as you call it. Even when he was the mayor, he governed by consensus."

"If you say so, honey."

"Don't call me that."

His eyes narrowed. "You don't want me as your enemy, Merry."

"We don't have enemies in Rudolph," I said. "We believe everyone working together for the good of the town makes each one of us better off."

"America's Christmas Town. Such a nice image. Doesn't quite match reality, though, does it? What happened in here, in your oh-so-charming little store, last July?"

"Obviously you know, or you wouldn't be asking."

"A man died. Murdered. While you and your Santa Claus were playing make-believe down at the harbor. And now another murder in Rudolph. At your parents' house, no less. Your father was in Florida when that happened, or so the story goes. Is that true?"

I floundered, speechless. Was this man threatening not only Rudolph's reputation but that of my dad himself?

"Thanks for your time, Merry," he said. "Let's talk soon. I have some ideas for next week's parade you'll find interesting. I'm thinking enough of this cozy small-town atmosphere. We're too late to line up corporate sponsorship for this year, but we can start working on next year."

"Why do you even want to be Santa?" I blurted out. "Jolly Saint Nick hardly suits the image you're trying to project here."

He grinned at me. "Good question. And because you asked it, I'll answer." He lowered his voice to a whisper. Almost despite myself I stepped forward in order to hear. "What else have I got to do with the rest of my life? As long as I'm stuck in this backwater, I might as well have fun with it." He raised his voice. "Jackie, what's your role in the parade?"

"I help Merry on her float."

"How about head elf?" he said. "You could be on Santa's float. Sit beside me. Would you like that?"

"Oh yes," she said. "But other than Alan, the head toymaker, and a parent to watch the children, Santa only has kids on his float."

"A more sophisticated, adult image would be nice for a change, don't you agree?"

"That's a great idea!" she said.

"Let's make it happen then." He touched a finger to his forehead and turned to leave.

The grin he gave me was not that of someone full of the Christmas spirit.

Chapter 20

"I have to go out," I said to Jackie.

She sighed heavily. "Again? I sometimes wonder if you work here, Merry. Good thing you have me. A less dedicated assistant wouldn't put up with all your comings and goings, you know."

I refrained from pointing out that any assistant, dedicated or not, would put up with whatever they had to if they wanted to be paid at the end of the week. "It'll be quiet for the rest of the afternoon. Everyone's at home getting ready for Thanksgiving."

As if to prove me a liar, the door opened and a mass of people streamed into the store.

"I want a promotion," Jackie said.

"To what?"

"Assistant manager."

"You're my only full-time employee. You'll be managing yourself."

"A promotion and a raise to go along with it. Can I help

you with anything, ladies? Those linens are lovely, aren't they? Perfect for your Thanksgiving table. Today's the last day they'll be available until next year, as we'll put the Thanksgiving things away tonight so we can start getting everything ready for Christmas on Friday."

"Then I'd better buy them today," a customer said. "I'll take the full set."

Jackie gave me a triumphant smile.

Jackie had her faults, and trying to trap me into a photo op with someone out to destroy my father was high among them, but she truly was an excellent saleswoman.

After talking to Wayne Fitzroy, I needed a shower. Instead, I marched down the street to the newspaper office. Dad had told me not to get involved in the matter of our town's Santa Claus. It would appear that I was involved whether I wanted to be or not. Wayne Fitzroy had involved me.

When I was growing up, the *Rudolph Gazette* was a big presence in our town. I'm only in my early thirties, but a lot has changed since my dad was the mayor and he would sometimes bring me with him when he visited the *Gazette* offices.

Back then, the newspaper filled most of an office building in the center of Jingle Bell Lane. Men and women with determined expressions on their faces, ink or typewriter ribbon stains on their fingers, and cameras around their necks ran in and out all day, in pursuit of the latest scoop. Inside, the building hummed with the clanging of typewriter—later computer—keys, the incessant ringing of phones, and the deep powerful voice of the editor in chief throwing open his office door and bellowing, "Get me rewrite!" There was an entertainment editor, a social (i.e., gossip) columnist, a sports reporter, news staff, and two full-time photographers, not to mention a team of copy editors, advertising salespeople, a receptionist, and personal assistants.

These days, the paper occupied the ground floor of the building, and the editor in chief didn't even have an office with a door, but a desk shoved into the corner. The editor in chief doubled as a reporter (the only full-time reporter) and he covered everything: news, high school sports, town events. The receptionist was also in charge of advertising.

And Kyle Lambert—Kyle Lambert!—was the photographer.

"I'd like to speak to Russ," I said to the receptionist.

"I'll see if he's in," she said to me.

"I can see that he's in. He's right there." I pointed. Russ was at his desk in the corner, head down, typing away at his computer.

"Formalities," she said, "have to be observed. He might be busy."

"This is important."

She picked up the phone on her desk and pushed a button. At the far side of the room, Russ's head came up. He looked over, saw me, and waved me in. Only then did he pick up the phone.

"You don't really need a receptionist," I said as I entered his office space. "Everyone who comes in can see you."

He grinned and leaned back in his chair. "What can I say? I like the image. What's up?"

"You can't keep Kyle Lambert on as a photographer."

"Yes, I can. But you can tell me why not."

"He's doing freelance work."

"That's not a problem. He doesn't work for me full-time. He has to find other jobs."

"Fair enough. But he's doing freelance while telling people he's with the *Gazette*. Which is probably bad enough, except other people are using him for their own ends."

"Such as?"

"Wayne Fitzroy set me and Mrs. Claus's Treasures up for a photo op, obviously wanting to show everyone that I'm on his side in the Santa Claus affair."

"I love this town. Only in Rudolph," Russ drawled, "do I not have to ask what the Santa Claus affair is."

"Wayne spun Kyle a story about how the paper likes to feature pictures of people enjoying Christmas."

"Why is that a problem? It's true. Photographs like that are the only thing that keeps this paper in business."

"You want photos of visitors, families, children, and grandparents, not Jackie and me, posing next to the Christmas tree in my own store. Kyle was there with his camera—your camera—and Jackie was dressed and made up for a photo shoot, when Wayne just happened"—I made quotation marks around the words—"to wander in to say hi."

"How does this reflect on the paper? Plenty of people take pictures and bring them in, hoping we'll run them. Sometimes we do."

"Kyle was using the camera you lent him and his supposed authority as an employee of the paper for someone's private ends."

Russ pulled a face. "Okay. I'll have a word with him."

"You do that. But, more to the point, we have to do something about Wayne Fitzroy. He's out to ruin Christmas."

Only in Rudolph would the editor in chief of a respectable newspaper not laugh. "How do you think he's going to accomplish that? And, more importantly, why?"

"Why? Because he's mean, that's why, and he thinks it'll be amusing. How? He's going to turn our wholesome image into some sort of adult-movie version of Christmas."

Russ's eyebrows came together.

"Corporate-sponsored adult Christmas."

His eyebrows rose.

"We have to stop him."

"I'll run any statement Noel wants to make, but otherwise, there's nothing I can do, Merry. Not unless your dad wants to make something out of it."

"He doesn't. He doesn't understand that Wayne doesn't simply want to be Santa because he wants to be Santa, but because he wants to use that position to take over the town. He's talking about corporate advertising for the parade. I'm sure some of that advertising revenue will manage to find its way into his campaign accounts when he runs for council."

"Then we'll expose that, when and if it happens. I can't run stories based on speculation, Merry."

I threw up my hands. "I know that. So let's be proactive."

"I'm all ears. I'm a newcomer to this town, but I'm beginning to love it as much as you do. Have a seat."

I sat down. "Okay, here's my plan. First, Mrs. D'Angelo's network says he was fired for embezzlement from his last job. You can investigate and expose that. Second, Wayne's blackmailing Sue-Anne into making him Santa because Sue-Anne's husband is having an affair. Which would be bad enough in itself, but he's supposedly having this affair with a town councilor from Muddle Harbor. To a true Rudolphite, that's equivalent to high treason."

Muddle Harbor was the town next to us. When Rudolph began to achieve some success and renewed prosperity after it made itself a year-round Christmas destination, the people of Muddle Harbor didn't take it well. The Muddites, as we called them, tried to make themselves over as Easter Town, which wasn't exactly a roaring success. Various other endeavors had been tried and failed over the years, leaving them without much other than a conviction that their town's economic collapse was caused by Rudolph's success.

"First, this is not the *Washington Post*, Merry. I don't have the resources to investigate anything that happened out of town, and I'm hardly going to ask Mable D'Angelo for a quote. Second, if it's true about some affair, and we don't know that it is," Russ said, "what can we do about it?"

"Blackmail Sue-Anne, too."

"Meaning?"

"Tell her if she appoints Wayne as Santa, we'll tell everyone about her husband. Maybe hint that you'll run an article in the paper."

"Which I won't. We're not a gossip rag, Merry."

"I wonder how Wayne plans to get the word out?"

"I'm also not a blackmailer. And neither are you. I don't think you've thought this plan through, Merry."

I had to confess, I hadn't. All I knew about Mr. Morrow's supposed infidelity was what I'd heard from Mrs. D'Angelo. Short of following Sue-Anne's husband to Muddle Harbor and lurking in the bushes with a camera hoping for a chance to take an incriminating picture, I had nothing.

What would I do, if I did get something? Sue-Anne had never done the slightest thing to harm me, and all she threatened to do to Dad was to stay out of the selection of Santa Claus. She might be cowardly, but she wasn't a bad person, and her husband's infidelities shouldn't reflect on her. Russ was right—I hadn't quite thought this plan through.

"I guess you're right."

"I am. The only person who can do anything about this is your dad, Merry. You'll have to leave it up to him."

I stood up. "Thanks, Russ."

"If anything incriminating about Fitzroy crosses my desk, I'll let you know. In the meantime, what's happening about the death of Karla Vaughan? I hear her husband's arrived in town."

"He has." I didn't say anything to Russ about what I knew about Karla and Eric's marriage. That didn't need a public airing. "Simmonds is going to decide later today if she can let the women go home. She'll have to, if she doesn't come up with anything new."

Russ nodded. "Lawyers have been calling me. They're threatening legal action against the Rudolph PD."

"Catch you later," I said.

"Happy Thanksgiving," he replied.

I didn't know what I wanted to achieve by talking to Russ, but whatever it was, I hadn't achieved it. I was feeling thoroughly miserable as I left the newspaper offices. On top of being told there was nothing I could do to stop Wayne Fitzroy from becoming Santa, the first step on his plan for eventual world (or at least the small part of it that was Rudolph, New York) domination, I'd been told to have a happy Thanksgiving.

Which was turning out to be anything but.

Outside the butcher's shop, a line was forming as Rudolphites waited to collect their fresh turkey or crown roast. "Happy Thanksgiving, Merry," a woman called.

I muttered something in reply.

Across the street, people were leaving Victoria's Bake Shoppe, carrying boxes containing cakes and pies, or jars of soup or condiments.

Vicky's bakery sits next to the municipal complex, containing the library, the town council offices, and the police station.

As I passed, I saw Wayne Fitzroy skipping down the steps of town hall. He buttoned up his coat and wrapped a scarf around his neck. He was smiling and looking highly pleased with himself indeed.

He caught me looking and flashed me a huge grin and a thumbs-up. I turned my head and hurried away.

Chapter 21

I debated telling Jackie not to have anything to do with Wayne, but I decided against it. She'd tell Kyle what I'd said, and Kyle would tell Wayne. And Wayne would then try all the harder to get her onto his side.

Jackie didn't have a mean bone in her body, but she sometimes didn't think things through to their logical conclusion.

All it would take to get her on Wayne's side would be a bit of over-the-top flattery. Like a lot of girls who'd been the prettiest one in their small-town high school, Jackie was spoiled. She was used to attention, and as the attention faded as she got older, she tried all the harder to draw it back.

Maybe it wouldn't hurt to make her assistant manager and give her a small raise. The store had had a good fall, and the holiday season was shaping up to be a profitable one. And, I had to admit, she had a point. I was spending more time on my personal business than in the shop.

All the more reason I couldn't tell her to stay away from Wayne. It would look as though the promotion and the raise were a bribe.

As I'd predicted, business was slow in the hours before early closing. While Jackie tended to the few customers who did come in, I began disassembling the Thanksgiving displays and getting the fresh Christmas ones ready.

At three o'clock, I flipped over the sign on the door. A few of the shop owners hurried past, having taken the opportunity to close early.

"Uh, Merry?" Jackie said.

I turned to see her studying her shoes. "What?"

"I was wondering if . . . well, I mean, do you have anywhere to go tomorrow? For Thanksgiving?"

"You mean for dinner?"

"Yeah. If you don't, I mean with your parents having guests and being under suspicion for murder . . ."

"My parents aren't suspects."

"Whatever." She lifted her head and the words tumbled out. "You can come to my mom's if you like. My sister and her family are coming, and some of the cousins. Not Uncle Jerry and Aunt Beatrice, who no one can stand, though. So that's a good thing. Kyle'll be there, too. You're welcome to have dinner with us. Mom's doing a turkey."

I felt a lump in my throat. "Jackie, it is so nice of you to think of me, but I've invited my parents around to my place."

"Okay." She went into the back for her purse and coat. "Happy Thanksgiving," she said on her way out. "See you on Friday."

I wished her a happy Thanksgiving, and then I got Mattie and we walked home. "Everything'll be okay," I said to my dog. "Wayne Fitzroy might have ideas for changing how we do Christmas, but this is Rudolph. We have our standards."

To myself, if not to the dog, I had to confess I wasn't so sure. Most of the members of our town council were a spineless lot. They lived by the principle that it was always easier to go with the flow and not make a fuss. On the other hand, some of the shop owners and other businesspeople wouldn't be too pleased, particularly not at the idea of "corporate sponsorship." Rudolph promoted itself as a family-friendly holiday destination. If cute preschool kids in cute costumes were kicked off Santa's float in favor of pretty young women in skimpy elf costumes, that reputation could disappear, and fast.

Time, I realized, was running out. If I wanted to stop Wayne, I'd have to start making calls tonight.

I let out a long sigh. *Why bother? Why was it up to me? If no one else cared, even Dad, why should I?*

No, tonight I'd enjoy a pleasant quiet night at home. I had to go out and get salad ingredients and wine for tomorrow's dinner, so I planned on a trip to the supermarket. I'd buy a chicken breast and the ingredients to make curry for tonight. I'd have a hot spicy curry and a glass of wine and watch something funny and silly on TV, then go to bed early with my book. Early to bed. What an indulgence that would be. Tomorrow, I'd enjoy a leisurely morning, maybe take Mattie to the path by the lake for a long walk, come back home for coffee and breakfast, and then tidy up for my guests.

I got the car out of the garage and ran my errands. I told myself I was looking forward to a do-nothing evening and then a do-almost-nothing day tomorrow.

Pure bliss.

I finished my shopping and arrived at home shortly after five. At this time of year, it gets dark early and the sun was dipping below the horizon as I pulled into the driveway. A curtain twitched in Mrs. D'Angelo's front room, but she did not come out.

I carried my shopping bags upstairs. I gave Mattie his dinner and he dove in, headfirst, while I put away the groceries. He didn't come up for air until the bowl was wiped clean.

I let out a long sigh as my resolution crumbled. "Okay, one more walk. Are you up to it?"

He wagged his tail and ran for the door. Mattie was always up to one more walk. The temperature had been dropping all day, and the forecast for tonight called for the first significant snowfall of the season. I decided to wear a warmer coat. I put it on, found gloves in the pockets, and we left the apartment.

Why was it up to me to do something?

It was up to me because Wayne Fitzroy had seriously overplayed his hand in front of me.

I doubted he'd let anyone know he had plans to change the entire nature of Christmas in Rudolph. All he wanted, he told anyone who'd listen, was a chance to involve himself in the community and take on the role of Santa.

He'd slipped up and told me he didn't have the interests of Rudolph at heart. He was bitter at being kicked out of his company, losing his home and place in the city, and bored with our small town. It would be amusing to watch us dance to his tune and then bring us all down with him.

He'd tried to charm me and get me on his side (and he'd hoped to have a picture to prove it) as a way of undermining any support Dad might have. When I didn't take the bait, he turned to Jackie, showing how easy it would be to get even the people close to me on his side.

Only one person could save Christmas in Rudolph.

And that person was Santa Claus.

Chapter 22

Once again, I headed to my parents' house. I'd been there so much lately, I might consider moving back in.

Thick clouds, heavy with snow, were moving in, blocking the light from the moon, but the strands of Christmas lights decorating some of the houses and trees went a long way toward breaking the gloom. I tried to walk briskly—a woman on a mission—but Mattie insisted on sauntering, pausing at every bush and lamppost to check out the news from the doggy neighborhood. We passed people taking dogs for their evening walk, and friendly Mattie insisted on greeting everyone.

By the time we finally turned into my parents' street, I was thoroughly impatient. "Will you hurry up!" I tugged at the leash as he found a fire hydrant of interest. "I should have left you at home."

He looked up and gave me a *you wouldn't dare* grin.

"See if I don't next time." Knowing that was an empty threat, he made no move to do as I'd said.

The lamp over the front porch at my parents' house was on, and yellow lights glowed softly from behind the curtains. As it was coming up to dinnertime, I might catch Mom or Dad in the kitchen or relaxing in the TV room, and so Mattie and I walked down the driveway, intending to come in the back. Tonight all the lights in the neighboring house were off, and the driveway, lined by a substantial hedge, was a long, dark tunnel closing around us. A trace of faint light leaked out from the kitchen windows, and the scent of tobacco drifted on the night air.

Mattie's ears pricked up, and he let out a soft woof. From around the corner, in the depths of the yard, I heard a muffled cry followed by a solid thump, and then a groan. Mattie barked, the sound loud and full of warning. My heart began to race.

"Who's there?" I yelled. "What's going on?" I fumbled in my coat pocket for my phone, so I could use the flashlight app, but my hands came up empty. I'd changed into a warmer coat and forgot the phone in the pocket of the one I'd been wearing earlier. I was almost jerked off my feet as Mattie took off, racing around the corner into the backyard, pulling the leash out of my hands.

I ran around the house. At first I couldn't see anything except Mattie, still barking his head off, streaking across the lawn toward the back fence. I stumbled after him. My eyes slowly became accustomed to the darkness and shapes took form. Something lay on the ground near the fence. Mattie stood over it, barking in an urgent tone I'd heard him use only once before. A foot away, a small but bright red glow burned in the grass from a fallen cigarette.

The shape on the ground came into focus, and I realized it was not something but someone.

Mattie whimpered and nuzzled the unmoving form. In the sudden silence, I heard a whoosh of expelled air, then footsteps, and the creak of protesting hinges.

When my siblings and I were children, we'd been friends with the kids who lived in the house behind ours, and our fathers put a gate in the fence so we could run back and forth between houses without using the street. Those kids had grown up, as had we, and the family moved away. The gate wasn't used anymore: the hinges were rusting, the wood rotting, the paint peeling. Dad talked occasionally about repairing the fence, but nothing ever came of it.

As far as I knew, the gate hadn't been opened in years.

Tonight, the old hinges squeaked and the wood creaked as the open gate swung back and forth.

I hesitated, unsure of what to do.

The kitchen door opened, and a blaze of light flooded the yard. "What's going on out there?" my father called.

"Call 911." I stomped on the burning cigarette. "I'm going after them."

"Merry, is that you? What's happened? Who are you going after?"

"Call 911," I shouted again as I ran through the gate. I emerged in the neighbor's yard and took off across the lawn. I skirted their swimming pool, closed for the winter, and rounded the house to come out on the sidewalk. I looked left and right but could see no running figure in the darkness. I tried to peer into the yards of the houses across the street. Again, nothing. All was quiet and all was dark. None of the houses on this stretch of the street had turned on their Christmas lights yet. A car drove slowly past.

As I stood on the sidewalk, trying to decide what to do,

a dark shape streaked past me. Mattie, dragging his leash, heading off to the right.

With no better idea of where to go, I chased after him.

Ahead of us, a shape passed through the warm puddle of yellow light cast by a streetlamp, and I saw a running form, a dark figure.

"Stop! Stop!" I yelled.

Mattie hesitated and half turned. "Not you, Mattie! Get him!"

Mattie loped off.

The person we were after took a sharp left, dashed across the street, and disappeared. The house on the corner was surrounded by a wall that ran next to the sidewalk on two sides.

I kept yelling, "Stop! Stop!"

I could hear sirens approaching. Dad would have called 911, but the hospital and police station are on the other side of town from the house. They wouldn't have any reason to come this way until Dad sent them after me.

Five minutes ago, the streets had been busy with people walking dogs, enjoying an evening stroll, coming home from work, or heading out to begin their Thanksgiving. Now it seemed as though the end of the world had arrived and no one had let me know. Not a soul was in sight.

I rounded the high wall and almost tripped over Mattie. He'd given up the chase and sniffed happily at the empty garbage can at the bottom of the neighbor's driveway. In this part of town, garbage pickup is on Tuesdays. You'd think people could bring their unsightly trash cans in after the collection truck had passed.

"Where'd they go, Mattie? Where'd they go?"

He lifted his head, wagged his tail, and gave me a grin and a soft woof of welcome.

"Shush." I strained to listen. Nothing but Mattie panting, the whoosh of cars in the distance, and sirens getting closer.

This was a short block with only three houses on it. I ran to the four-way stop at the next intersection. From here, the person I was after could have gone in three different directions. More, if they'd taken shelter in a yard. Most of the houses had lights switched on inside and out, but no one was around.

I studied the ground, but I didn't know what I was looking for. A dropped driver's license maybe or an arrow painted on the sidewalk saying "this way." The ground was dry. If the snow had come earlier, I might have been able to follow footprints, but I was no tracker—trained to read signals in a bent leaf or the movement of the wind. A gray squirrel emerged from the undergrowth and dashed up a maple tree. I read nothing into that: squirrels are always running up trees and across roads.

"Anything?" I said to Mattie.

His big body quivered. He took a step to the right and then another. He broke into a run. I ran after him. My heart was pounding, and from far more than the sudden burst of exercise. He ran across the lawn of a house on the corner. At the far side of the building, a motion light came on. I tensed and prepared myself for a confrontation.

I'd run blindly, instinctively, not stopping to think about what I was doing. Someone had been attacked in Mom and Dad's yard, and I'd chased the assailant. Could the attacker be armed? Even if he was unarmed, I might be no match for him.

Bring it on. I clenched my fists and planted my feet

firmly on the ground, legs apart, knees slightly bent. I took a deep breath. I sent a quick thought out to Alan Anderson, and I remembered that he'd used the L-word.

The first thing I'd do when next I saw him—I'd say it again.

Now I was ready for whatever I had to face.

Chapter 23

Tap. Tap. Tap.

An elderly gentleman came slowly around the side of the house. His back was bent, his right hand gripped his cane. A Pomeranian trotted at the end of the leash held in the man's left hand. Mattie barked in welcome, and the small dog began wagging his tail so enthusiastically I feared the force of the wind would knock his frail owner over.

"Good evening," the man said. "Can I help you?"

The dogs greeted each other excitedly. In other circumstances I might have laughed. Mattie weighed 170 pounds, and the little dog probably topped the scales at 6. Maybe 6½ after a big meal. But they were both dogs, and they recognized each other as such.

"Did you see anyone in your yard a moment ago?" I asked.

"Excuse me?"

"My friend is . . . uh . . . playing a trick on me. She's got my keys, and I have to get home."

"No, I didn't see anyone," the man said.

"Thanks. Come on, Mattie. Matterhorn! Come!"

Reluctantly he said good-bye to his new friend and followed me to the street.

"Happy Thanksgiving," the man called after us.

"Same to you," I said.

Mattie and I walked quickly back to Mom and Dad's house. Flashing blue and red lights filled the street, and once again, neighbors were gathering on their porches. As we approached, an ambulance pulled away, lights flashing, sirens screaming.

"Nice of you to show up," Candy Campbell said to me. She stood on the sidewalk at the edge of the property, turning the curious away.

"Coulda used some help," I replied.

She glanced at Mattie, standing calmly at my side. "Walking your dog is not in my job description."

"There she is!" My mother's screech could have been heard in the back row of the upper balcony at the Met. She hurled herself down the path and wrapped me in a deep embrace. "When Noel said you'd gone after that . . . that . . ." My mother wasn't often at a loss for words.

"I'm okay, Mom, as you can see."

She stared deeply into my eyes. "So you are."

We walked up the path together. "Your father's in the backyard with Detective Simmonds."

"What happened? Is someone hurt?"

"Don't you know?"

"I don't have a clue, Mom. I saw what I thought was someone being attacked and I ran after them. After the attacker, I mean."

"It's Ruth. She's been taken to the hospital."

I thought about the sirens and the ambulance pulling away fast. That meant she wasn't dead. Didn't it? "Is she going to be okay?"

"I don't know, dear. I'd like to take you upstairs and put you in a hot bath and tuck you into bed, but Diane will want to talk to you."

We went into the house and through the living room, heading for the kitchen. The only people around were police officers. "Where's the rest of the quarrelsome quartet?" I asked.

"Who?"

"Your friends."

"They went out this evening. Only Ruth stayed in. She was upstairs in her room, reading. Your father and I were in the conservatory watching TV. Ruth must have gone out for a cigarette or to get some fresh air."

We emerged into the backyard into a blaze of light. Every light both inside and outside the house had been turned on, and police officers were using powerful flashlights to search the ground. Diane Simmonds squatted on her haunches at the back fence, examining the ground. My dad stood over her, watching, while another cop held his flashlight up so she could see. Mattie saw his idol and leapt forward with a joyous cry.

"Stay!" Simmonds said without even turning her head. Mattie dropped immediately to a sit.

"Go inside." Simmonds pointed to the house.

Mattie stood and trotted away, the end of his leash dragging behind him.

I stared after him, openmouthed. "How do you do that?" I asked when I'd recovered some of my senses.

She didn't bother to answer. "Aline, would you mind putting the dog in Noel's study so he doesn't disturb the scene? As well-meaning as I'm sure he is."

Mom went into the house after Mattie.

"Are you okay, honeybunch?" my dad said.

"I'm fine, Dad."

"Noel says you went in pursuit of whomever you saw here," Simmonds said. "That wasn't wise, but never mind that now. I assume you didn't catch him or her."

"Obviously not."

"Do you know who it was?"

"No."

"Did you see anything familiar about this person?"

"No."

"Go in the kitchen and wait for me there. I need another minute here and then I'll join you. Why don't you put the coffee on? I could use a cup."

"Sure. But first, Mom said Ruth . . ."

"A blow to the head," Simmonds said. "She was knocked unconscious, but she was beginning to come around when the paramedics got to her."

"She's going to be okay," Dad said to my enormous relief. I went into the house and made coffee. While the water dripped into the pot, I stood at the kitchen sink staring out into the backyard. Simmonds spoke to police officers and pointed at various patches of grass. A man called to her, and she went over to him. She crouched down and studied whatever he was pointing at. Then she nodded and pushed herself to her feet as he wrapped it—a rock, I thought—in an evidence bag.

She came into the kitchen.

"Coffee'll be a minute," I said.

"Thanks. Take a seat." She dropped into a chair. Detective Simmonds looked, I thought, exhausted.

I also sat down. "Someone attacked Ruth."

She nodded. "So it would appear. Person or persons unknown. Tell me what you saw."

I did. I also told her that I'd seen no identifying characteristics on the person I chased. "They wore a dark coat that came to about midthigh, but everyone would have been warmly dressed tonight. I can't even say if it was a man or a woman. Not too short, not too tall. Not noticeably obese."

"Gloves?"

I tried to remember. "I think so."

Mom came into the kitchen and sat down. "Poor Ruth. I can't believe it."

"Where are your friends this evening, Aline?" Simmonds asked. "Noel said they were making plans to leave tomorrow but have gone out."

"Eric moved to the Carolers Motel this afternoon. Noel was able to get him the last empty room. Barbara said she was going for a walk. She does that a lot. Constance wanted to be alone and didn't invite anyone to join her. Genevieve left about an hour ago. I don't know where either of them went."

"They went their separate ways?"

"Yes."

"On foot?"

"Except for Eric. Noel drove him to the motel. Other than that, it's not far to town, so no one needed a ride. The only one of them who brought their own car is Barbara, and she usually likes to walk everywhere." Mom groaned. "I want this to be over."

I got to my feet and poured coffee for Simmonds and

myself. I didn't bother to offer Mom one. She drank one cup a day, at breakfast, and said any more made her edgy. She was edgy enough right now.

"Do I have a killer staying in my house, Diane?" she said.

"At this time, it's too early to come to any conclusions. It might have been a random attack."

"As if there has ever been a random attack in Rudolph on a woman standing in her garden at six in the evening," I said.

"Always a first time," Simmonds said.

She didn't believe that, and neither did I.

"Aline, can you call your friends and ask them to come back?" Simmonds said. "Tell them I want to talk to them but don't say why. I'd prefer to send officers to pick them up, but I don't have sufficient manpower."

Mom pulled out her phone, but before she could use it Barbara burst into the kitchen. "What the heck is going on now?" She was dressed in a midthigh-length black wool coat and hiking shoes. She peeled her gloves off and stuffed them into her pocket.

Simmonds glanced at me. I shrugged. The person I'd chased might have been Barbara. It might not have been.

"Your friend Ruth was attacked a short while ago, when she was outside having a smoke," Simmonds said.

"Attacked? What sort of town is this? Thank heavens I'm getting out of here tomorrow."

"I'm afraid not," Simmonds said.

"What does that mean? You phoned us not more than two hours ago and said we could go. I would have left on the spot, but I don't like driving on the highway at night, and it's supposed to snow later."

"In light of tonight's developments," Simmonds said, "you'll have to stay awhile longer."

Mom groaned.

Barbara said, "I don't believe this. Where is Ruth anyway?"

"At the hospital," Simmonds said. "An officer is with her now, and I'll be going there shortly."

"Is she badly hurt?"

"It would appear she was lucky. Thanks to Merry."

Barbara glanced at me but didn't ask what I had to do with it.

"Where have you been?" Simmonds asked.

"I went for a walk. I'm restless here. I need to be back home and back at work. My cases are piling up, I've missed court dates thanks to you, and my law partner's struggling with the workload. Walking helps me relax."

"Barbara's a keen hiker," Mom said.

"Where did you walk?" Simmonds asked.

"Into town, down to the lakefront, and along the hiking trail that follows the shore. I've been there before, so I knew the way in the dark." She pulled a flashlight out of her pocket. "And I'm always prepared."

"Did you see anyone you know while you were out?"

"No. It's fairly quiet in town. Thanksgiving Eve, I suppose. I assume you mean did I see Ruth, Constance, or Genevieve, and I did not. Before you ask, I don't have an alibi, either. It's dark, and I didn't see anyone on the trail. The restaurants are open in town, but all the shops are closed, so not many people are on the sidewalks. Of the few people I did pass, no one paid me any attention, and I didn't speak to anyone."

"Thank you," Simmonds said. "Please leave that flashlight on the table."

Something moved behind Barbara's eyes. But she said nothing and did as she'd been told.

"I need you to stay in tonight," Simmonds said. "I might have more questions."

"Tomorrow," Mom said, "if you can't go home, move to a hotel. I can't take any more of this."

"We'll see about that." Barbara stomped out of the kitchen.

I watched her go.

"Merry?" Simmonds said. "What are you thinking?"

I wondered if I was as easy to read as a dog. "The only one of Mom's group who's made friends with Mattie is Barbara."

"What of it?" Mom said.

"Mattie ran after the person tonight. I wonder . . ."

"Did you begin the chase first, or did he?" Simmonds asked.

"I did. I remember Mattie tearing past me and going after them. I had no idea what direction to go in, so I followed Mattie."

"If you began the chase, then you signaled to the dog that it was something to do," Simmonds said. "Unlikely he was specifically running after his friend, but it's something to keep in mind. Good thinking, Merry."

I almost sat up straighter, raised my paws, and hoped for a biscuit.

Simmonds turned to Mom. "Noel tells me you were watching television when you heard a commotion in the yard. Is that true?"

"Yes, we were," Mom said. "Noel went to check, and I

heard him yelling, so I followed him. We found Ruth, and I called 911."

"What were you watching on TV?" Simmonds asked.

"A documentary on Pavarotti," Mom said. "We'd DVRed it to watch when we had a quiet moment. There's been precious few of those around here lately."

"Your husband enjoys opera also?"

I studied Mom's face. She didn't seem to realize that Simmonds was asking her for *her* alibi. I was my dad's alibi. I'd seen him standing at the back door when Ruth's attacker bolted for the gate.

"He likes opera as much as I like his fishing programs," Mom said, "meaning not one tiny bit. But we enjoy spending time in each other's company." She smiled at me. "Even after all these years."

"Neither of you left the den in the minutes before you heard Merry and Mattie outside?" Simmonds asked.

Mom shook her head. "Fortunately, the program had reached a quiet moment. Mr. Pavarotti was resting at his home, not singing. Otherwise, we might not have heard anything. He does have a powerful voice."

Simmonds's phone rang. She reached for it as she said, "Call Mrs. Westerton and Ms. Richmond, please, Aline." She answered the phone and walked outside. She hadn't touched her coffee.

"Is this ever going to end?" Mom said.

"It will," I said, with absolutely no conviction whatsoever. Someone attacked Ruth in my parents' backyard. To think that had nothing to do with the murder of Karla required a stretch of imagination I wasn't prepared to take.

Ruth must know something the killer was afraid of her revealing. And so the killer decided to silence her. She was lucky, very lucky, that Mattie and I arrived in time to scare the attacker away.

Earlier, I'd thought Karla might have been blackmailing Genevieve, and Genevieve killed her to keep her secret. Now I had to wonder if it was possible Ruth was blackmailing the killer?

I tried to think of anything Ruth had said or done that might indicate she knew more than she was telling the police.

I came up totally blank.

"I don't care if you've just ordered another drink," Mom snapped into the phone. "The police are here, and if you don't come voluntarily, they'll be sending someone around to get you."

"Who's that?" I said.

"Constance. She's in a bar somewhere." Mom placed the next call. "Genevieve, this is Aline. It's important you come to the house the minute you pick this up. The police are here."

"Voice mail?" I asked.

"Yes," Mom said. "That doesn't mean anything. If she's in a restaurant or at a movie, she might have turned it off or not hear it ringing."

Simmonds came back. "That was the officer I sent to the hospital. He was able to talk to Ruth in the ambulance, but she was confused and disoriented and had no idea what he was asking her or what had happened to her. The doctor said the injury is not severe, but she needs to rest. She's been stitched up and given a bed and a sedative. I won't be able to talk to her until the morning."

"Not a good way to spend your Thanksgiving," Mom said.

"My daughter's used to sudden callouts. My mother's in charge of the dinner, and I'll be home for that. No matter what happens." Simmonds's phone rang again. She listened, said, "Get back here," and hung up.

"Drink your coffee," Mom said.

Simmonds gave her a tight grin and took a sip as Dad came into the kitchen. "Noel, how long do you estimate it would take to walk at a brisk pace to the Carolers Motel from here?"

"Twenty, thirty minutes," Dad said. "Why?"

"That call was from the officer I sent to the motel. He found Eric Vaughan in his room. It took Mr. Vaughan some time to answer the door. He claimed he was asleep. He said he hadn't left his room since you dropped him off earlier, but that means nothing. All the room doors on the first floor—where he is—open directly onto the parking lot. They don't go through the lobby."

"You think Eric came here, attacked Ruth, and then ran back to the motel?" Dad asked.

"I don't think anything," she said. "I'm merely commenting. More than half an hour has passed since you called 911. But, it's important to note, Mr. Vaughan is not in the best physical shape."

I agreed. I couldn't see that overweight, red-faced man running two miles across town.

"What's happened now?" Constance came into the kitchen, pulling off her gloves and stuffing them into her pocket. She tossed her thigh-length black leather coat onto a vacant chair. "I hope you're here to tell me I can go home and to apologize for inconveniencing me so much. Did you catch the person who killed Karla? Any wine in the fridge, Aline? I'd say that calls for a drink."

"Where were you this evening?" Simmonds asked her.

"Me? Out. What does it matter?" She opened the fridge door and peered in. "Aline called and told me to get back here, and fast. So I did." She emerged with a bottle of white wine.

"Out where?" Simmonds asked. "And with whom?"

Constance glanced around the kitchen. At last she seemed to read the expressions on the faces of the people in the room. "What's happened?"

"Answer the question, please," Simmonds said.

"I went to town. As pleasant as this visit has been, it's long past becoming confining. I couldn't bear another night in with that bunch. Sorry, Aline, but I'm sure you agree. I went to a bar for a quiet drink."

"What bar?" Simmonds asked.

"The one across the street from her store." Constance pointed at me.

"A Touch of Holly," I said.

"Yes," she said.

"Have you been there over the last hour?" Simmonds asked.

"Yes."

"Were you alone?"

"I was. I was hardly in the mood for company, which is why I went out."

Meaning she had no real alibi. The bars and restaurants would be crowded tonight, the staff on the hop. Jingle Bell Lane was a five-minute walk from the house, easy enough for someone to slip out of the bar unnoticed. If the waiter stopped to ask if the patron wanted another drink and found the seat empty, they'd assume she was in the restroom or had gone outside for a cigarette.

I glanced at Simmonds in time to see her give my dad a slight nod.

"Ruth was attacked earlier this evening," he said.

Constance gasped. "Attacked? You can't be serious. Is she okay?"

"I'm very serious," he said. "Fortunately, the assault was interrupted, but the person got away. Ruth's fine, but they're keeping her in the hospital overnight for observation."

When she'd come in, Constance's face had been ruddy from the cold. Now, all the blood drained from it. She put her hand on the back of a chair to steady herself. She shook her head. "This is too much, I can't take it all in. I'm going to lie down. I managed to get a flight, at considerable expense, leaving Rochester at ten. I'll call a taxi to take me and be out of your hair first thing in the morning."

"You can go up to your room," Simmonds said. "But I'm afraid you're not leaving town tomorrow. I'll have more questions after I've spoken to Ruth."

"I can't bear to stay here another day."

"Believe me," Mom said. "I don't want you to."

Dad said nothing. His expressive face said it all.

"Call Ms. Richmond again, please, Aline," Simmonds asked.

This time Genevieve answered. Mom simply told her she was to come back to the house now, or the police would find her and pick her up. She hung up as Genevieve shouted questions. "She got my earlier message but decided not to answer. She had dinner at A Touch of Holly and has just left. She says it's embarrassing enough having dinner alone the night before Thanksgiving, never mind being stuffed into the back of a police car."

"I'd think embarrassment would be the least of her worries at the moment," Dad said.

I wondered, but didn't say, how Genevieve, if she was so broke, could afford dinner at the most expensive restaurant on Jingle Bell Lane.

"That's the same place Constance says she was," Simmonds said. "Is it possible they didn't see each other?"

"Very possible," I said. "If Constance stayed in the bar and Genevieve was in the dining room and they didn't arrive at the same time. The two areas are completely separate. Are you aware that Constance has been the object of police attention before?"

"You mean in the death of her husband?" Simmonds replied. "I'm familiar with the case. I've been in contact with the police who handled the situation."

"What?" Mom said. "You mean Constance really is a killer? I went to his funeral, for heaven's sake. He'd been killed in a robbery. That's what we were told. One of the women—I forget who—muttered something about it the other day, and I assumed she was making something out of nothing to get a dig in at Constance."

"I'm not saying Constance killed him, or anyone. Her husband was murdered in what appeared to be a break-in at their home. No one was ever charged with the crime. It's natural enough for immediate family members to be investigated."

"Because," Dad said, "sadly enough, they're usually the ones responsible."

"Which brings us to Eric Vaughan," I said.

"'Usually,'" Simmonds said, "doesn't mean 'always.'"

I cleared my throat. "Speaking of police attention. Genevieve?"

"Has a shoplifting conviction," Simmonds said. "I am aware of that."

Mom groaned again.

"If she's as broke as she claims to be," I said, "I'm surprised she went to A Touch of Holly for dinner."

"I wouldn't read much into that," Simmonds said. "People who get themselves into a lot of debt often can't control their spending. Particularly in times of stress. Which is why they are drowning in debt. They usually have at least one credit card that hasn't been closed on them yet."

A few minutes later Genevieve came into the kitchen. Another black coat, another pair of gloves. She was, I thought, taller than the person I'd chased. Genevieve was the tallest of them all, including Eric Vaughan. I glanced down at her feet. She was wearing high-heeled boots that added a couple of inches to her height. The person I'd chased had run easily and smoothly. Could Genevieve have changed her footwear after the attack on Ruth? Tossed a pair of running shoes into the garbage somewhere? Without the high heels, her height would be closer to normal.

If she'd taken an extra pair of shoes with her, that would mean she'd gone out with the intention of coming back and attacking Ruth and had tossed the running shoes once the deed was done.

I thought back to what the other women had been wearing on their feet: Barbara had on her usual hiking shoes, and Constance's ankle boots had low heels.

Dad told Genevieve what had happened. She expressed shock and then anger when she was asked to account for her movements tonight. Simmonds simply looked at her until she calmed down and said, "I went to that nice restaurant in town. I ate dinner. I'd just finished when Aline called the second time."

"Did you leave the restaurant at any time before that?" Simmonds asked.

"I went to the restroom. That couldn't have taken more than a minute or two."

"Thank you," Simmonds said. "You can go now."

"Where are Barbara and Constance? Are they back yet?"

"Upstairs," Mom said.

"I don't suppose either of them confessed?" Genevieve asked.

No one replied.

Simmonds repeated that the women were not to leave Rudolph.

"I'm going to be stuck here until I die," Genevieve moaned.

"Genevieve," I said, once she'd left the kitchen, still moaning, "is a professional actor."

"She might be," Mom said, "but she was never a good one. I think she was genuinely shocked when we told her about the attack on Ruth."

"Perhaps," Simmonds said.

"Did you see her shoes?" I asked the detective.

"I did. What of them?"

"The person I chased was not wearing such high heels. I can be pretty sure of that."

"Easy enough to change shoes," Dad said.

"Officers will be searching the neighboring properties," Simmonds said. "I'll tell them I'm interested in any shoes they might find that have been tossed into a patch of bushes. I'll also have the trash checked at the restaurant." She got to her feet. "I'll be off. I have a long night ahead of me.

You'll call me if you think of anything, anything at all? At any time."

"Of course." Dad walked with her out the back door.

Mom and I sat in silence until Dad came back.

"I want them gone, all of them, tomorrow," Mom said. "When Ruth's released from the hospital, she'll need rest, so she can stay here for a day or two, until her family can take her home. You definitely saw someone attacking her, Merry?"

"You mean did she hit herself?" I shook my head. "I saw someone, all right. I chased someone down the street."

"So Ruth didn't kill Karla."

"We don't know that. It's possible Ruth killed Karla and one of the other women—"

". . . or Eric," Dad said.

". . . or Eric, attacked Ruth for other reasons."

"The only one with any sort of alibi for tonight," I said, "is Genevieve. Unlike someone sitting in a corner in the bar, if she had a table in the restaurant, left for the time it took to come here, attack Karla, and then go back to her seat, the waiter likely would have noticed. Even in a busy place."

"Maybe not," Dad said. "There are nooks and crannies in A Touch of Holly, and the staff are trained to be respectful of their guests' privacy. Unless they have their eye on the clock, it's unlikely they can say exactly when she left."

"I assume Simmonds will be checking all that out," I said.

We sat in silence for a long time, each of us wrapped in our own thoughts. Police officers moved around in the backyard, but eventually they left, and the last of the cars drove away.

Once they'd all gone, I stood up. I stretched and said, "I'll get Mattie and be on my way."

"What brought you here tonight anyway, dear?" Mom asked.

I glanced at Dad. "For a while there I forgot all about it. Wayne Fitzroy will not make a good Santa. He has no intention of being a good Santa. He's talking about, of all things, corporate sponsorship for the parade. I—"

My father lifted his hand in the universal stop gesture. "All moot now, honeybunch."

"We can do something. No one—"

"While your mother and I were enjoying the singing of Mr. Pavarotti, only moments before we heard that commotion in the yard, I got a text from Sue-Anne." He paused. "I've been fired."

Chapter 24

Santa Claus.

Fired by text.

On the night before Thanksgiving.

I opened my mouth to argue, but Dad shook his head. "Sue-Anne doesn't have an easy time of it. She aspires to rising further in politics, but that husband of hers is an anchor around her ambitions. He's not only totally uninterested in giving her and her career any support, but he has a reputation that doesn't reflect well on her, even though it's not her fault. I feel sorry for her, to tell you the truth."

"But . . ."

"No buts. Good night, honeybunch. Rudolph is a strong town, full of strong people. We survived Fergus Cartwright as mayor; we can survive an unsuitable Santa. Wayne Fitzroy will tire of his games soon enough and go on to bother someone else."

I wasn't so sure, but there was no point in arguing anymore.

Vicki Delany

By the time Mattie and I left Mom and Dad's house, fat, soft snowflakes were falling gently from the night sky. I usually love the first snowfall of the year, but tonight my mood was as black as the sky above my head.

Never mind the whole ridiculous Santa Claus business, I'd seen the heaviness in my mom's face, the deep circles under my dad's eyes.

They needed this to be over, and they needed Mom's friends out of the house. Mom wouldn't kick an ailing Ruth into the street, so who knows how much longer Ruth would stay.

I had no doubt Mrs. D'Angelo would have heard all about renewed police activity on my parents' street, and she would be poised to waylay me when I got home.

Luckily, last summer I discovered a secret access route into my yard I hadn't known about. I'd intended to make sure it was sealed, but had never gotten around to it. Tonight I was glad of it.

Mattie and I crept, under cover of falling snow and darkness, through the back neighbor's yard to the adjoining fence. That is, I crept. Mattie danced across the grass, snapping at snowflakes. I pulled at the loose boards, made enough of a gap for us to squeeze through, and emerged into my own yard.

We tiptoed up the back stairs. That is, I tiptoed. Mattie charged ahead.

I filled the kettle and put on my pajamas. I hadn't had anything to eat since breakfast, but I wasn't hungry. Mattie, however, was, and I filled his bowl.

I made a mug of hot tea, added plenty of sugar, and

carried the drink to the couch. I curled my legs up under me and called Alan to tell him the news about Dad as Santa Claus.

Earlier, thinking I was about to single-handedly confront a cold-blooded killer, I'd promised myself I'd tell Alan I loved him again. Instead, a sudden bout of shyness had me just blurting out the news. "Sue-Anne texted Dad to tell him he was fired. She didn't even have the nerve to talk to him in person."

"Sue-Anne isn't known for her bravery," Alan said. "And, if what you suspect is true, she didn't want to get rid of him but felt she had no choice. How'd Noel take it?"

"Not too badly. He's got a lot of other things on his mind right now." I went on to tell Alan what else had happened tonight.

"I don't like the sound of that, Merry. You don't think your parents are in any danger, do you?"

"The guests are leaving tomorrow."

"Simmonds is letting them leave Rudolph? After what happened tonight?"

"They have to stay in town, but Mom's kicking them out of the house. All except Ruth, who's still in the hospital."

"Is dinner still on for tomorrow? I'll understand if you don't feel like entertaining."

"It's still on. I'll enjoy having you all over. The only stipulation is that we do not talk about murder. Or about Santa Claus in Rudolph."

Alan chuckled.

"It seems strange to me," I said, "that Wayne Fitzroy could blackmail Sue-Anne over something everyone knows."

"Something everyone suspects, Merry. I don't know that

anyone's ever seen Jim Morrow with this supposed paramour of his. No one even knows who it's supposed to be. Three women are on the Muddle Harbor town council."

We talked for a while longer before saying our goodnights. I gathered my courage around me and said it . . . the L-word. I could hear the smile in his voice as he said, "And I love you, Merry. I always have."

I let Mattie out for his evening patrol of the yard and then we went to bed.

I didn't get to enjoy my day off for long. Mom called at nine, when I was sitting down with my first cup of coffee. I was so surprised to see her cell number on my display that I shouted into the phone, "What's wrong now?"

"Wrong?" she said. "Nothing's wrong. Not here, anyway."

"It's nine o'clock in the morning. Why are you up?"

"Because I am determined not to have houseguests for a moment longer than is necessary. Noel's on the other phone trying to find empty hotel rooms, which seems to be a problem. At least Barbara has her car. She can sleep in that."

"Are you kidding?"

"No. I'm going to the hospital shortly to see Ruth. Diane Simmonds called to tell me Ruth is awake and conscious and able to have visitors. Would you like to come with me?"

"Sure. Do you know if she had anything to tell the detectives about what happened last night?"

"Diane didn't say. I'll be there at ten."

"I'll be ready."

And I was.

Rather than stand on the sidewalk, as any normal person would do when waiting to be picked up, I lurked around the corner of my own house, peeking out whenever I heard the approach of a car.

About an inch of snow had fallen in the night, just enough to give the grass and trees a fresh coating of white. The sky was the rich shade of blue it gets the day after a snowfall, and the sun shone cheerfully in a cloudless sky: a perfect Thanksgiving Day. The Wilkinsons would do their best to enjoy it, but it wasn't going to be easy.

Mom's car turned the corner, and I dashed down the driveway as fast as I could in the slippery coating of snow. I wrenched the passenger door open and leapt in. "Drive, drive, drive!"

"What on earth?" Mom said.

"Step on it! Here she comes."

Mrs. D'Angelo's front door flew open, and she bolted out of the house. She ran down the path in her robe and mule slippers, waving at us.

Mom pulled into the street, wheels spinning, snow flying in our wake.

"Close one," I said.

"Aren't you overreacting, perhaps a tiny bit?" said the opera diva.

"You have no idea," I replied.

The Rudolph Hospital is about the only place in town that doesn't try to be all Christmas, all the time, but they had attempted to give the place a Thanksgiving air, with pumpkins and cornucopias (containing real vegetables) on the main reception desk, and paper pilgrim hats and cutout turkeys hanging on the walls behind the nurses' stations.

Mom asked the receptionist for Ruth's room, and she

replied, "Admittance is restricted. Can I have your names, please?"

Mom gave them, the receptionist typed them into her computer, told us where to go, and asked us to check in with the nurse first.

Eventually we found Ruth's room. The door was half-closed. Mom knocked lightly, and we pasted smiles on and went in.

Ruth had been given a private room, and that, plus the limits on visitors, was probably on police orders. It was a nice room, too, bright and sunny, overlooking the woods behind the hospital rather than the parking lot. Ruth was in bed but sitting up, propped against a pile of pillows. Her face was pale and her head was wrapped in miles of bandages. A stack of paperbacks lay on the table, next to the remains of a cup of tea. A woman I didn't recognize sat in the chair next to the bed. She didn't smile as we came in.

"Good morning," Mom said, trying to sound bright and cheerful. "It's so nice to see you awake." She bent over the bed and brushed Ruth's cheek with her lips.

"I've been up since before dawn," Ruth said. "The police wanted to talk to me."

"Hi," the young woman said.

Ruth made the introductions. "Aline, Merry, this is my daughter Becky. Becky, this is my college friend Aline and her daughter Merry, who I've been telling you about."

"Nice to meet you," Becky mumbled. She looked a great deal like Ruth: the thin frame, the prominent cheekbones, the small chin. She got to her feet. "There's only supposed to be two of us in here at a time, so I'll let you chat with your friends, Mom. I'm going to the cafeteria. I won't be long." She left.

"How nice of your family to come," Mom said.

Ruth smiled. "Becky's a marvelous girl. She wanted to bring the kids, but I suggested they stay home and enjoy their Thanksgiving. My husband, Pete, is around here somewhere. He went for a walk. Pete doesn't handle emotion very well." She smiled at the thought and then her face settled into serious lines as she looked at me. "Detective Simmonds said I have you to thank."

"I saw someone, and I yelled and scared them off. That's about it."

"You might have saved my life."

"I'm glad you're okay."

Mom took the visitor's chair and folded her hands in her lap. "Detective Simmonds has told the others they can't go home yet, but they'll be moving into a hotel this morning. You're . . . uh . . ." She choked out the words. ". . . welcome to come back to my house to recover when you're released from the hospital, but as your husband and daughter are here, they'll probably want to take you home. Rochester isn't far if the Rudolph police need to talk to you."

"All I want," Ruth said, "is to go home and be with my family. I did enjoy our weekend, Aline. The part that involved spending time with you, anyway."

Mom took Ruth's hand in hers. "I'm so sorry about what happened."

"All's well that ends well," Ruth said. "Thanks to Merry, it did."

"More thanks to Mattie, I think," I said. "Detective Simmonds spoke to you this morning. Could you tell her who attacked you?"

Ruth started to give her head a shake, but stopped with a grimace of pain. "I don't remember anything. I was in my room reading, the other women had gone out, and Noel and Aline were watching television. I wanted a smoke. I remember getting my cigarettes and heading down the hall. The rest is all a blank. I can't remember anything more until I woke up in here this morning. It gave me quite a fright, I can tell you. The nurse told me that happened last night. Meaning today's Thanksgiving."

"That's right," I said. "Do you have any thoughts about what might have happened? Who might have wanted to . . . hurt you?"

"The police asked me that, but I could only tell them I have no idea. It was dark out, but I don't mind the dark, and I must have gone to the bottom of the garden for my smoke. Maybe whoever it was mistook me for someone else."

Mom and I exchanged a glance. That was an angle I hadn't considered. Could one of the other members of the quarrelsome quartet—even my mom—have been the intended victim? The women didn't look much alike, but wrapped in a coat standing out of range of the house lights? That could have happened. The only other one of them who smoked was Genevieve.

"You said something the other day about secrets," I said. "That all mystery novels are about secrets. People hiding things, and other people either knowing them or trying to find out. Is one of your friends holding a secret they don't want you to reveal? Something to do with Karla, maybe?"

"I can't think of anything like that," Ruth said. "I don't know any secrets, about anyone. I've tried to think like Lord Peter Wimsey, but"—she gave a short laugh—"real life isn't quite so neat, is it? If any of our friends are keeping secrets, I don't know them." She glanced at Mom. "Do you have any ideas, Aline?"

"Nothing I can think of. Nothing at all. If one of the women has such a secret, she's kept it to herself. As she should have. Not many of us have lives that are an open book. I might have committed a few small indiscretions when I was singing. There was the time that Latvian tenor, who shall remain nameless, deliberately trod on my toe during our duet at La Scala. He'd wanted his lover, a totally underwhelming singer who was married at the time to someone else, to get my role. I might have mentioned to the woman who cleaned the dressing rooms that—"

"Perhaps we can talk about that another time. Ruth, you were saying?" If a Latvian tenor arrived in Rudolph and my mom ended up dead, I'd have something to work with. But Mom's reminiscences didn't exactly have anything to do with the matter at hand.

"I haven't seen some of those women for almost forty years," Ruth said. "We haven't all been together as a group since college. We lead completely different lives, and the only thing we have in common anymore is a few fond memories of our long-lost youth." She looked at my mom. "I guess I should say that was something we used to have in common. Turns out none of us were ever fond of the others, and our youth wasn't as great as we've always pretended it was."

"I'll admit," Mom said, "this weekend might have been a mistake."

"If you do know a secret—if any of you do—then it has to be something that happened when you were in college," I said.

Mom threw up her hands. "Nothing happened when we were in college. We were young and foolish, and then we went our own ways in life. For heaven's sake, what sort of a secret would be so important you'd kill someone a lifetime later over it?"

"Some of us," Ruth said, "did better than others in life, as Constance keeps trying to remind me. But all Constance sees are the material things. I might not have the money to buy fancy trinkets in Merry's nice store or go out for expensive dinners, and my husband might be a handyman, not a business executive, but he's here now. He came when I needed him. My daughter left her family Thanksgiving to be with me. She brought a bunch of books for me to read and had her children write me notes." She pointed proudly to sheets of paper covered with childish scrawls and colorful drawings. "My son called me as soon as Becky let everyone know I'd woken up. Even before I ended up in here, my children were concerned enough about what's going on to call me every day for updates. Constance's son didn't seem to be all that worried about her being under police investigation. Not bothered enough to come and be with her, anyway." Ruth let out a long, deep sigh. "Constance is the poor one, not me."

Mom gripped her hand tighter, and they smiled at each other.

A nurse came into the room. "I need you ladies to wait in the hallway, please, while I run a few quick checks on Mrs. Nixon."

Mom stood up. "We won't stay any longer. You need your sleep, Ruth. The offer's still open; if you can't go home for any reason, come back to the house."

Ruth smiled at her as her eyes began to droop. "Thank you, but my family's here now."

We left the room.

"I think," Mom said, "Ruth's going to be just fine."

"I think you're right."

We walked down the long hospital corridors, across the parking lot, and drove back to town.

"Are you still inviting us for dinner tonight?" Mom asked as she turned into my street.

"Yes. It'll do us good to get our mind off everything that's been happening. Mom, what do you think about Dad being fired as Santa?"

"'Fired' is a strong word, considering he wasn't being paid a red cent." She let out a long breath. "Being Santa isn't all that important to him, Merry, although he enjoys it. It's the town and people of Rudolph and everything Christmas in Rudolph represents that's important to him. If Wayne Fitzroy makes a good Santa, then so be it."

"Alan doesn't trust Fitzroy, and he won't be toymaker to him. Will you be in the parade?"

"I have no choice, dear. Even if I wanted to drop out, I can't. My classes expect it. Some of my parents send their children to me specifically with the aim of them marching in the parade and singing at the post-parade reception. The younger ones in particular cannot sing without me leading them. You, my dear, will be in the parade also."

"I don't know."

"I do. The town is what matters. Christmas is what matters. Not Wayne Fitzroy or Sue-Anne Morrow and her fool of a husband."

"Do you know anything about what Jim Morrow is supposedly doing?"

"Nothing I haven't heard from the usual town grapevine. Don't change the subject. You'll have a float in the parade no matter what your personal opinion is. You should try to talk Alan into being Santa's toymaker again. For the good of the town."

"He's going to be on my float. We're doing Saint Bernard rescue dogs in the Swiss Alps."

Mom pulled up in front of my house. She turned to me with a smile. "Excellent. Alan and you will be supporting the town but subtly expressing your disapproval at how the issue of Santa Claus was handled. Would you like to borrow some children?"

Meaning kids from her vocal classes.

"Sure. Children add so much to a float. Wayne Fitzroy is going with pretty young women."

Mom groaned.

Chapter 25

"Your father and I are thinking of going on a cruise in January," Mom had said as we drove back from the hospital.

"Where?"

"The Caribbean. I can't be away for too long, I have my classes, but I can take a week."

"That would be nice," I said. I wasn't thinking quite so far ahead. All I was thinking about was the rest of the day. I intended to relax and try to enjoy what remained of my day off. My guests were coming at six, and all I had to do before that was tidy up and lay out glasses, dishes, cutlery, and napkins. As I don't have a dining room, or a dining room table, we'd be serving ourselves buffet style and eating on our laps. Not quite my mom's standards for the holiday meal, but she'd have to put up with it.

At least I was having a holiday meal.

I was determined not to spare another thought to Karla or Ruth or the rest of the quarrelsome quartet. Let the police do their job and let me enjoy my Thanksgiving. Tomorrow it was full speed ahead into the holiday season.

Dad had clearly stated that he was not going to fight for the Santa Claus position, so that was settled. Let the candy canes fall where they may.

My determination not to so much as think about all that had happened didn't last long.

Mom let me off at the curb, and I bolted up the driveway. A call of "Merry Wilkinson!" had not followed me, and my landlady did not appear on the front porch in a puff of smoke like a mule-shod wizard clutching an iPhone.

I hesitated. *Should I check on her?* I'd have expected her to be on the lookout for me. No doubt Mrs. D'Angelo had contacts at the hospital who'd have told her Mom and I had visited Ruth.

Maybe this was some new ploy of hers, a way of getting me off-footed and thus vulnerable to being dragged into the house and interrogated.

Maybe she wasn't home. Surely even Mrs. D'Angelo had to go out sometimes? Come to think of it, I'd never seen her outside the boundaries of her own property. She must have shopping to do, doctor and dentist appointments to go to, friends to visit. Didn't she?

I stood in front of the door at the bottom of the back stairs, indecisive. *Peace and quiet versus checking on a lonely woman.* At that moment the door opened, and Steve and Wendy came out. Steve carried Tina in his arms, and upstairs Mattie barked.

"Happy Thanksgiving, Merry." Steve put Tina down. She wore a pretty red velvet dress adorned with ribbons and bows under a matching red sweater.

"Same to you," I said. "Going to your folks'?"

"Yup," Wendy said. "Mom's expecting forty-two of us this year."

"How on earth do your parents manage?"

"We eat in shifts," Steve said.

Tina spotted one of Mattie's balls and toddled for it.

"Don't get your dress dirty!" Wendy scooped her daughter up, and then she turned back to me. "Sorry about what happened with Noel. I hear Sue-Anne asked him to step down as Santa."

I shrugged. "He's good with it."

"I don't trust that Wayne Fitzroy," Wendy said. "There's something nasty under all that fake charm."

"Sue-Anne," Steve said, "needs to get a backbone. But first of all, she needs to read the riot act to her husband."

Wendy smiled at him. Tina struggled to get down. "Like I do to you," Wendy said.

"All the time." Steve winked at me.

"Does everyone in town know Jim Morrow's business?" I asked.

"Sure," Wendy said. "Although, far as I know, it's nothing but rumors."

"And this house is rumor central," I said. "Speaking of which, Mrs. D'Angelo didn't leap out at me just now to ask what's going on. Not only with the Santa Claus stuff but with the death of my mother's friend."

"She's gone away," Steve said.

"Away? Where?"

"To her niece's," Wendy said. "She'll be back tomorrow. She called to let us know. Didn't she call you?"

"My phone's off." I'd switched it off when we went into the hospital and hadn't turned it back on as part of my intention to enjoy a quiet day.

We wished each other a happy Thanksgiving, and I gave Tina a big sloppy kiss on her plump cheek. She laughed in delight, waved her pudgy hands in the air, and they went on their way.

I ran up the stairs, cheered on by an eager Mattie, and turned on my phone. One voice message: Mrs. D'Angelo telling me she was going out of town for the day.

I imagined all the phones in Rudolph falling silent.

Unfortunately, my phone wasn't one of them. It rang. Diane Simmonds. I opened my apartment door with one hand and answered the phone with the other.

"Happy Thanksgiving, Merry," she said.

"Is it?" I asked.

She didn't reply. "I'm calling about what happened last night at your parents' home. Have you thought of anything you didn't tell me at the time?"

"Nothing, sorry. All I can say is, I saw a shape in the yard, and I chased it down the street and lost it."

"You're sure this person you saw is the one who attacked Ruth?"

I thought. "Pretty sure. I mean, I heard a grunt and then a heavy sound, like someone falling. When I came into the backyard, I saw someone standing over someone else. Oh, they, the standing person, was holding something in their hand. They threw it down when Mattie and I arrived and ran off. I saw you bagging a rock. Was that what they used to hit Ruth?"

"Very likely," she said. "I've sent it to the lab. I can't keep your mother's guests in Rudolph any longer. I tried to argue that once they've dispersed it will be too hard to question them if I learn anything new, but Mrs. Westerton and Ms. Shaughnessy have some powerful legal friends. I have to tell them they can leave today."

"I understand," I said.

"The hospital tells me Ruth Nixon will likely be released once the doctor has given her one more check. Her family has arrived, I understand, so they'll be taking her home."

She hung up without saying good-bye.

Now that I was, once again, thinking about all that had happened, I couldn't stop thinking about it. I made a pot of coffee and pulled a chair up to the kitchen table.

I dragged a piece of paper and a pen toward me and wrote five names:

Ruth
Genevieve
Constance
Barbara
Eric

I put a dotted line though Ruth's name. I decided not to even consider that Ruth had killed Karla and a different person had attacked Ruth. That might be what happened, but right now it would only complicate things.

The person who attacked Ruth must have thought she knew something about the death of Karla. Something she, Ruth, claimed not to know.

Claimed not to know. Did she, in fact, know exactly what had happened and why? Was she keeping that information to herself for blackmail or other purposes?

I thought of the soft smile on her face when she talked about her family. Ruth knew money didn't buy happiness.

I believed her.

Therefore, for the time being, I'd remove Ruth from the

list of suspects, leaving four. Plus, of course, person or persons unknown.

I studied the list, and then I drew a stroke though Eric's name. He might have attacked Ruth—he was in town and in walking distance of the house—but he wasn't here for the death of Karla. He was nothing more than a small-town guy who owned a family business and was going through a nasty divorce. If he had the wherewithal and the contacts to get on a plane, cross the country and back again incognito, or the knowledge of the underworld to arrange a hit on a troublesome wife, Simmonds would find it.

I did not believe Eric murdered Karla.

She was not killed by any random passerby or in mistake for someone else. A guest at that potluck dinner had made a curried egg salad specifically to disguise the taste of ground peanuts. That same person had hidden the EpiPen. It had been a deliberate, and successful, attempt to murder Karla.

It had to have been someone who'd been at the potluck dinner.

I hadn't done it. My mom hadn't done it. Vicky had absolutely no reason to have done it. Therefore, it could only have been one of the quarrelsome quartet.

What had Ruth said about her mystery novels?

Secrets. Secrets.

I drew squiggles on the paper, but no pattern emerged.

I supposed it might be possible that the killer was Mom, but aside from the fact that she's my mother, she wouldn't have invited the group for the weekend if she was keeping a secret, something so terrible and important she'd concealed it all these years.

Then again, why would the killer come for the reunion

weekend if she didn't want to see Karla and risk her secret being exposed?

Had something happened to force her hand?

Had something lingered large in her mind for almost forty years, something that was now in danger of being exposed?

I sucked in a breath.

That had to be it.

But what that something might be was the question. A question I was unlikely to be able to answer. I didn't know these women well—no more than what had been revealed in a few overheard snatches of conversation.

I wrote Karla's name on the right side of the paper in thick block letters.

Those snatches of overheard conversation might be important. What had I learned about the four women—and Karla—in the time I'd spent with them?

Genevieve was a failed actress and a petty thief.

Barbara was on her second marriage; she liked dogs and the outdoors and was an environmental lawyer.

Constance's family was wealthy. Her husband had died five years ago, leaving her with one son, who ran the family business.

Ruth had given up a promising acting career to care for her mother, but she had a husband, children, and grandchildren who loved her.

Karla had been a bitter woman. Angry at life, angry at her husband for leaving her, apparently angry with her adult children for not being closer to her, trying to pretend in front of her "friends" that everything was perfect.

Karla was also, I'd been told, the one who kept the group together. Without Karla, they would have drifted apart long ago.

Karla cared about her old friends so much, she carried a photo of Constance with her when she traveled. She might have had pictures of the others among her things that I hadn't seen when I searched her room.

Poor Karla. Had life been such a disappointment to her that one year at college, so long ago, had been the highlight?

She hadn't even graduated, but quit in her junior year and went home to Minnesota, where she'd remained. Had she regretted not graduating that much? I remembered being told neither Karla nor Constance had finished.

Mattie slurped at his water bowl and then lifted his head to give me a wet, dripping grin. I smiled back at him. Dear Mattie. Born on the wrong side of the blanket, as Vicky put it. Hard to imagine life without him these days. I turned my attention back to the paper in front of me and drew lines between the names, trying to find something they had in common other than college. Something that would have lingered, even grown, since their heady youth in New York City.

And then I had it. I drew a solid line between two of the names on the paper in front of me.

I called Diane Simmonds. It went to voice mail.

She'd told me she'd have to allow the quarrelsome quartet to go home today. She might not have informed them they were free to go yet. She hadn't at ten o'clock when Mom and I went to the hospital: Mom had said Dad was calling around, trying to get them hotel rooms.

My next call was to Dad. "Are Mom's friends still there?"

"No, they've left. Thank heavens. I had to contact almost every hotel and B&B in a fifty-mile radius, but I finally got three rooms in the Muddle Harbor Best Budget.

Constance wasn't at all happy about that. A Best Budget is not quite up to her standards, apparently, but at this point, I do not care about her standards. Why are you asking?"

"I want to talk to them."

"They left about an hour ago. Barbara drove them over. Your mother didn't even come down to wave them off."

I glanced at the clock on the stove. To my surprise I realized I'd been sitting there for almost two hours. I studied the paper in front of me.

"Can I talk to Mom?"

"Here she is."

"Hi, Mom. I have an idea as to what might be going on. I have a quick question about your friends and what happened when you were all in college."

"I'll answer if I can," she said. "Although my memory of those years seems to be not quite what I thought it was. I can't imagine why I thought this weekend was a good idea. Perhaps I'd forgotten that the only one who was actually friends—as in *friendly*—with them all was me. Even then, the rivalry and petty jealously was strong."

"Which brings me to my question." I asked it. I waited.

Silence stretched between us. "Yes," she said at last. "That is entirely possible. But after all these years, why does it matter?"

"Secrets, Mom. Secrets. They fester in the dark. Put Dad back on."

My father took the phone. "What's going on? Have you learned something?"

"No, but I'm about to. I'm going to Muddle Harbor. Do you want to come?"

"If you know something important, you have to call Diane."

Vicki Delany

"I did. I got voice mail. She's going to tell them they can go home today. Once that happens, I'll have no chance to confront them. I need Mom to call them and tell them we're on our way. Have her suggest they meet us in Barbara's room."

"I'll pick you up," my father said. "Five minutes."

"Bring Mom," I said.

Chapter 26

"Sorry, Mattie, but you can't come."

His face collapsed into a picture of disappointment. His ears drooped, his tail hung limp, and he let out a long, low whine.

"If all goes according to plan," I said, "we'll have a houseful of guests tonight for Thanksgiving dinner."

He didn't look as though that promise made up for being abandoned.

"Sorry," I said again. I slipped out of the house and waited at the curb for my parents. It felt strange to know that piercing eyes weren't focused on my back, itchy fingers ready to call everyone in town and tell them what time I was leaving for work or taking my dog for a walk.

Dad pulled up, and I hopped into the backseat. "I called Diane," he said. "I also got her voice mail, and I left a message for her to call me back immediately."

Mom twisted in her seat to look at me. "Are you sure of

this, dear? Don't you think it would be better if we wait until the police can join us?"

"All we're going to do is talk," I said. "I have a theory, but that's all it is. If I'm right, we'll leave, and I can tell Diane what we learned and let her take it from there."

"I agree with your mother," Dad said, "but if we tell you to wait for the police, you'll go by yourself."

"Probably," I said, meaning *definitely.*

We drove down the highway to Muddle Harbor. Like Rudolph, Muddle Harbor lies on the southern shore of Lake Ontario and had once been a highly prosperous shipping port. As they had in Rudolph, the ports had closed or shrunk into insignificance when lake shipping declined. Unlike Rudolph, Muddle Harbor hadn't been able to re-invent itself. Many of the grand Victorian houses had been converted into apartments or boarded up and allowed to fall into ruin. The handful of shops on Main Street strug-gled to stay open. We drove through town and out the other side to the Best Budget Motel. The motel was fairly new, part of a franchise operation, and nicely maintained. Much of their business came from Rudolph overflow.

I thought, not for the first time, that Muddle Harbor would be better served helping to promote Rudolph and hoping to attract some of our visitors. Instead, they'd put up a virtual wall between us. No one from Rudolph ever went to Muddle Harbor, and the Muddites came to Rudolph only if they were out to make trouble. They'd prefer to drive all the way to Rochester rather than be seen shopping on Jingle Bell Lane.

Today, the motel parking lot was almost full. Two empty spots were close to the doors, reserved for unloading cars. My dad never parked where he wasn't supposed to, so he drove through the lot searching for a place. He found one around the corner from the lobby. First-floor rooms opened directly onto the parking lot, and an open hallway ran along the second floor. Mom grumbled about having to walk so far when we were only going to be here for a few minutes. Dad gave her an indulgent smile, and we got out of the car.

"What room?" I asked.

"One-two-five," Mom said.

The lobby was empty except for a young man standing behind the reception desk. He couldn't possibly have looked more bored if he tried. He blinked as the doors whooshed open and said hopefully, "Good afternoon. Are you checking in?"

Mom passed him in a swirl of her red cape, trailing the scent of Chanel No. 5. "Just visiting friends. We're expected." She marched down the hall, heels tapping.

"Happy Thanksgiving," Dad said to the clerk.

We trotted after Mom.

Room 125 was situated next to the elevators. We hadn't needed to have been given the number. As we approached, we could hear the whine of high-pitched voices.

"Still at it, I see." Mom hammered on the door with a red leather–gloved hand.

Barbara opened the door. She didn't bother with preambles. "Okay, the gang's all here. One last time. What's this about, Aline?"

The Wilkinson family walked into the room. It was a standard budget-chain-motel room. Double bed, desk, mass-produced prints on the wall above the bed, tea and coffee things on top of a tiny fridge, cheap furniture. Barbara had not unpacked. Her suitcase stood next to the door.

Genevieve sat in the desk chair, and Constance stood at the window, looking out over the parking lot.

"We've decided to leave, never mind what that cop has to say about it." Constance turned. "My father's lawyer advised against it, but I've made up my mind. She can arrest us if she wants, but I'm not staying in this"—she shuddered—"place a moment longer."

"One for all and all for one," Genevieve said. "If Constance leaves, we're going to go, too. Barbara and I are heading for the city and dropping Constance at the Rochester airport."

"I thought your father was sending a private plane?" Mom said.

Constance flushed. "As his lawyer advised me not to leave, my father won't help me."

"Never mind that," Genevieve said. "Whatever you have to say, Aline, say it now."

"You meant well by trying to get us all together for a reunion," Barbara said. "Not your fault it didn't work out."

"That's the understatement of the year," Constance said.

"I have nothing to say except good-bye." Mom turned to me. "But my daughter does. Merry?"

Dad hadn't immediately followed us into the room, but now he came in, pulling the door behind him. He leaned against it, his arms crossed over his chest. Mom perched on the edge of the bed. She didn't take off her gloves or unfasten her cape.

I cleared my throat. All eyes were on me, and I was suddenly unsure of my conclusions. It had made sense in my mind and on paper. Now, looking at the faces of the watching women, I wasn't so sure.

Constance let out a long sigh of impatience. Genevieve

studied her fingernails and pretended to stifle a yawn. Barbara said, "Get on with it."

"Secrets," I said. "This is all about secrets. Ruth was right about that when she said secrets are at the heart of any mystery novel. The heart of almost any novel, come to think of it. But one of you thought she wasn't making a general observation. One of you thought she was talking specifically to you. I was there when she said it. You all were." I remembered how Ruth had made a simple statement sound like a declaration. How she looked at each of the women in turn.

"She spoke as though she knew something. She didn't, but as the saying goes, 'The guilty run when no one pursueth.'"

"What of it?" Barbara said. "Ruth is always nattering on about her tedious books."

"And her tedious life," Constance said.

"Merry and I visited her in the hospital this morning," Mom said. "It would be nice if you did also. She's awake and allowed to have visitors."

"As we said, we're leaving town," Genevieve said. "We don't have time to go, but we sent flowers."

"I sent them, as in paid for them," Constance said. "I let you put your names on the card."

"Wasn't that nice of you," Genevieve said.

"I thought so," Constance replied.

I was losing control of the conversation here. "One of you has a secret, a secret so important Karla had to be killed to protect it. That person then thought Ruth had either guessed the secret or figured out who killed Karla, and so she had to be silenced in turn. That person probably thought that as Ruth hadn't gone to the police with what she knew, she was intending to use the information for black-mail."

"Hey!" Genevieve said. "You promised not to tell any-one about that."

"About what?" Mom said.

I turned to Genevieve. "I'm not. This is about something other than what we discussed, but you've just proven my point about the guilty running for no reason."

She flushed and looked away.

The other women, including my mom, gave her curious looks.

"And," I said, "as this person had already killed once to keep her secret, meaning Karla, she decided it would be necessary to get rid of Ruth also. Fortunately for Ruth, I happened along and interrupted the attack. None of you have alibis for that time."

"I do," Genevieve said. "I was in a restaurant."

"But the waiter can't say positively what time you left." I didn't actually know if that was true. Simmonds hadn't shared the results of the alibi checks with me.

"I didn't slip out early and attack anyone," she snapped. "The whole idea is preposterous."

"I was having a walk. By myself, as I like it," Barbara said. "If I'd known I'd need an alibi, I would have marched up and down Main Street with a sign."

"Jingle Bell Lane," Dad spoke for the first time.

"What?" Barbara said.

"Our town's main street is called Jingle Bell Lane, not Main Street."

She threw up her hands. "Whatever."

"Among all the bickering and backbiting you five, in-cluding Karla, engaged in this week, two things stood out,"

I said. "Constance never stopped needling Ruth about not having any money."

"I was hardly needling," Constance said. "I was trying to be a friend. I didn't want her to feel left out because she couldn't do some of the activities the others of us did."

"Needling," I said. "Making her feel inadequate. Embarrassing her. You never lost a chance to remind her that you have money and she does not."

I stole a quick glance at Genevieve. She was intently studying the pattern in the veneer on the desk.

"That's true," Barbara said. "But what the heck. That's the way Constance is. Her bragging about something she had nothing to do with is her way of compensating for all her other inadequacies."

"As this seems to have turned into a bash-Constance session, I'm outa here." Constance's Michael Kors bag lay on the desk; she picked it up and headed for the door. "I'll find my own way to the airport."

Dad didn't move to get out of her way. "Why don't we let Merry finish?"

She hesitated for a moment, and then she turned around to face into the room. "If I must."

"The other point of contention," I said, "was the issue of children. Ruth and Karla have good-sized families."

"Believe me"—Constance shifted her purse from one hand to the other—"we know. Boy, do we know."

"Not that that seems to have made Karla at all happy," Barbara said. "She lied to us about her marriage."

"Yes, she did. She lied because she had something to prove. Even to herself. Most of all to herself."

I looked directly at Constance.

Mom, Dad, Barbara, and Genevieve glanced at one another.

Constance stared back at me. Something moved in the depths of her eyes.

"Karla only agreed to come on this weekend because you wrote and told her you were coming, Constance. She told me that. I thought nothing of it, assuming she wanted to catch up. A little stroll down memory lane. But from the very beginning, I didn't see anything at all close between the two of you."

"If you're going to rehash all of Karla's petty grievances," Constance said, "I'm going to demand you let me leave. Keeping me here against my will is called kidnapping, you know."

"I'm almost finished," I said. "Are you aware that Karla kept a picture of you with her at all times, Constance?"

"What? That's rather creepy."

"Why would she do that?" Barbara asked. "Constance and Karla weren't close, even back then."

"Good question," I said. "But when I thought about it later, I remembered that Constance isn't the only one in that picture. There's a young man with you. Your son, I assume. He's a good-looking man."

"Thank you," Constance said. "I'm very proud of him."

"He's quite a bit shorter than you, though. Children are generally taller than their parents, particularly sons and mothers. But not always."

"I have absolutely no idea where this is going," Barbara said. "I hope you're not going to tell us Karla has been nurturing a secret crush on Constance all these years. She was an unhappy woman."

She had to convince herself that she hadn't made a mistake in giving her son up for adoption all those years ago. Giving him to you, Constance, to raise."

Barbara sucked in a breath, and Genevieve let out a low whistle.

"Oh yeah," Barbara said. "That would work."

"Something Mom said put me on the track."

"Me?" My mother glanced up, startled. "I didn't know anything about it until you started asking me earlier today."

"'A secret you'd kill a lifetime later over' are the words you used when we were speaking to Ruth at the hospital this morning. It hasn't been your entire lifetime since college, has it? But it has been for Karla's baby."

Constance's eyes darted around the room. "What of it? Is that all you bunch have to do? Dig up old dirt?"

"Karla got pregnant in our junior year," Mom said. "At first, she tried to hide it, but of course we all knew. This was the 1970s. An unmarried pregnancy wasn't the scandal it might have been ten or twenty years earlier, but to some families, it was still a matter of disgrace."

"She quit college and went to stay with an aunt. Or so she told us," Barbara said. "She intended to have the baby adopted when it was born. Isn't that what happened?"

"Yes, it happened like that," I said. "But what you didn't know is that Constance adopted him. Karla didn't keep a picture of *you*, Constance. She kept a picture of her son."

Constance said nothing.

"I don't mind telling you that I checked into your backgrounds on the Internet," I said.

"That was rude," Barbara said.

"It's public information. I was looking for a reason that would turn a woman into a killer. Constance has one son, and that son would have been conceived at the time you were all still in college."

"I, unlike Karla, got married before I had a child," Constance said. "Not that that's any of your business."

"One day, right out of the blue," Genevieve said, "you announced you were quitting college and going back to California to marry Frank, your boyfriend."

"I remember," Barbara said. "It was a mighty quick wedding; none of us were invited. I also remember we weren't entirely surprised when we got a birth notice from Constance a few months after that."

"Only Ruth, Barbara, Aline, and I were left of the original six to finish college," Genevieve said. "We said at the time that Constance's baby and Karla's would have been born very close to each other. Now you're saying there was only one baby. Wow."

"Why on earth," Barbara said, "would someone go into a shotgun marriage if she wasn't pregnant? Constance, as I recall, was always reading magazines, nattering on and on about the grand society wedding she planned to have one day. Even then, all she ever talked about was spending money."

"What surprised us most, Constance," Mom said, "was that you were going to marry the odious Frank. He was studying philosophy, and he thought he was God's gift to women. Earlier in the year you were thinking of breaking up with him because you suspected he had another girlfriend on the side. Then, all of a sudden, you announced an engagement and quit school. Naturally we assumed there could only be one reason for that."

"He was extremely good-looking," Genevieve said. "As I remember."

"Constance and Frank had one child, Edward," I said. "He was born six months after the marriage. But then, no more children." The look Constance gave me would melt ice at the North Pole. She could have demanded Dad get out of her way and left. He wouldn't try to physically stop her. That she stayed, to hear me out, told me I was on the right track.

"That, of course, is absolutely none of my business," I continued. "But, as Karla was murdered in my mother's house, I decided to make it my business. I also learned that once you'd settled in California, Frank went back to university and switched to a business degree at UCLA. After graduating, he took over as your father's heir apparent in the business and got full control of the company ten years later, when your father had to step down after a stroke. Five years ago, Frank died in an apparent, and unsolved, home invasion."

I paused. I knew all this from simply reading Constance's bio on the Stewart Industries website and other bits and pieces I'd collected off the Internet. Everything else was largely conjecture on my part, helped by snippets of Mom's memory as to what had been going on when the group was in college. There had to be a reason Constance and Frank had no more children, and I could assume, judging by Constance's reaction to other women's talk of children and grandchildren, that it wasn't a voluntary decision. "You mentioned your son's allergic to peanuts. Like Karla."

"Exactly like Karla," Barbara said.

"When Karla talked about her peanut allergy, she said she was grateful that none of Eric's and her children inherited it. I thought nothing of it at the time, but then later I realized that—particularly as she and Eric were fighting a bitter divorce—she would be more likely to say 'my children.' But she added the qualifier. So I asked myself why she'd done that."

"It's all starting to come back now," Barbara said. "You were worried that Frank had another girlfriend on the side in college. I knew, but I never told you because I didn't think that would be helpful, that it was Karla. Frank got Karla pregnant, not you. But you married the guy."

"Karla came into my shop without the rest of you one day," I said. "She called Frank a slimeball. At the time I thought that a strong word for someone she'd barely known forty years before, but it turns out she had good reason to remember him, didn't she, Constance? And not at all fondly."

"It makes sense," Barbara said.

"You're talking nonsense," Constance said. "Why on earth would I have done something like that if he was cheating on me?"

"Because you loved him," Mom said. "Why else? Love forgives a lot of sins, but it can't withstand that sort of betrayal, can it? If a man fools around before you're even married, he's not likely to stay faithful to his marriage vows. I doubt your marriage was a happy one."

And then Frank died. Getting rid of a bad husband and giving Constance control of the business.

Constance had been suspected, or so the papers said, of being responsible for her husband's death, but nothing was ever proven.

"It wasn't happy," Constance said slowly. "The honeymoon period didn't last long. You're right in one thing only:

love doesn't last, not if it's all coming from one side. I asked Frank to marry me, not the other way around. He was willing enough. Why wouldn't he be with all the extras he got as part of the deal? And it was a deal. Love and eternal happiness for me. A job for life and a rich father-in-law for him."

I held my breath, willing no one to interrupt. If I was right, Constance had been carrying this secret for a long, long time. She must be desperate to let it out at last.

"Adopting Karla's baby was part of the deal. Frank had been horrified when Karla told him she was pregnant. She wanted to get married, of course, but not only did he not love her—he didn't even like her much—he had no intention of joining the working classes to support a family at that stage of his life. Frank wasn't all that smart, I have to say, and he thought I was doing it for him when I said we could adopt Karla's baby. His baby."

"I still don't understand why," Mom said. "Why would you want to raise your husband's child by another woman? Why pretend it was yours?"

"My father has some old-fashioned ideas about the roles of women. My brother and my mother died in a car accident when I was in high school, leaving my dad with only me—a girl—as his heir to both his money and his company. That would never do, not in my father's eyes. If he didn't have a son, he wanted—needed—a son-in-law and a grandson. After my mom's death, he started bringing young, and not-so-young but unmarried, men around to the house to meet me. Each one of them more dreadful than the last. That's why I went to Steinhardt. To get as far away from him and his endless parade of supposedly suitable men as I could. I had some idea of being an actress and cutting ties with my father, but I soon realized that wasn't going to work."

"More like waiting on tables while waiting for the big break to come wasn't going to work," Genevieve said, "while you got older and older and time passed."

I doubt Constance heard her. She was talking as much to herself now as to us. "He rewrote his will after my mother's and brother's death, to say I'd get the full inheritance only if I was married and a mother. Otherwise, everything went to some distant nephew. What Dad didn't know—and to this day he doesn't know—is that I can't have children. I've known that since I reached puberty. My mother knew, of course, but she never told Dad."

"Oh my dear," Mom said under her breath.

"I arranged to take Karla's baby—she didn't want it— and to marry Frank. What harm did it do? Dad was happy, and it wouldn't have even mattered if the baby had been a girl. Dad's will only said I had to be a mother. Frank had his son, and he was part of a wealthy family, which was about all he ever wanted in life. Frank got his business degree, but Dad wouldn't hear of me going back to college, not with a baby at home. I studied beside Frank every step of the way. Without me, he wouldn't have gotten a word of it into his thick head. Without me, constantly reminding him that Dad would cut off his allowance if he didn't get the degree, he wouldn't have dragged himself home from the bars at night in order to study."

We'd all fallen silent. Outside the windows, a car drove past. A door opened in the corridor and shut again. A woman laughed.

"So that's my story," Constance said. "And now you know the secret of my life." She lifted her head and looked at each of the women in turn. "What happened to Karla was most unfortunate, but it had nothing to do with me." She turned to face my dad. "I want to go now. Please get out of the way."

Dad glanced at me. I nodded. *Let her go.* I'd uncovered a motive for Constance to kill Karla, and the police could take it from there.

But before Dad could move, Genevieve flew across the room. Her face was wild, her arms outstretched, her long red nails reaching for Constance's face. "You killed Karla. You can't just walk away and expect us to forget all about it."

Constance whirled around. She lifted her bag and swung it through the air. It hit Genevieve full in the face. Genevieve cried in pain and surprise. She staggered backward and fell onto the bed, collapsing into my mother.

Mom screamed and struggled to push the other woman off her.

"Hey!" Dad said. Constance turned again, putting all her strength into keeping her bag moving, as though she were swinging a baseball bat. It was a big bag, decorated with metal hoops and rings, packed full with things she'd want on her flight. Dad ducked and tried to move to the left; he tripped over the suitcase by the door and fell hard against the wall.

"Noel!" Mom flailed at Genevieve, trying to get her off.

Barbara yelled, "You won't get far, Constance. Not this time."

Constance threw the door open and burst into the corridor. I took off after her. No, she wouldn't get far, but who knows what a desperate woman might do when she was cornered.

"Mom," I shouted, "call 911."

I emerged from the room in time to see Constance run directly into the waiting arms of Detective Diane Simmonds. Constance was so surprised she hesitated. Simmonds grabbed her, flipped her around, and twisted one arm up and behind her.

Chapter 27

"It was her," I gasped. "Constance. She killed Karla. She tried to kill Ruth."

"You're out of your tiny mind," Constance shouted. "You and your mother made something out of nothing in an attempt to blackmail me. Well, I'm not paying up. So there. Let me go, Officer, or I'll sue you for everything you're worth." Constance hissed and spat like a cornered cat.

"Which isn't much," Simmonds said. "You can come with me back to Rudolph, and we'll have a nice long chat. I'm due to join my family for dinner shortly, so you'll have to wait at the police station until tomorrow. I'm sure we can find you a nice cell."

Constance struggled, but Simmonds held her fast.

A uniformed officer rounded the corner from the lobby. He took Constance from Simmonds and snapped handcuffs on her wrists.

One by one the rest of the women came out of room 125,

shock written on their faces. Dad limped, ever so slightly, and rubbed at his hip.

Constance's eyes were narrow with anger and suppressed rage. She spoke directly to Genevieve. "Do you ever want to act again? I have contacts, lots of contacts, important contacts, in Hollywood."

Genevieve lifted her chin and stared the other woman down. "Is that so? Too bad you never used them to help me when I could have used the help. Don't try to bribe me now."

Barbara put her arm around Genevieve's shoulders. Mom joined them, and the three women hugged one another tightly.

Simmonds nodded to the officer, and he led Constance—protesting, shouting, still making threats—away.

"That was a lucky one," I said. "You couldn't have timed your arrival better if you'd tried, Detective."

"Luck?" she said. "I never rely on luck. Thanks, Noel."

"Anytime." Dad took his phone out of his pocket and lifted it up. "Diane returned my call moments after we got here. I put the phone on speaker to hear better and must have forgotten to switch it off."

"I've been standing here," Simmonds said, "listening to every word."

"Can we go home, Detective?" Barbara said. "Please. I promise I'll be back whenever you need me."

"Sure," Simmonds said. "I have everything I need for now." She followed her colleague and his prisoner.

"I'll say good-bye for now," Mom said to Barbara and Genevieve. "You'll be back to make statements and then for the trial, so please let me know when you're going to be in town. Perhaps we could go out for dinner or something."

My dad and I exchanged glances. He wiggled his eyebrows at me. Noticeably, Mom had not invited them to stay at the house.

"Are you ready to leave?" Barbara asked Genevieve.

"Yes, I am."

The women fell into a circle and hugged again. When they separated, tears filled three sets of eyes.

Dad and I walked away. He was limping slightly, and I took his arm while Mom once more said her good-byes. "Are you okay, Dad?" I asked.

"Yeah," he said. "Nothing damaged."

"Have a nice day," the bored clerk called.

Mom caught up to us as we left the motel. "Thank heavens that's over."

"It might not be," Dad said. "Constance never confessed to killing Karla or to attacking Ruth. All Merry did was force her to reveal that she had a reason. It's up to Diane to get a confession out of her."

I dropped Dad's arm and fell into step beside Mom. "It's over for us, and that's all that counts."

My mother gave me a radiant smile.

Still rubbing his hip, Dad led the way across the parking lot. He rounded the corner of the building, heading for our car, and came to a halt so abruptly I bumped into him. He leapt backward with an agility that belied his injuries, dragging us with him. "Quick! Hide."

"What?" I said.

"What is it now?" Mom said. "I can't take any more drama."

Dad hurried to the side of the building, and then he leaned out as far as he could without falling over. He peered around the corner. Mom and I did likewise.

"Oh my gosh. Is that who I think it is?" I asked.

"Shush," Dad said.

"They can't hear us," Mom said.

"Shush," Dad repeated.

We watched as Wayne Fitzroy, the newly appointed Rudolph Santa Claus, flicked the key fob for his car and an Audi with the license plates KINGROY1 blinked in response. He opened the door and then turned to look at the woman who'd followed him out of the motel room. She was tall and slim, in her early forties, long shiny blond hair tumbling around her head, dressed in a short tight dress and bare feet. She lifted one hand and ran her fingers down Wayne's cheek.

She was not Mrs. Fitzroy.

My dad lifted his phone and snapped a picture.

Wayne got into his car and the engine roared to life. He drove away, watched by Mom, Dad, me, and the unknown woman. She waved good-bye and then turned and went back into the room. The door shut behind her.

Chapter 28

B y quarter to six I'd walked Mattie; tidied my apartment; made a huge bowl of salad; laid out glasses, cutlery, and dishes; and dressed for company. I was ready to receive my dinner guests and delighted that Thanksgiving was back on track. I'd have to do without the turkey and all the trimmings, but it was still a Thanksgiving celebration in the company of the people closest to me.

Mom and Dad arrived first. Dad came up the stairs with a bit of a limp, a result of being knocked over by Constance. He greeted Mattie enthusiastically while Mom slipped out of her coat. She'd dressed for the holiday dinner in a knee-length ice-blue cocktail dress with dangling earrings of twisted silver and a diamond-studded silver bracelet. Dad was in another one of his Thanksgiving-themed sweaters: orange with brown trim on the sleeves and collar and a picture of a roast turkey on a platter across the front. The contrast with his Santa beard and belly was startling. The contrast between my parents might have been even more startling, but I was used to it.

"What's happened?" I asked.

"Why do you think something's happened?" Mom said.

"You're fifteen minutes early. You're never early, so I assume you have something you want to talk to me about before the others arrive."

"I'm always early." Dad headed for the fridge.

"When you're on your own," I replied.

He chuckled.

"Is your float going to be ready next weekend?" Mom asked.

"It should be. I've been thinking of the mountain rescue dog idea, and I think it'll work. Mattie's well enough behaved not to try to jump off the float, and he'll enjoy being the center of attention. Hopefully he'll get us the trophy this year."

"That's nice, dear," Mom said, "but Alan won't be able to stand with you. Tell her why, Noel."

My dad came back from the fridge with a beer bottle for himself and glasses of wine for Mom and me. "Looks like I've been rehired." He lifted the bottle in a toast, and we clinked glasses. "Sue-Anne had a change of heart and gave me the role back. I'd like Alan to be head toymaker again."

"Did you tell her what we saw in Muddle Harbor?" I said.

"All this talk about secrets and how they fester in the dark got me thinking. I paid a call on Sue-Anne this afternoon and found her preparing for Thanksgiving dinner. Jim was not at home."

Mom snorted.

"I laid it out straight," Dad said. "I told Sue-Anne that

everyone in town's talking about her husband, but as far as I'm aware, no one actually *knows* anything; it's all just gossip. The state of her marriage is none of my business, but Rudolph is. I said if she let Wayne influence her decisions as mayor because he had something on her, or she thinks he has, then she needs to deal with it, whatever it is, and deal with it now. Or Wayne'll have it hanging over her for the remainder of her political career. And his demands will soon get a lot more damaging than wanting to play Santa Claus and having the biggest float in the parade."

"What did she say to that?"

"She pretty much broke down and started to cry. She said she didn't know what to do. She admitted that she and Jim were having some difficulties."

Mom snorted once again.

"Sue-Anne said Wayne hadn't actually blackmailed her, but he broadly hinted that he could make trouble for her with rumors about her husband if he wanted."

"Sounds like blackmail to me," I said.

"I then told her what we saw in Muddle Harbor earlier today, that Wayne himself isn't entirely squeaky-clean. I also suggested that the story of Wayne choosing to take early retirement might not be the exact truth."

"How do you know that?" I said.

"Russ Durham talked to me about it, and I made a few calls. I still have some contacts in the business world, Merry. My point is, if Sue-Anne needs my support, if Wayne Fitzroy tries to act against her, she has it."

"What are you going to do with that photo?" I asked. "The one you took at the motel."

"Unlike Wayne, I'm not a blackmailer, and I don't intend to reduce myself to his level. I don't care about Fitzroy, but his wife doesn't deserve to be humiliated in public. I deleted the photo off my phone, but first I sent Sue-Anne a copy. If he attempts to smear her publicly, she'll be in the position to fight back." Dad grinned. "And so I have the job once again."

"Congratulations," I said.

"Which is somewhat ironic, as I'd decided I didn't want to be Santa anymore. It's time for someone else to take on the role, and now I'm stuck with it for another year. But Rudolph's important, and as long as Sue-Anne's the mayor of Rudolph, she has my help and support if she needs it."

"I'll drink to that," Mom said, and we clinked glasses once again.

Mom and I took seats on the couch, and Dad wandered into the kitchen to check on dinner preparations—of which there was precious little.

"One thing I've been thinking about," I said in a low voice.

"What's that, dear?" Mom said.

"Paul the Doll."

Her eyes opened wide. "I believe his name came up at one point last weekend. What about him?"

"Just wondering. The women said you had a big thing for him. You don't have to tell me if you don't want to."

Mom laughed. "Noel! Merry's asking me about Paul."

Dad came back, munching on a cracker. "Oh yes, Paul. I guess you and your friends talked about him over the weekend."

Paul the Doll was obviously no secret between my parents.

"Paul was my boyfriend in college," Mom said. "We called him Paul the Doll because he was not only incredibly handsome and a very nice man, but it was a play on his name."

"What's he doing these days?" Dad said. "I sort of lost track of him after he got the second Oscar."

"Did he name his dogs Oscar?" I asked.

Mom laughed again. Dad smiled at her, his warm blue eyes full of love. "He might have," she said, "for all I know. No, he won two Academy Awards."

"Really?"

"You might have heard of him," Dad said. "Paul Dollheimer?"

I gasped. "You mean the actor? The man who everyone called the next Robert Redford or Paul Newman? He was your boyfriend?"

"For a while." Mom patted her hair. "He was madly in love with me." She returned my father's smile. "But I always felt something was missing in our relationship. We broke up when I met your father. I knew that very day which of them was the man for me."

My parents were smiling at each other, so much so I felt like an outsider.

No secrets there, and that was definitely a good thing.

At that moment, the doorbell rang, and Mattie charged for the stairs.

Chapter 29

"We need more greenery."

"Any more greenery," Alan said around a mouthful of nails, "you won't be able to see anything but greenery."

"You can never have too many trees in a forest," I replied.

"Yes, you can." He gave the wreath a tug, and it did not come free. He leapt off the flatbed. "We're done here, Kyle."

Kyle Lambert put down his hammer.

Jackie said, "Best-in-parade trophy for sure."

I rubbed the top of Mattie's head. While Kyle and Alan had been assembling the forest scene on what would be my float—stumps of birch to sit on, pine branches sticking out everywhere, wreaths on the pillars, and a couple of Christmas trees nailed to the floor—Jackie and I had put the finishing touches on the painted backdrop of a mountain scene. The kids in Mom's classes who would sit on my float were going to dress in green and brown. I'd dispense with my normal Mrs. Claus getup and wear a dirndl dress with my fake spectacles and gray wig. Jackie refused to make herself a new costume, so I gave in and agreed to let her wear the turquoise and green elf costume. She was disappointed enough when told her presence on the Santa Claus float was no longer required.

On my float, Mattie would be the star of the show. He'd sit on a platform in the center, surrounded by kids. Alan had rigged up a few pieces of cardboard to look like a wooden barrel, which we'd tie under the dog's chin. He hadn't looked entirely happy when we'd tried it out, but encouraged by praise and pats and a handful of dog treats, he gave in.

The four of us, five including Mattie, stepped back and admired our handiwork.

"A prizewinner for sure," Alan said.

"Best in show," Jackie said.

"Don't jinx it," I said. "I'm sure Vicky's coming up with something even better." Vicky had not been invited to help me with my float, nor I with hers. In this one thing only, we were rivals.

It was the Sunday after Thanksgiving, less than a week before the Santa Claus parade, and my parents had moved their cars out of the garage so we could convert a rented flatbed truck into a remote outpost in the Swiss Alps. True to his word, Alan had arranged for George Mann and his World War II–era tractor to pull it.

"It's almost noon," I said. "I'd better be going if the store's to open on time."

"Catch you later, Merry." Kyle lifted the case of beer that was his payment for the morning's work. "Coming, babe?"

"Sure," Jackie said. "I'm stopping at my place to change and then I'll be right there. You can take your time if you want, Merry. I can open the shop today."

"I'll be there," I said. "On time."

"Alan," she said, "did Merry tell you I've been promoted?"

"No, she didn't," he said. "Congratulations."

She puffed up her chest ever so slightly. "Assistant manager." Kyle bumped her hip with his. "With a salary to match my new responsibilities." Kyle high-fived her, and they left.

Alan, Mattie, and I took another minute to admire our handiwork and then we walked out into the beautiful, but cold, sunshine. A layer of fresh snow sparkled in the sun, and it looked as though it was going to stay. Alan pulled down the garage doors.

A BMW pulled up to the curb, and Diane Simmonds got out. She'd called me a few minutes before to say she had some news. Mattie ran toward her and greeted her politely. She touched the top of his head, and they walked together up the path.

"Morning, Detective," Alan said. "If you've come for a sneak peek at Merry's float, you can't have one. It's a surprise."

She smiled. "I can't wait to see it, but I guess I'll have to."

"Is your daughter going to be in the parade?" I asked.

"No. We're going to be spectators."

"If she'd like to ride on my float, there's room. All she needs in the way of a costume is something that looks sorta woodsy."

"Woodsy? That shouldn't be hard. Thank you, Merry. Charlotte will love it."

"What's up?" Alan asked.

"I thought you'd want to know I've charged Constance with the murder of Karla. I have enough to take to court, and I'm pretty confident we can get a conviction."

"She confessed?"

"No, but the L.A. police searched her home office and computer and came up with a great deal of interesting correspondence. They found a series of e-mails Karla had sent to Constance over the past six months. All of them had been deleted, but it's easy enough for the techies to access deleted e-mails. Basically, Karla wanted to meet her son. She claimed that enough time had passed, and he deserved to know the truth about his parentage. At first Constance simply refused, but Karla got more and more insistent. She said he was an adult, and she didn't need Constance's permission to meet with him."

"Which was true enough," I said.

"At that, Constance's tone changed. She became more consolatory, saying she'd arrange something, but right now he was traveling or busy with work. She arranged a date for Karla to come to California, even made the flight bookings herself, but the day before Karla was to leave, Constance claimed an emergency at work had taken Edward out of the country, and she canceled the flight. She was, I believe, preparing to get rid of Karla and her demands once and for all. Constance booked a flight for herself to Minneapolis, which she canceled a few days later. In that time, the invitation from Aline for the reunion weekend in Rudolph arrived."

"Good timing," Alan said.

"For Constance," I said. "Not for Karla."

"Constance immediately wrote to Karla and said they

would use the weekend as an opportunity to get to know each other again, and then they could talk to Edward together."

"Karla told me she came because Constance was coming," I said. "I think we can assume Constance had no intention of taking Karla to meet her son."

"Probably not. The way I read it, Constance was terrified of her father finding out Edward is not his biological grandson."

"Surely after all these years?" Alan said.

"Mr. Stewart is known to have some out-of-date ideas about the importance of family bloodlines. Whether he would have accepted the news about Edward or not doesn't matter. The only thing that matters is that Constance believed he wouldn't. Edward is the CEO of Stewart Industries, a role he took on after his father's death. Constance's father, Mr. Phillip Stewart, is physically incapacitated as the result of a stroke, but he's mentally as astute as ever. He owns the majority of shares and controls most of the board. He could get rid of Constance and Edward if he wants to. He could also write them both out of his will."

"So Karla and her secret had to be silenced," I said.

Simmonds nodded. Mattie sat at her feet and smiled up at her. She rested her hand on his head.

"And Ruth?" I asked. "Can you pin the attack on Ruth on Constance?"

"We're not having much luck there," Simmonds said. "No one at the bar can positively say where Constance was at the time. Ruth had been struck by the rock we found lying nearby, no doubt about that, but we couldn't get any prints off it. It was a cold night; most people would have been wearing gloves. These things have a way of coming to light when other questions are being asked."

"All you have is still only conjecture," Alan said. "You can't prove what was going on in her mind, and any lawyer will argue that thought doesn't necessarily lead to action."

The slightest of smiles lifted the edges of Simmonds's mouth. "As I told you, we've had officers going around town with your mother's friends pictures, particularly to food stores. Constance bought a bag of peanuts and a tiny amount of curry powder, enough to make one dish, in the supermarket on Saturday. We hadn't been able to find the clerk before now because she went out of town the next day for a pre-Thanksgiving visit to her parents', so she didn't get back to work and hear that we were hoping to speak with her until yesterday."

"Ha!" Alan said. "Gotcha."

I wasn't so sure. "A store clerk remembered that? They must have been busy in the week before Thanksgiving. Most of the time the clerk in the supermarket doesn't even look into my face. She passes the goods over the scanner and tells me the price at the end."

"That's usually true," Simmonds said. "But in this instance, the clerk remembered Constance quite clearly. The scanner didn't read the bar code on the bottle of water she also bought. The clerk had to send someone to check, and for some reason that took a long time. Constance had what is commonly called a hissy fit."

I laughed. "She would."

"She's well-dressed, well-groomed, attractive. Her clothes and appearance speak of money. Thus, she's someone who would be remembered, particularly after she drew attention to herself by being difficult. I won't mention the word the clerk used to describe her, but she's prepared to testify in court that it was Constance. Ironically, Constance got impatient with the waiting, thinking there was now more of a chance of someone recognizing her and going to the police later. Instead, she got angry and thus ensured she'd be remembered."

"What about the death of Constance's husband?" I asked. "If she killed Karla, I can't help thinking this was a woman who did what she thought she had to do to people who got in her way."

"That case will be reopened. The L.A. police were never satisfied that Frank Westerton's death was the result of a random robbery, but they simply had no proof. The timing of his death is interesting. He was the CEO of his father-in-law's company, and the business was struggling under his leadership. He'd made some bad decisions. He and Constance were increasingly arguing in public, both at the office, where she worked, and in their private life. The night before his death, they'd been at a dinner at Mr. Stewart's home. Witnesses told the investigating officers that Frank Westerton had a substantial amount to drink, and when Constance told him to slow down, he said he'd had enough of her bossing him around. Mr. Stewart then said that Frank should be happy to have a wife as good and as honest as Constance, and Frank replied that he knew things Mr. Stewart might not want to know. He then walked out of the house."

"And he died the next day," I said.

"And he died the next day," Simmonds said. "I stopped in because I thought you'd want to know how the case is progressing. I also want to thank you for your help, Merry.

But please, please don't do anything like that again. That scene at the motel could have gone badly wrong. I believe I told you not to interfere; I can't imagine what you would have done if I'd asked for your help. In the future, please bring your suspicions to me, and let me take care of it."

Alan put his arm around me. "I'll see she behaves herself."

I stuck my tongue out at him. "No need. I have absolutely no intention of getting myself involved in a murder case ever again."

Mattie barked in agreement.

Ready to find
your next great read?

Let us help.

Visit prh.com/nextread

Penguin
Random
House